MURDER IN THE DUNES

A SMILEY AND MCBLYTHE MYSTERY

Murder in the Dunes
© 2021 Bruce Hammack
All rights reserved.

Published by Jubilee Publishing, LLC
ISBN- 978-1-7373443-8-4

Cover design: Streetlight Graphics
Editor: Teresa Lynn, Tranquility Press

This novel is a work of fiction. Names, characters, organizations, places, events and incidents are either products of the author's imagination or they are used fictitiously. All characters are fictional, and any similarity to people living or dead is purely coincidental.

All rights reserved. No part of this book may be reproduced, or stored in a retrieval system, or transmitted in any form or by any means, electronic, mechanical, photocopying, recording, or otherwise, without express written permission of the publisher.

MURDER IN THE DUNES

A SMILEY AND MCBLYTHE MYSTERY

BRUCE HAMMACK

Books by Bruce Hammack

The Smiley and McBlythe Mystery Series
Exercise Is Murder, Prequel
Jingle Bells, Rifle Shells
Pistols and Poinsettias
Five Card Murder
Murder In The Dunes
The Name Game Murder
Murder Down The Line
Vision Of Murder
Mistletoe, Malice And Murder
A Beach To Die For
Dig Deep For Murder

The Star of Justice Series
Long Road to Justice
A Murder Redeemed
A Grave Secret
Justice On A Midnight Clear

The Fen Maguire Mysteries
Murder On The Brazos
Murder On The Angelina
Murder On The Guadalupe
Murder On The Wichita
Murder On The San Gabriel

See the latest catalog of books at brucehammack.com/books.

1

Steve was already on the edge of his beach chair when Heather opened her eyes. "Someone's in trouble," he said. His voice carried a certainty she'd come to know and trust.

"There," said Jack. "In the surf to our right. Someone must have gone under."

By this time, Heather was out of her rented chair. "Come on, Jack, let's see if there's anything we can do."

They took an angle toward the water to get out of the soft sand of South Padre Island. Once on the water-packed beach, they ran to a growing throng of people sixty yards to their right.

A lifeguard raised an air horn and pierced the screeching laughter of gulls. He sprinted to the surf with a red float trailing behind, shouting and motioning for swimmers to get out of the water. Parents waded into the surf-churned brine to retrieve children who didn't understand why they had to leave their fun. The blare of approaching sirens overrode the sound of pounding waves. Crying children and voices in Spanish and English rose in volume.

Another lifeguard arrived on a four-wheeler with balloon tires. He made a last transmission on his radio, grabbed his float, and followed the first into the curling waves.

Time seemed to slow down as Heather and Jack followed the last instruction by the lifeguard to keep everyone out of the water. Long minutes later, another four-wheeler arrived pulling a Jet Ski. The female passenger dismounted the four-wheeler and ran into the waves as the male driver backed the trailer into the shallows. The woman climbed on the Jet Ski, backed it off the trailer, and whirled it around in one smooth move. Heather shaded her eyes and watched the machine cut a path through the waves, going completely airborne at one point. City police and sheriff's department trucks reached the location and closed the beach to swimming a hundred yards in each direction. They gave clear instructions for everyone to leave the immediate area unless they saw the swimmer go under or knew who it was.

Heather walked, hand in hand with the man who was rapidly winning her heart. The promise of a cloudless day and spending a working vacation with Jack was now tainted by a cloud of death looming overhead. When they arrived back at their shady spot, Heather took her seat next to Steve while Jack retrieved a bottle of water. Kate was the first to speak. "I can tell by your expressions this doesn't look promising."

"Not at all," said Jack.

Steve let out a soft moan but remained silent otherwise. Words seemed feeble. The waves and birds made their own soundtrack, like they did every day, with or without an audience or an impending tragedy.

Heather took inventory of the group and how they were reacting. She was still on stable ground. Her experience as a police officer and a detective in Boston brought her into contact with a wide variety of situations, including death. Steve also was on an even keel, at least for now. The mid-fifties former Houston homicide detective wore a blazing orange button-up Hawaiian-style shirt that covered most of a baggy rainbow-striped bathing suit. The colors clashed, but what could you expect from a blind guy who shopped at Goodwill and consignment shops? He was no stranger to death, but some tragedies affected him more than others. Memories weren't always his friends.

Heather cut her eyes to Jack and took in his profile. He had a good face and trim physique. A head taller than her, she was well aware that he cut a fine figure in either a suit when he appeared as attorney for the defense, or in casual wear. He also was no stranger to death, but after the fact. Trial preparation sometimes meant becoming intimately familiar with coroner's reports and gruesome photos of crime scenes.

Then there was Kate. She was the wild-card in the group as to how she'd react to watching what might be the recovery of a body.

This was Heather's second experience of being around Kate. The more she knew, the more she liked the woman. It probably had to do with her taking Steve under her wing and giving him new meaning to his life. Or, was learning to write novels only a hobby for him to fill his days? Either way, both seemed content to stay a safe distance away from each other, but she wondered if the relationship might blossom. The successful author's distant past hadn't been revealed to satisfy Heather's curiosity, but staying in Kate's apartment with her might be a good time for girl talk.

Steve broke the silence. "Anything new going on? It's been fifteen minutes since I heard the first screams."

Heather's focus shifted back to the scene. "Nothing but the Jet Ski making passes where the waves are first breaking. The lifeguards with floats are working their way toward us."

"It's a recovery," whispered Steve. His voice took on a new intensity. "When you and Jack were swimming earlier, did you feel a pull from right to left?"

"Not particularly strong, but steady," said Jack. "Where we swam it was mainly a pull out to sea, but it only lasted until the next wave broke."

"Rip current," whispered Steve.

"Do you mean rip tide?" asked Heather.

"Most people call them rip tides, but they're rip currents. Rip tides occur near jetties or places where rivers flow into the gulf, or the natural cuts into the bays. A rip current can occur anywhere along a beach. Look at the waves. Most of the time they come more or less straight in or at a consistent angle, and go out straight. The in-and-out causes the sand to pile up into sandbars. Water will take the spot of least resistance to flow back from the shore. Sometimes it cuts a trough in the sand bars, and the water will flow out at a speed that an Olympic swimmer can't outrun."

Heather traded glances with Kate before she directed her question to Steve. "When did you get to be such an expert on rip tides and rip currents?"

"In high school." His voice had a somber tone. "A carload of us drove from Houston down to Surfside Beach in Brazoria County. We helped form a human chain and recovered a child in only four feet of water. It convinced me I needed to study tides and currents."

Steve unbuttoned his shirt. "The longer a body bounces against the sand, the worse shape it will be in. Most people don't realize how unforgiving the sea is. Who's up for going with me?"

"Going where?" asked Heather.

"To find the body."

Jack rose from his chair, but not Heather. "There's a lot of water out there. Where are you going to look?"

"You don't look. You go where you think the body is going and wait."

Kate pushed up on the arms of her chair. She looked nice in her one-piece. Actually, she looked darn good for a fifty-something-year-old woman who spent most of her time banging out novels on a laptop.

"You don't have to go," said Steve. "I seriously doubt we'll—"

"I'm going," said Kate in a way that didn't brook debate. "Besides, I'm probably the strongest swimmer in the group. I was on my high school swim team and I still try to do laps every morning."

Heather noticed more and more people, especially parents, were leaving the water. "We can't swim here. The deputies are telling everyone to get out of the water. They put flags in the sand in both directions to mark the no-swim areas."

"We need to go farther up the beach," said Steve as he sought Kate's arm. "Fifty feet on the far side of the flag should be right if the current is still pulling in that direction." He took in a deep breath. "I imagine all we'll end up doing is having a nice swim. The pros will probably find the body in deep water."

The quartet set off at a brisk pace up the beach. Heather corralled her auburn hair with a scrunchy and wondered if Steve was downplaying their chances of finding the ill-fated swimmer. Soon, they turned right and walked through water that came to her ankles before a wave surged against her and scurried to shore. Before long, the water's force pulled in the opposite direction.

"Sand bar," said Steve as he and Kate led the way.

The water level fluctuated between slightly below her calf to above the knee as they progressed. The seabed once again rose, but as it did, the waves broke higher. Steve didn't need to call out that they'd reached another sand bar.

"Not too much farther," said Steve.

The four pressed on, and didn't stop until Steve held up his hand like a traffic cop. "Jack, you're the tallest. Link arms or hold hands with Heather." At that moment, a wave curled over them. Had it not been for Jack's hand gripping her wrist, Heather would have been sent tumbling. As it was, the wave smacked her square in the face and bowed her over backward.

"Keep your eye out for the waves," shouted Steve. "If it's too big, duck under it."

Heather rubbed stinging saltwater from her eyes. "Now he tells me."

"Can't we all get up on the sandbar?" asked Jack. "I'm standing in waist deep water until a wave comes along."

"Trade places with Heather. If the body comes this way, it will come from the direction of the rescuers and will be pulled along by the current. Can everyone feel the water pushing you to the side?"

"I can," said Kate. "It's not strong enough to take my feet out from under me, but it's stronger than usual."

They stood relatively stationary for several minutes and became accustomed to the capricious waves. Some came with fury; others, as unambitious surges of water that tilted the four toward shore, only to relent.

The scream came from Kate somewhere near the twenty-minute mark. By the time Heather turned to look, Kate was face down in the water, digging in with powerful strokes, kicking with practiced beats, and headed to shore. Steve was nowhere to be seen. Jack dove under a wave. She saw it building, but the distraction of Kate's scream kept her from reacting to it. When she came up for air, Steve had his arm under one arm of a brown body, while Jack had the other. She half-walked, half-swam to them but there was nothing for her to do but watch as the two men moved out of the trough and pulled the body through surf that crashed one final time over a young face and twisted his body for spite.

Kate ran through shallow water, facing the closest first responder with arms above her head, forming one X after another. Time had no meaning for the young man now, but emergency personnel abandoned their posts and rushed to where he lay on the beach. They gathered around with downcast eyes. First responder sometimes meant first mourner.

After the police took statements, the four trudged back to their chairs and umbrellas. Steve summed up the mood. "What a way to start a vacation. I don't know about anyone else, but I need a shower, a sandwich, and a bed."

Heather knew what he left unsaid. Steve needed time by

himself in his dark world to come to grips with what should have been for the young man, and for his own life. What could she and Jack come up with to bring him around?

Her thoughts went to Kate. It would be good for Kate to go to bed tonight thinking about something besides death. In fact, that would be good for everyone's mental health. But what could it be?

2

The four doors of the rental SUV closed at almost the same instant. Heather looked across the hood and winked at Jack as he slipped the keys into the pocket of his shorts. He acknowledged her with a wolfish smile as they waited for Kate to round the back of the car.

"I don't know what the big secret is," said Steve. "Even a blind guy can tell we're going to a restaurant on the bay side of the island."

Kate's voice had a hint of a tease to it. "Always the detective, spoiling the surprise."

Music from a live band spilled out from the restaurant as Heather jogged across the street well ahead of the others. She walked under a series of garish signs giving the restaurant's name and the name of an additional business operated at dockside.

In a low tone, Heather addressed the hostess. "Sunset cruise?"

The cheery voice of a young woman with tattoos covering both arms pointed. "Follow the walkway past the bar, turn left, down some steps, and you'll see the catamaran docked. Sarah is there to confirm your reservations and get you on board."

The others caught up as an October sun sat above the horizon. Once past the bar and through a maze of tables they arrived at dockside. Sarah, a perky blond, checked the foursome in and said, "Thanks for coming a few minutes early. The catamaran can be a little tricky to get on and off, but if we take our time, it won't be problem."

Heather guessed the woman to be in her early-to-mid-twenties. She had one of those flawless faces, making it hard to guess her age. A knit shirt with the name of the boat embroidered on the right side, shorts, and flip-flops seemed to be the business' uniform. Typical dress code on this tropical island.

"I'll help our special guest get on board. What's your name, sir?" asked Sarah.

"Steve. Where do we sit?"

Her smile and voice invited conversation. "The most popular seats are on the bow. You have your choice since you're the first to arrive. You can sit by the rail with pillows, on what's called the trampoline, which is really a tightly woven mesh net, or we have a few bean-bags."

"I'll take a bean-bag. It'll remind me of my apartment furniture in college."

The young woman's giggle reminded Heather of Jack's niece, a sophomore in high school with a disposition as sunny as their day had been.

A voice came from the boat. "Welcome aboard. I'm Miguel."

Heather turned to see a young man with black hair and eyes just as dark. He carried himself with confidence on a small frame she guessed to be five-foot-five and one-hundred and thirty-five pounds. His attire matched Sarah's.

"If you'll help Steve climb the steps and cross the gangway, I'll help him down and get him to his bean bag," said Miguel. "There's an ice chest with water and soft drinks. Help yourself."

It wasn't long before Miguel had Steve safely seated, narrowly missing a bump on his head from the frame covering a canopy over the middle section of the boat. The back third of the vessel was for crew only. The ship's steering, a row of ice chests, and a propane-fired cook-top grill filled the deck at the stern.

With Steve settled and drinks passed out, the four breathed in the smells of Laguna Madre, a vast bay separating mainland Texas from the barrier island with the Spanish ecclesiastical title of Padre. More specifically, they were on South Padre Island, not to be confused with North Padre that ran from Corpus Christi south until it reached a natural break called the Mansfield Gap.

The band in the restaurant launched into an up-tempo number in Spanish. Kate moved her lips to the words but wasn't one to try to out-sing those being paid for their talent. She grabbed a bean bag, pushed it next to Steve, and placed her hand on his arm. "How is your revision of the short story going?"

"Slow. I've listened to a hundred podcasts on showing instead of telling and that story still sounds like a witness statement."

"Keep at it. One day soon it will click in your mind and your stories will come alive."

"If you say so." He had his bottle of water almost to his lips when he added, "Right now it's DOA."

"See," said Kate. "That's the type of line you need to include in your stories. It's spontaneous, clever, and shows the reader your voice."

The arrival of six college-age girls put an end to the conversation. They stripped off their cover ups, grabbed bottles of pre-mixed piña colada, and slithered onto the trampoline. It wouldn't have been uncomfortable if the red-head had worn something besides a thong. Heather stared at Jack with eyebrows raised and a scowl across her face. She hoped he understood the Foster Grants resting on his nose wouldn't save him if she caught him ogling. He promptly turned around and dangled his feet off the side of the boat. He stayed looking at the band until one of the young ladies said there was no hope of tanning this late in the day. The gaggle reached for their cover ups and Heather whispered to Jack that it was safe to turn around. His reward for good behavior was a kiss on the cheek.

Heather knew from the website that the boat held forty-nine guests. They'd scored the last tickets for the evening cruise. She watched as a flood of touristy-looking people filed on board. While she was at it, she counted crew members. Sarah checked people in while Miguel scurried about, helping a broad-shouldered man wearing a chef's coat with long pants. They greeted guests the best they could in between loading large ice chests. She looked around but didn't see anyone else.

Things soon got cozy as the ship filled. Many brought their own small ice chests, plastic bags, or flasks containing their favorite adult beverages. The two-hour sunset cruise promised to be well lubricated, and it didn't take long before introductions passed among strangers. A woman carrying a guitar case boarded and worked her way to the bow where a microphone was set up in front of a short barstool. She plugged in, did the usual microphone check, introduced herself, and told everyone there was a restroom on board and that they would be underway soon.

Kate talked to Steve about his short story as a movement on shore caught Heather's eye. A dark-skinned man plowed a path through the restaurant and sprang from the dock to the boat. He wore the same shirt as the crew, only a different color. A neatly trimmed salt-and-pepper beard hid his face. Standing behind the wheel of the catamaran, he pointed to Miguel. With that lone gesture, the deckhand leapt from the vessel and untied fore and aft. The singer clicked on her mic. "We're beginning our world-famous sunset dinner cruise. Sit back, relax and if you need anything, let one of the crew know." She began her first song which set the tone for the cruise—a slow ballad about lost love with the hope of something new.

The boisterous laughs and crude jokes dwindled as the burbling sounds of water striking the twin hulls had a soothing effect on the crowd. Heather's fears that the journey would be a booze cruise slipped away as the boat's engine chugged almost noiselessly somewhere far behind them.

Jack entertained a lad of about six by telling silly jokes. With multiple nieces and nephews, he had a way with kids that she sometimes envied. So far, she was sadly lacking in the maternal instincts department. She and Jack would need to discuss this, perhaps before they left the island.

With a southeasterly breeze behind them, it wasn't long before aromas found Steve's sensitive nose. "Do I smell shrimp on the grill?"

"Appetizers," said Jack. "The website said chicken and beef fajitas for the main course, followed by grilled fish. Sound good?"

"Sounds good and smells great. They're gilling onions and bell peppers and jalapeños, too. The lunchmeat sandwich I had for lunch is long gone."

The run on shrimp was fast and furious, but Sarah and Miguel brought platters until everyone slacked off and began to enjoy the scenery. Heather didn't know what to expect from the cruise in terms of where they would go. It turned out they didn't venture very far out into the expanse of water. Instead, the boat hugged the shoreline, which took it past open-air restaurants, many with live bands, homes built along canals that cut water streets into the island. One building in particular caught Heather's eye. It rose four stories high and gave balcony views to the bay. It was small in comparison to the mega condos, apartments, and hotels on the beach side, but looked peaceful, the kind of place that would attract stable residents who cared for their property. Pelicans perched on top of dwarf telephone poles that formed the skeleton of piers for a small armada of shining new boats. Heather leaned toward Kate and pointed at the building. "What do you know about that place?"

Kate shook her head. "Not much, but I can ask Connie. She's the owner of the complex where I leased for the winter. She claims to know every inch of the island and what goes on here." Kate pointed to boat docks and Jet Ski ramps. "This side of the island is so different from the Gulf side. More retirees and long-term leases. The people who live on this side of the island tend to be older with most of the party animal in them tamed."

"My speed and my kind of people," said Steve. "The beach scares me. No offense, Kate, but I like this side of the island better."

"None taken." She patted his hand. "I wish I'd known before I signed my lease."

The catamaran chugged on. The volume of voices onboard increased when several people cried out, "They're so cute!" Steve turned to Kate and said, "What's everyone looking at?"

"We passed a business that rents novelty boats. They're made of fiberglass and seat up to four. We're passing one that's a giant version of a yellow duck bathtub toy. There are also boats that look like race cars or limousines. All of them have fiberglass awnings and seem to be propelled by some sort of hidden trolling motor. You can walk faster than they can travel."

"Now you're talking," said Steve. "I might be game for an early-morning ride on one of those."

Steve couldn't see it, but Kate shook her head. "You're on island time. There's not much of anything open before noon. We could come for lunch and take one out after that." She looked at the sky. "Weather permitting, that is. I heard there's a chance of thunderstorms, but I can't remember if they said tomorrow or the next day."

Talk of boats that looked like bathtub toys and the weather ended when the singer announced fajitas were on their way. Once again, Sarah and Miguel worked the crowd with an efficiency that looked like a well-choreographed dance. His hand on the small of her back and her smile told Heather the young couple danced in places other than on the boat.

A soft whistle from the rear of the ship brought Miguel's head up. He handed Sarah his bowl and took sure steps between bodies to answer the call. Curiosity got the best of Heather, so she stood and stepped to the ice chest, where she grabbed four replacement drinks. The captain moved to one side and surrendered the wheel to Miguel. With the captain pointing, the young man made a lazy turn into a canal.

The interaction of the two sailors reminded Heather of a father teaching his adult child how to take over the family business. She wouldn't know what that was like personally since she and her father hadn't been on speaking terms for ten years. Only recently had their relationship come onto somewhat level ground. Thinking of the improved relationship brought a half-smile to her face as she regained her seat and enjoyed the view of waterfront mini-mansions.

Sarah came around with a platter of grilled fish. Despite the quality, takers dwindled. The feeding frenzy of fajitas on top of fresh gulf shrimp put a severe damper on appetites. Steve and Jack had a fillet each, but Heather and Kate had already reached their limit.

Miguel steered the boat to the end of a canal and swung it around under the watchful eye of the captain. They faced the setting sun at the precise moment it sat on the horizon, resting on still waters. Phones came out of purses and pockets and snapped photos until the orange orb dipped out of sight and the craft changed course to return to its watery bed at dockside.

Conversations softened as they seemed to glide across the still lagoon. The singer's music remained at the same volume, but became much clearer. She had talent, but like so many artists, worked mainly for tips. As the boat glided to a stop at dockside, she made sure everyone knew she was a starving artist and gave instructions on where the tip jars were located. She ended the cruise by saying, "On behalf of the captain and crew of the *Maria Elaina*, we want to thank you for sailing with us this evening.

Kate gasped when she heard the name of the catamaran. A look of near panic crossed her face.

The singer kept talking. "It was our pleasure having you aboard. If you enjoyed yourself, please tell a friend."

"What's wrong?" asked Steve.

"I need off this boat," Kate's words came out rough and ragged.

"We're at the dock now," said Heather. "It won't be long."

Being first on meant they were last off. Kate grew more agitated the longer they waited. Heather couldn't understand her sudden change. As for herself, she could have easily gone on a private cruise at that moment. Jack had closed the gap between them when the sun made its final farewell. She spent the last hour of the voyage enjoying the feel of his thumb massaging the back of her hand.

The spell was broken when Kate jumped up and reached for Steve's hand. "It's our turn."

The four of them made their way toward the middle of the boat.

"It sounds like we're bringing up the rear of the line," said Steve.

"We saved the best for last," said Sarah. "Be sure to bend over as much as you can to avoid the canopy, Steve. Come back to see us."

Miguel took over and helped Steve find the steps up to the gangplank. He made it up with no problem and waited for Kate once he reached the dock.

For the second time in one day, Kate screamed.

3

The vice-like grip of the captain's suntanned hand pulled Kate into his chest. She jerked back, but to no avail. Too stunned to move, Heather heard the bearded man speak through clenched teeth. "At last, Maria Elaina. You've come back to me."

"Let her go," shouted Jack.

The narrow confines of the boat made it impossible for Jack to get around Heather without climbing on a seat.

Heather stood behind Kate and glared at the burly man. "You heard him. Let her go!"

The captain paid no attention. His words changed to Spanish, and he sprayed them in Kate's face.

"Don't touch me, Ricardo." Words rose from a place of deep hatred. "You've already broken that arm once. Are you going to do it again?" She struggled against his grip with no success.

His gaze narrowed. He took a wide stance and pulled Kate even tighter into his chest. "I'll do whatever I have to, *mi esposa*."

Heather had heard more than enough. She stepped around Kate as much as she could, raised her sandal and stomped the top of his foot with all her might. It wasn't enough to take him down, but it did stun him enough that he released his grip. She wasted no time in placing herself between Kate and the man claiming to be her husband.

A claw-like hand grabbed Heather's shoulder as she pushed Kate toward the gangplank. To release his grip, Heather used her off hand to separate the middle finger from the rest and bent it back. The self-defense and martial arts classes she'd taken throughout her career paid off. The captain's knees buckled, and he cried out.

Turning to face Kate, Heather said, "Get out of here."

By this time, Jack had climbed over a bench and had his arms wrapped around the captain. "Go with her. I'll hold him."

Steve's voice came from below the gangplank. "What's going on?"

Heather was on the gangway when she heard the sound of a fist striking flesh behind her. No time to worry about Jack. She had to take care of Kate and get Steve out of harm's way. Kate staggered like an inebriate into the restaurant, giving no indication she even saw Steve as she passed him. Heather grabbed Steve's arm. "Come on. I'll explain later."

Heather hadn't taken three steps on dry land when a force drove her face down onto a table. She looked up to see the captain headed for Kate. A beefy man wearing a blue jean jacket without sleeves came from the area of the bar. He held out his hands until the captain ran into them. "Ricardo. What's going on?"

Kate spun around. Her voice cracked like a whip. "Come near me again and you're a dead man. Understand?" She repeated the threat in Spanish.

Instead of answering, the captain tried to get around the man blocking his path. Heather suspected the man to be a bouncer because he didn't back down. Instead, he took a step to block the captain. For the first time, Ricardo relaxed. It was a ploy. The punch Ricardo threw landed on a thick shoulder. The bouncer's muscled arm wrapped around the captain's throat when Ricardo tried again to get around him.

"Settle down, Ricardo. Do you want to go to jail?"

The captain might have responded if the choke-hold hadn't been so tight.

A soft hand on Heather's arm preceded Sarah's pleading voice. "I'm so sorry. I don't know what got into Captain Ricardo. If you'd like, I can take the lady home. You have your hands full with Steve and your boyfriend. Miguel's taking care of him."

"Is he hurt?"

"Just the wind knocked out of him."

Heather considered the responsibility of caring for three people and found the task more than she could handle. "Yes. Take Kate home." She pulled some bills from her clutch purse and extended them to Sarah. "This is for your time and kindness."

"You don't have to pay me. If you're staying on the island, it can't be far."

Heather looked to the boat, where Miguel guided Jack over the gangplank. "Take Miguel out to eat someplace special."

"Thanks, I will."

Heather watched as Sarah worked her magic on Kate, who didn't question leaving the group she came with.

"Is all the excitement over?" asked Steve. Heather couldn't help but notice the melancholy pitch to his voice.

"We'd better get out of here before the boys in blue show up."

"Where's Kate?"

"Sarah's taking her home."

Steve's huff of exasperation had an eloquence all its own. It spoke of his frustration with not being able to protect Kate, and how that weighed heavily on him. She wondered how many bad memories of a similar event would haunt him tonight.

Jack arrived with a hand over his stomach. "Sorry. I must have missed the class in hand-to-hand combat in law school. How's Kate?"

"Not good," said Heather. "I've seen a lot of angry ex-wives. She's right up there with the best of them."

Steve groaned.

"Come on, you two," said Jack. "The thought of filling out statements in a police station tonight doesn't appeal to me."

They'd almost made it past the bar when two uniformed officers came toward them. The hostess with the inked arms pointed. "That's them."

Jack's words echoed in Heather's thoughts. "Looks like we aren't going home any time soon."

STEVE SAT IN THE RECEPTION AREA OF THE SOUTH PADRE Island Police Department with his cane between his feet. He imagined those coming and going doing double takes. Heather and Jack were somewhere in the bowels of the building, giving their statements. The reception area had the new building smell until the door opened and the sea breeze brought in the distinctive odors of exhaust fumes mixed with decaying seaweed and whatever else the gulf dumped on its sandy shores.

Footsteps approached. "Mr. Smiley? Come with me, please. Chief Giles would like for you to wait in her office."

He stood. "This will be easier if I can put my hand on your arm or shoulder. No need to walk slow; I can keep up."

A small hand took his and placed it on the shoulder of a woman wearing a shirt with an epaulet.

"You haven't been on the force long, have you?"

A buzzer sounded along with a metallic click. The officer opened a door.

"Less than a month. How did you know?"

"The uniform. It has the feel of new material."

The officer walked on and turned to the right after commenting, "It's not just new, it's hot and scratchy. I'm glad to be inside this evening."

They came to a halt. Keys jangled and one scraped against metal. Another click and cooler air escaped to welcome them as footsteps came from the opposite direction.

"Thanks, Cindy. I'll take Mr. Smiley from here."

Steve waited until the mature voice said, "Three steps forward and one to your right. There's a chair with arms. Can I get you some water or a cup of coffee?"

"No, thanks," said Steve. "The coffee in police stations will make you go blind." He found the chair with no problem and lowered himself, while the woman acknowledged that the coffee in the squad room was best left alone.

Chief Gloria Giles self-identified and gave him a pat on the shoulder as she passed by. "I answer to almost anything except G.G. You've had quite an eventful day, Mr. Smiley." The voice wasn't harsh like that of a two-pack-a-day smoker, but it wasn't soft and gentle either.

"Steve. Call me Steve."

"Then you can call me Gloria. It's not every day a blind former homicide detective finds a drowned swimmer. How did you know where to search?"

"Lucky guess."

"That's not what I read this afternoon. The statements from the two lawyers with you said you knew where to look. That's not to mention Kate Bridges' account. Her version of your heroics with the drowning victim reads like one of her books."

"Kate's a great writer," said Steve. "Have you sent someone to get her statement about tonight? As upset as she sounded, they may not get much."

"Do you think it's best we not press her?"

"You'll get less emotion if you wait until tomorrow morning."

"Tell me about tonight."

The open-ended question was exactly what he expected. Gloria knew her business. She'd softened him up with conversation and friendly banter, had even done him a favor. What she needed now was an accurate account of what happened on the boat and at the dock. She'd also already proved her finger was on the pulse of the island by reading the day's reports.

Steve stalled for time, not wanting to go into a long narrative of the cruise until he knew Kate was all right. The chief must have read his mind.

"Don't worry about Kate. We won't get her statement until tomorrow. I'll try to find someone who can spell." She chuckled at her own joke. "I called in a favor from a retired psychiatrist on the island. She's with Kate now and I'll wager the shrink will have her knocked out until noon tomorrow. An officer will stay with Kate until Ms. McBlythe gets back."

Steve dipped his head and brought it back up. "Thanks. Where do you want me to start?"

"When you arrived at the boat."

"Heather and Jack thought we needed a nice, calm, dinner cruise to get all our minds off the young man drowning today. They surprised Kate and I with a voyage on the *Maria Elaina*. They didn't know it, but that was Kate's name before she had it legally changed after she divorced Ricardo."

"A messy divorce?"

Steve nodded. "It was a bad marriage with lots of documented spousal abuse by Ricardo."

"You seem to know a lot about Kate."

"I'm inquisitive." Steve launched into a fact-by-fact account of the cruise, what he heard from the gangplank, and after Heather led him to the restaurant.

A sigh came from the other side of what Steve assumed was a desk in front of him. "Sorry I can't give you more," he added as a post-script.

"There are a lot more facts in your account than what I usually get."

"I had practice... once upon a time."

A fifteen-second moment of silence passed before Gloria asked, "Why are the four of you here?"

"The surface reason for Heather is that she's considering buying apartments."

"Singular or plural?"

It was Steve's turn to laugh. "Singular, if you're talking about the entire complex. She comes from a long line of Boston McBlythes that would rather buy a hotel than rent a room."

"She has that kind of money?"

"And more every day. The only time she takes a break from making deals is when she helps me work a murder case."

Steve heard papers move on Gloria's desk. "You're not working on a case now, are you?"

He held up three fingers of his right hand. "Scout's honor. This is a business trip, with a little pleasure thrown in. I'm here so Kate can help me polish some short stories. I'm trying to learn how to write. And, as I said, Heather's here to check out an apartment complex."

"Which one?"

"The one we're staying in. I think it's called Playa Del Ray."

"That's interesting."

Something about the way Gloria said it struck an out-of-tune note. Steve tilted his head. "What's so interesting about Heather checking out that particular complex?"

"Are you sure it's for sale?"

Answering a question with another question always made the little hairs on Steve's neck start to tingle. He played it straight. "Kate told her it was a rumor going around. Heather's supposed to start snooping tomorrow morning to see if there's anything to it."

"If she finds out for sure that it's for sale, give me a call. If it's not, don't worry about it."

Steve knew better than to press too hard the first time around. He'd tell Heather to dig deep on this one.

Gloria broke his concentration. "Something tells me you being on the island involves more than buying expensive property."

Steve tapped a finger on his thigh. "For Heather and Jack it's time to get away, grab more than a few hours together and see if they still like each other as much as they think they do."

"What are their chances?"

Steve answered with a shrug. "I'm learning to write mysteries, not romance."

"And what's below the surface of the famous homicide detective and one of my favorite authors?"

Steve stood. "I thought it was clear skies and a following wind until tonight. Today's storms caught me off guard. I wasn't expecting a possessive ex-husband to pop up. That goes double for Kate. Bumping into a dead teen in the surf and being grabbed by a violent ex-husband on the same day is too much for anyone, let alone a confirmed introvert." He sat back down. "And speaking of, what are your plans for Captain Ricardo?"

"Are Jack and Heather going to throw a fit if I decide to handle this incident informally?"

Steve shook his head. "After a night to cool down, they'll defer to Kate and do what she wants."

"Then I'll let everyone catch their breath and tackle this tomorrow... or the next day. Remember, we're on island time. Things tend to move slow around here."

"What about tonight?"

"Ricardo will be my guest in a cell until tomorrow afternoon. Longer if he acts out. That way everyone will get a good night's sleep."

"One night at a time," said Steve, and then whispered the phrase again.

4

A blast of cold air hit Heather as soon as she tugged open the restaurant's door. She hugged the thin top of her exercise outfit and looked up at Jack. "I should have worn a parka."

"Get a table. I'll grab my windbreaker out of the car."

She took several steps forward and stopped in front of a sign that read: PLEASE WAIT TO BE SEATED. Jack returned with the flimsy jacket before one of a group of three employees broke their huddle and came to the counter. "Two?" she asked.

Heather nodded but wondered if the hostess had problems counting past one. She shook off the uncharitable thought and chalked it up to a traumatic yesterday, a short night, and a sub-par pre-dawn workout. The equipment at the complex's workout room left a lot to be desired, although it might have been a blessing in disguise. The previous night's spicy fajitas and a grilled jalapeño had their revenge at one-thirty in the morning.

Once seated, she gave a brief glance at the menu, then let it drop on the table. Coffee first.

"How do you do it?" asked Jack.

She tilted her head. "Do what?"

"Look so good at seven-thirty in the morning while on vacation."

She shook her head in denial. "You'll need to get your eyes checked when we get back to Conroe. I saw myself in the mirrored wall of the workout room. This is my no sleep, sweat, and spandex look. The good news is, I don't look much worse without needing hospitalization."

He flashed a smile. "I could get used to seeing you in the morning."

Her gaze shifted to the menu. It was way too early to be playing verbal lover's tag. In spite of the windbreaker, a shiver went from head to waist. She wondered if it was from the cold or the thought of a commitment that would last a lifetime.

Condensation on the windows ran down to puddles on the ledge beside their booth. "It must be forty degrees in here."

"It's chilly," said Jack as he folded his arms across his chest. "I'd say around sixty-five."

He seemed to be waiting for her to respond, but all she wanted was hot coffee.

Undeterred by her silence, Jack asked, "What do you want to do today?"

Heather turned in the booth until she spied the same three employees, huddled again, talking with their hands as much as with their mouths. She turned back to face Jack. "A cup of coffee would be a good start."

He slipped out of the booth and walked to where the trio stood and cleared his throat loud enough for her to hear him halfway across the empty restaurant. Seconds passed... then more. Finally, one of the servers looked over and spoke to Jack. In typical Jack fashion, his voice was calm, controlled and low enough she couldn't make out his words. If it had been her who approached them, there would have been no ignoring her. There was no excuse for sloppy customer service, even on island time.

Jack returned with a smile parting his lips. "They confirmed my suspicions."

"Oh?"

"They work on island time. That means they don't start brewing coffee until the first customer after daylight asks for it."

Heather looked at the menu again. "This says they're open twenty-four hours a day."

"They are, but that doesn't mean people are up and about yet. They dumped the night's left-over coffee twenty minutes ago." He threw an arm over the back of the booth. "Relax. We're on vacation and the coffee will be fresh and hot."

She took in a deep breath, allowed it to seep out, and closed her eyes. Inhaling deeply, she prepared to allow more stress to flow, but the clank of a glass on the Formica table top caused her eyes to fly open.

"Here's your water," said the server, a young woman with wide eyes and a substantial gap between her two front teeth. "Coffee is almost ready. Do you want to order now? It might be a good idea if you're in a hurry."

"No hurry," said Jack before Heather could speak.

She bit her lip, wishing Jack had asked her first about ordering breakfast. She was ready to escape this igloo. By the time coffee arrived, she was sitting on her hands.

As she sipped and used the cup as a finger-warmer, Jack spoke. "You didn't answer me a while ago. What would you like to do today?"

She pulled her left hand off the mug and began to make a list of her fingers. "First, I need to call the office and check the progress of the deal at Lake LBJ. Next, I need a shower." She held up a third finger. "After that, I'm expecting a call from a start-up software company in North Dallas. I read their prospectus last night. It's some exciting stuff and the call might last an hour or more." She tilted her head and raised another finger. "It should be getting close to noon by then and the pills the doctor gave Kate last night will probably have worn off. Who knows how long she'll want to talk. Then, I need to track down the woman that owns the building we're staying in and pump her for information."

A sliver of sarcasm accompanied Jack's question. "Is that all?"

"I'll need to check with Steve. He may need some help to research Kate's ex-husband."

"Wasn't this supposed to be a vacation for us? I didn't hear my name in anything you said. Did I miss something?"

She leaned back, not really liking the cross-examination tone Jack had taken with his last question.

The server arrived with more coffee and an order pad. "Ready to order?"

"Yes," said Heather, with more force than necessary. "Oatmeal, one piece of whole wheat toast, and keep the coffee coming."

Jack took his time. "Everything looks great. Bring me the sampler breakfast."

"Anything else?"

Jack shook his head while Heather added to the order. "Make that two samplers, but don't put the order for the second one in until you serve ours. I need it to go."

The waitress ambled away as Jack looked a little embarrassed. "I forgot all about Steve. I'm glad you remembered him."

"Did you make coffee for him before you left?"

"Sorry. Didn't think about it."

"There might be a mess on the counter when you get back, but he should be able to figure it out."

Jack looked out the window to an empty parking lot, save the one SUV they'd rented at the airport in Harlingen. "Steve's lucky he has you living next door."

Heather reached across the table, but Jack ignored her gesture by pretending he was interested in something outside. She pulled her hand back. "I know I'm a workaholic. Overachievement is as natural to me as swimming is to fish. I'm trying to cut back, but it's not easy. You have no idea what it was like for me growing up. My crib came equipped with an appointment calendar."

He turned his gaze back to her. "You find time to work with Steve whenever he needs you."

"That's just it. He doesn't need me but a few times a year. It's a forced vacation, but one that completely consumes me until he untangles all the loose threads." She tilted her head. "Are you jealous of Steve?"

He put his elbows on the table. "Don't you understand? This isn't about Steve."

Jack turned to look out the window again, then he scooted out of the booth. "I'll settle the check on my way out. Make mine to go along with Steve's. I'll eat when I get back." A set of keys for the rental rattled on the table. "I need to think. A long walk on the beach is what I need."

INDISTINCT WORDS OF A MORNING NEWS PROGRAM COMING from Steve and Jack's apartment told Heather her part-time business partner was awake. Steve opened the door and let out a sound she'd come to recognize as his pre-coffee growl. She moved past him and headed for the kitchen. He lifted his head as she passed.

"Is that breakfast for me?"

"One of them is. The other's for Jack. It may take a while for him to return."

"Ah."

Heather began the task of putting things back in the cabinet, locating a canister of coffee in the freezer, and checking the controls of the coffee pot. It looked to have been designed by an engineer getting paid by the hour. The only thing Steve had accomplished was putting water in the glass pot. "Whenever you can't find coffee, check the freezer."

"Should have known. Coffee, illegal drugs, and wads of cash wrapped in aluminum foil go in the freezer."

"Good to see you remember where to look in a drug dealer's

home." It was nice to banter with Steve. The disastrous conversation with Jack took its toll, and she needed something to splice her emotions back together.

"What's for breakfast?" he asked.

"They call it a sampler platter. I think an underemployed cardiologist came up with it. Guaranteed to harden your arteries."

Steve rubbed his hands together in a sign of excitement. "Sounds great. I'll worry about my arteries tomorrow."

It didn't take long before the aroma of strong coffee joined those of bacon, gravy, fried potatoes, scrambled eggs, and biscuits. She arranged everything on a plate and gave it thirty seconds in the microwave. She checked it and decided another twenty seconds would have everything piping hot.

Steve felt his way to the table and seated himself. His brown hair stuck out in multiple directions, which wasn't unusual. It did, however, give evidence he'd had a fitful night's sleep. "You forgot to comb your hair this morning."

"Didn't realize I'd have to stand for inspection."

She brought him a mug of coffee and released a sigh. "Don't pay attention to me. I woke up on the wrong side of the island this morning."

"I thought I had that market cornered." He took a tentative sip and put down his mug. "Do you know Jack snores?"

"Yeah. How bad was it?"

"Not bad, and it didn't matter. I'm worried about Kate. Jack told me how Ricardo went after her. It sounds like he's real trouble."

The microwave's bell dinged. Heather retrieved the plate and placed it in front of Steve. "I'll get your silverware."

She returned and said, "Eggs at six o'clock, bacon at nine, biscuits and gravy at three, and hash browns at twelve."

He nodded and located a strip of bacon. "Did you kick Jack out of the car or was it his idea to walk?"

"His, but I can't blame him. I should have left the SUV for him and ridden my broom."

It took a lot to make Steve laugh, but her comment earned a chuckle. "How far does he have to walk?"

"About four miles. He said he was taking the beach route."

A bite of eggs kept more questions at bay until he swallowed and chased it with a full swig of coffee. "Exercise will do him good. Whenever I really messed up bad, Maggie would go for a run. I'd time her to determine how big of an apology I needed to make."

It was the first time Steve had spoken his deceased wife's name on the trip. It gave Heather a clue of how he'd spent at least part of his night.

He plowed back into his breakfast. She wondered if he might be trying too hard to pretend last night's assault on Kate hadn't brought back memories of a bad night in Houston when Maggie died and he lost his sight.

Out of the blue, Steve said, "Take Jack fishing."

"What?"

"It doesn't have to be fishing, but do something fun and unexpected with Jack. Make it something he likes."

"I can't. I have a full day planned."

Steve waved a fork at her. "You always have a full day planned. What have you done now to ruin your vacation?"

She bristled at the accusation, but rattled off her schedule.

He located another bite of eggs but didn't lift his fork. "Your afternoon is free. If Kate's up to it, we'll investigate this complex and the woman who owns it. I didn't tell you last night, but Gloria took a special interest in this complex."

"Gloria?"

"Gloria Giles. The chief of police. She interviewed me." He picked up another piece of bacon. "There's something about this complex, or the owner, that Gloria's interested in."

Guilt for how she'd treated Jack at the restaurant gnawed away at Heather, but she wasn't ready to give up her afternoon quite yet. "What about Kate's safety? I'm afraid Ricardo might find out where she lives and come hassle her. Abducting her crossed my mind, too."

Steve waved off the excuse. "Gloria's keeping him locked up until this afternoon. Because we're on island time, he'll be released with only enough time to make the evening dinner cruise. You and Jack can have the whole afternoon to yourselves." He paused. "Besides, I need time alone with Kate to go over my short story. She can come here as easy as I can go to her. Even if Ricardo gets out of jail early and can find out her address, she'll be here with me."

Heather retrieved the coffee pot and topped off Steve's mug. "Parasailing would be more fun than fishing, or we could rent Jet Skis."

"Do both."

Heather nodded, the excitement building in her. "I'll call Jack after I get everything set up."

"Be home by dark," said Steve. "Ricardo may be more dangerous than we think."

5

Steve stopped dictating notes into his laptop when he heard the key slide in the door's lock. Jack's words came out in short bursts as he tried to catch his breath. "Steve. Heather said my breakfast is here. I'm starving."

"Did you run all the way from the restaurant?"

A deep breath preceded the sound of Jack flopping on the couch. "I'm so out of shape it's pitiful. It must have been a ten-mile walk. I thought I'd be a stud and run up the stairs. I only made it three of the six flights."

Steve didn't have the heart to tell him Heather clocked the distance from the restaurant to the apartment and it was a little under four miles. "Catch your breath. She put everything on a plate for you."

It didn't take long before Jack could speak in more complete sentences. "I'll get a bottle of water first. Can I get you something?"

"If you don't mind, look in my room on the nightstand and bring my phone charger. I forgot to plug it in last night."

Steve heard the slight squeak of the couch as Jack rose. His footsteps became fainter before they squeaked back into the kitchen.

"Your shoes are wet."

"How did you know?"

"They weren't squeaking on the tile floors when you left this morning. Now they are."

"No wonder Heather says you have ears like a bat."

Steve shifted in his chair. "There should be an open plug on or near the bar. I might be on the phone quite a bit this morning."

"It's plugged in and sitting on the bar. Are you working on a case?"

The clicking sound of the cap of a water bottle being unscrewed came from the kitchen. "Sort of. The local chief of police is interested in this complex. I have some calls in to people who might know why."

"People?" He paused. "Does that mean individuals who carry guns and badges?"

Steve chuckled. "Some have badges." He left unsaid that a couple of the calls he made went to characters who probably had a pistol in their waistband, but they tried to stay clear of badges. He changed the subject. "What are your plans for this morning?"

"Shopping for waterproof shoes. There's no shortage of souvenir shops on the island. It should be easy enough to find flip-flops or slides."

Steve considered what the day might bring. "Pick me up a pair of size tens of something inexpensive. Don't worry about the color."

The refrigerator door opened then shut, as did the door on the microwave.

"Are you planning to go down to the pool today?" asked Jack.

"We both are, if the property owner is there." Steve added, "Don't worry, I'll have you back in plenty of time for your date with Heather."

"What date?"

"Heather's cooking up something for the two of you to do this afternoon."

A series of beeps from the microwave sounded and the motor and fan engaged. A minute later came a loud triplet of beeps. A barstool scraped across the tile and Jack settled at the bar with the aromas of breakfast filling the apartment for the second time. He spoke between bites. "Do you know the name of the owner?"

"She goes by Connie. I did a little snooping this morning and found out her legal name is Consuelo Diaz. While you were soaking your tennis shoes in the Gulf I was making phone calls."

"The wave caught me by surprise."

Steve couldn't help but think of the fickle nature of the beach. It could be a place of awe-inspiring beauty and peaceful relaxation, or a place of sudden calamity.

"You're quiet again," said Jack. "Worried about Kate?"

"Yeah. If Ricardo turns out to be the type of man I think he is, we might all be leaving the island before we planned. Kate included."

"Do you really think he's out to harm her?"

Steve's gut clenched. "He already has. When they were married, it was physical as well as psychological. Last night he left a bruise on her wrist, but that wasn't the real wound." Steve tapped his head with his index finger. "He messed with her mind. No one should have to put up with that, especially someone like Kate."

"Do you want me to file a restraining order? I can do it today."

Steve shook his head. "Not today, but we need to keep a close eye on Kate."

Steve's first phone call came from a man he'd never met. "This is Texas Ranger Mike Moreno with Company C out of Weslaco. Is this Steve Smiley?"

Steve confirmed he was and thanked the Ranger for calling him. "Did Leo tell you what this is in reference to?"

"I didn't speak with Leo, but to Captain Lewis from Houston. He told me to call and find out what kind of trouble you're getting into this time. He filled me in on your background. Very impressive."

Steve ignored the last comment and went right to business. "I'm staying on South Padre and through an unfortunate series of events, I ended up having a conversation with the chief of police last night. When I mentioned the complex we're staying in might be coming up for sale, she seemed a little too interested. It's owned by a woman named Connie Diaz."

It was subtle, but the quick inhalation of a breath by the Ranger caught Steve's attention.

"Are you considering buying the complex?"

"Not me. My business partner in our private investigator firm might be. Her name is Heather McBlythe and she collects properties and businesses like some people collect butterflies."

Steve made out the sound of either a pen or a pencil scratching down notes. "Is there anything you can tell me about Connie Diaz?"

"Are you sure the complex is for sale?"

For the second time in as many days, a law enforcement official asked the same question. Steve knew he'd baited the hook, and some big fish were nibbling. "I'm going to try to speak with her today and find out."

The words had no more left his mouth when Ranger Moreno said, "Call me if it is. There's an open murder investigation, and up to now Ms. Diaz hasn't been cooperative."

After Steve committed himself to calling the lawman back, he closed the conversation. Then, he spoke loud enough to get Jack's attention. "I have a job for you this morning after you get back from shopping. Can you help me?"

"My morning is free."

"Kate told Heather the owner goes to the pool every day at eleven if it's sunny. I need us to find an excuse to talk to her."

"That's it?"

"Yeah. Heather says you're quite a hunk. I need you to break the ice and introduce me."

"How will I recognize her?"

"Kate told me she's hard to miss. Look for a shapely woman poured into a skimpy bathing suit."

WITH HIS NEW FLIP-FLOPS UNDER A PLASTIC CHAIR, STEVE left his T-shirt on. Jack brought him to the shallow end of the pool and made sure he had a grip on the metal bar. "Three steps down and you'll be in thigh deep water."

Steve nodded. "Is she here?"

"There's only three women under the age of thirty and two of them are with children."

"What does Connie look like?"

"Expensive."

"Interesting descriptor," said Steve. "Can you be a little more explicit?"

"Blond hair."

"Ah," said Steve. "She could be of Spanish heritage. What else?"

"Five-nine, a hundred and forty well-distributed pounds, tanned to a golden glow, and fifty cents worth of material in a hundred-dollar bathing suit."

Steve took a step into the water. "Where is she?"

"By the deep end. About twelve feet away from the water on a lounge chair. There's a ladder on the left side of the pool not far from her."

"I'll give you five minutes before I head your way. Talk loud enough for me to hear you. I'll come out of the water when I know you've broken the ice."

Steve eased around the shallow end until his internal clock told him it was time to go to deeper waters. He sidestepped around squealing children and worked his way slowly along the pool's edge until his hand brushed the chrome ladder. He went a little further and listened while holding on. His clue to exit came when Connie regaled Jack with her résumé as an actress in a Mexican soap opera.

Jack said, "Connie, there's someone I want you to meet."

Steve was already out of the water. He took his seat in a deck chair that Jack directed him to. Jack nudged him with a towel and took care of the introductions.

"Jack says you're a writer," said Connie. Her voice had a silky, sultry quality, made more so by the heavy Spanish accent.

"Aspiring writer. Kate Bridges is the real thing. She's trying to teach an old blind man new skills. I'm afraid she doesn't have a very good pupil."

"She's a nice lady," said Connie. "I understand she has company staying with her."

"Yes, Heather McBlythe, my next-door neighbor. I take care of her cat most of the time."

"Her cat?"

"He's a Maine Coon named Max. His coat feels like mink. Since Heather's so busy acquiring new properties and businesses, he and I have become good friends."

The blond bombshell now had all the information she needed to do a computer search for Heather.

Connie's voice sounded like a purr. "Jack, would you hand me my robe? I've had enough sun for the day." While she completed this act of modesty, footsteps approached and a man's rough voice interrupted.

"Mrs. Diaz, we need to talk."

"What is it this time, Mr. Zelinski?"

"The children. I require absolute quiet if I'm to get anything done. I made that clear when I signed the lease."

Connie's next words came with a thicker accent and bore an edge. "*Los niños* always make noise. Keep it up, Mr. Zelinski, and I'll turn the music to the pool back on."

Heavy footfalls carried the man away but not before he said, "One of these days, Mrs. Diaz, and you'll be sorry."

A period of several quiet seconds passed before Connie

asked, "Is Ms. McBlythe interested in purchasing property here?"

Steve tilted his head to the left. "What do you think, Jack? You know her better than I do."

Jack's chair made a tiny shifting sound, indicating he either leaned back or sat straighter. "She's always interested in investments that will yield a good return." He paused. "Heather and I are both attorneys. I do a little of everything, but she deals exclusively in mergers and acquisitions. She's always interested in a bargain. Do you know of any complexes that might be for sale here on the island?"

Steve hoped Jack hadn't pushed too hard or too fast. He needn't have worried. Their fish took the bait hook, line and sinker.

"As a matter of fact," said Connie. "I'm considering selling this place. I want to be in movies and on television again."

Steve had the information he needed, but wanted more. "Jack, why don't you call Heather and ask if she has time to meet Connie?"

"Is that all right with you?" asked Jack.

Seconds passed before Connie said, "Let me change. Can she come to the penthouse in thirty minutes?"

"I'll check," said Jack. "I know she's working on a big development at Lake LBJ this morning, but she's always looking for new projects."

Jack didn't have to stretch the truth when it came to Heather's commitment to expanding her portfolio. The phone call produced the results both Steve and Jack knew it would.

An hour and fifteen minutes later, Heather returned to Kate's where Steve and Jack waited. "It's official. Connie wants to sell, but she insists it be a cash deal, and I don't mean a bank draft or a cashier's check."

Steve picked up his phone and told it to call Gloria Giles. She answered on the second ring. "Gloria," said Steve. "Connie Diaz is interested in selling. Cash deal only."

She emitted a low groan. "Anything else?"

"I'm calling Mike Moreno to fill him in as soon as I hang up."

"You're living up to your reputation, Steve. It will save me a phone call if you tell Mike what you've learned."

Steve repeated the information when the Ranger answered the call. Steve added, "Gloria indicated you'd be the one that's most interested in Connie selling."

"I talked to my captain, and he gave me permission to clue you in. Connie Diaz's husband was found floating face down in an irrigation canal nine months ago. He was the main mouthpiece for the cartel in the Lower Rio Grande Valley. The complex you're staying in was a present to Mr. Diaz for many years of faithful service to the cartel. He was a sharp lawyer and got all kinds of bad guys off with reduced sentences, cases dismissed, and people released on bond. Most of his clients who bonded out were never seen again this side of the border."

"You must suspect Connie had something to do with it," said Steve.

"There's not a speck of evidence to suggest it, but there was a big age difference between the two of them and he wasn't much to look at. She had to have married him for the money."

Something occurred to Steve. "The cartel might not be happy with Connie if they find out she's looking for someone to dump a pile of cash on her desk so she can run off to parts unknown."

"And we would lose someone we might be able to turn into a gold mine of information."

Steve had one more question. "Do you want us to keep digging with Connie?"

"Let me get back to you on that. I'd hate to have two former cops wind up in a canal."

"Not as much as we'd hate it."

6

A dockside seafood restaurant seemed the ideal place to end a near-perfect day with Jack. Heather imagined what she looked like after an afternoon of sun and water sports, but it didn't matter. He'd seen her in much worse shape. She touched her bottom lip. The scar, a souvenir of a prior murder investigation with Steve, barely showed. More importantly, she and Jack were back on track.

The restaurant, bearing the catchy name *Shortboards*, had a vibe all its own with tables and a long bar made from discarded surfboards, cut to size, and re-fabricated. Beach-themed music poured from speakers while the walls bore enlarged photos of surfers shooting the curl or facing imminent catastrophe by wiping out. To add even more ambiance, vintage beach paraphernalia was scattered among the photos and suspended from the building's exposed metal skeleton. Lawn chairs, umbrellas, brightly colored children's buckets, metal ice chests, life jackets, and a full collection of first-generation bikinis made a captivating collection of wall and ceiling art.

Jack chuckled as he played the gentleman and helped Heather with her chair. "It wasn't that funny," she said. The lift in her voice contradicted her words.

"The look on your face was priceless. You were ready to give someone a verbal thrashing."

Heather looked back to where the hostess stood, greeting six more customers. One of the women stood before a round cage, four feet in diameter and at least eight feet tall. Inside, perched on what looked like a trapeze, swung a parrot with vibrant plumage. The woman cooed and said the line the bird must have heard a thousand times. "Polly want a cracker?"

Without hesitation, the bird replied, "I shot Polly. Bring me rum."

Jack had to turn away to keep from laughing out loud. Heather managed to keep a fairly straight face. "That's better than what it said to me."

"He spoke the truth," said Jack, trying hard to hold it together. "You do have nice legs."

"That's not all he said, and you know it."

While Jack enjoyed another laugh, their server arrived. He looked to be about thirty with dark hair corralled into a man bun. "Salty is in good form tonight. He's one of the biggest celebrities on the island." The man had a winning smile. "I'm Zeke and I'll be taking care of you tonight. Could I start you off with something from the bar and an order of fresh calamari?"

"White wine for me," said Heather.

"I'll take whatever beer you have on tap," said Jack. "Calamari sounds great."

After Zeke left, Jack leaned toward Heather. "Our server lives in the same complex we're staying in. He stopped by the pool this morning and let Connie know he didn't appreciate the noise the children were making in the pool. He said she'd be sorry if she didn't start taking him seriously."

Heather cast her gaze toward Zeke and then back to Jack. "Did Connie provoke him?"

Jack placed his palms flat on the table made from sections of two surfboards. "Connie needs to work on her people skills, but it seemed this wasn't their first point of contention."

While keeping an eye on Zeke, Heather said, "It doesn't surprise me. An hour with Connie today was all I wanted. She and Narcissus could be brother and sister."

She placed her hand over Jack's. "Tell Zeke you remember him from this morning when he confronted Connie. I want to see how he reacts."

"Why?"

"He may have more to say about Connie that will give me an idea of how she treats the tenants. I need to know what to expect if I decide to purchase the complex."

The growl of distant thunder rolled across the watery expanse of the Laguna Madre. The room grew quiet, but only for a few seconds. As if by magic, Zeke set their drink orders in front of them on cardboard coasters, along with a plate of steaming fried calamari with two white ramekins of dipping sauce. "Don't worry about the weather. It's slow moving and won't hit here for almost an hour. Are you ready to order?"

"What do you recommend?" asked Jack.

"If you like things Louisiana spicy," he pointed to a selection on the menu, "the blackened redfish or a bowl of étouffée is perfect. For fried, you can't beat speckled trout." He looked around and knelt between them, ready to divulge a secret. "We specialize in cooking what customers catch. It's not uncommon for them to bring us more than they can eat and donate the extras. There's two flounders fresh off the boat and available if I get the order in quick. You can have them plain, stuffed with crab, grilled, blackened, or fried."

"Stuffed and grilled," said Heather.

"Same, except fried," said Jack.

Zeke completed the order and scurried to the kitchen.

Heather made a point of watching Zeke work his tables while she savored their appetizer. He moved with no wasted motion, yet never seemed rushed. His ability to read the customers bordered on clairvoyance. The table next to theirs was occupied by a rather dour couple. The sunburned man stared at a television over the bar and quaffed two mugs of beer in eight minutes. The woman didn't look up from her phone and barely touched an exotic drink with a tiny umbrella sticking in it. No conversation. Zeke had the man's timing down and brought a third mug without the man having to flag him down.

Laughter rolled from Zeke's table of six, and he matched his mood to the good times.

Zeke checked back at the precise moment Jack finished his beer. "You two look like you spent the day on the water. Let me guess. You went parasailing?"

"And we rented Jet Skis for a couple of hours," said Jack.

"You'll sleep tonight," said Zeke, as if he had all the time in the world to chat. "How 'bout a fresh brew?"

"One more, and that's all."

Tired of waiting on Jack to ask what she needed to know, Heather put her hand over her half empty wineglass and looked up at their server. "Jack tells me he saw you this morning at the complex we're staying in. Have you lived there long?"

His friendly smile didn't change. "Two years. I looked up and down the island for the perfect place and the unit I'm in gives me the best combination of view and light."

"Light?" asked Heather.

He gave his head a firm nod. "I paint. Oils on canvas, and only daybreak beach scenes. It's a niche market, but I guess you could say I've been captured by the waves. Every day they speak to me and show me something different." He looked to the kitchen. "Your food should be ready by the time I get back with that fresh brew."

Another roll of thunder came across the water, but still no sign of lightning. The meal followed the delivery of Jack's second beer, just as Zeke said. A feeding frenzy with sparse conversation marked the next fifteen minutes.

After clearing the platters, Zeke returned with a single pre-cut slice of pie. "Key lime with mango. If you don't want it, I'll put it back in the cooler."

Jack pointed to a spot between him and Heather. He looked up. "Something tells me you brought two forks with you. Just in case."

Zeke placed the forks on each side of the pie, and placed the bill on Jack's side of the table. "I don't want to rush you, but the storm's getting close. You should get back to your apartment with a few minutes to spare before it hits."

Even though Heather thought she couldn't eat another bite, the explosion of flavors from the pie changed her mind. Moans of satisfaction came from Jack as he pretended to swoon after taking the first bite.

Heather pictured herself waddling, more than walking, from the restaurant and across the parking lot. She climbed into the SUV and buckled up. Lightning split the dark horizon, but the expected boom didn't occur for several seconds. "Let's get home before the bottom falls out."

Jack had the vehicle running and rolling in seconds. "Zeke sure was different tonight than this morning. I can't remember when I've had better service. He earned the extra tip I left him. Between what he makes from his paintings, and his restaurant gig, he should be doing all right."

Heather shrugged. "Could be, but businesses here are seasonal and I bet there are a lot of starving artists around."

Jack punched in the code that gave access to the gated parking lot. Driving rain pelted them before they could park. "Zeke missed his perfect streak of predictions by two minutes."

"We'd better say goodnight here," said Heather as the rain intensified. "I'll look like a drowned cat by the time I get to the door."

Jack looked at her with a single eyebrow raised. "Maybe if we sit here for a while it will slack up."

She looked out the door's window as sheets of rain danced across the parking lot. "I don't think so, and I need to relieve Steve." When she turned her head, Jack's face was only inches from hers.

"Steve and Kate wouldn't want you catching a cold."

His hand slid behind her neck and gave a gentle tug, bringing her closer. "I guess we could wait awhile and see if it slacks up."

He gave another tug. She didn't resist.

THE FIRST KNOCK ON HEATHER'S DOOR BARELY REGISTERED IN her brain. Stuck in the land between dreams and awake, she struggled to determine if the noise had its origin in the here-and-now, or if it emanated from a more ethereal world. The second triplet of knocks and Kate's strained voice gave context to the situation. The door opened and Kate appeared, fully dressed.

"Steve called. He told me to wake you."

"Wh..." Her voice cracked and Heather had to take another run at asking the one-word question. "Why?"

Kate answered while wringing her hands. "Something's happened. Police are swarming the parking lot like so many ants."

Heather grabbed a light summer robe, slipped it on, and put a half hitch in the belt. "Can you see them from the balcony?"

Kate nodded a wordless reply.

Quick, barefooted steps took Heather to the sliding door that separated the living room from the balcony. It was already open a few inches, so she hooked her hand in the metal frame and gave the door a push. Once at the rail, she had a seagull's view of a scene below. Emergency lights of red, blue, orange, and white winked, blinked, and bounced off reflective surfaces, giving the scene a kaleidoscopic appearance. Crime scene tape made irregular boxes at two locations. The first was in the parking lot. It didn't rate much attention.

Heather visually followed a wooden walkway that led to the beach. Halfway down was the place of heightened activity. "Bring me the binoculars on your bookshelf."

Kate came back in seconds. Heather made the necessary adjustments to sharpen the focus. "There's a body lying face down. If there was any sign of life, they'd be working on him, or her."

"Do you think it could involve foul play?" asked Kate.

Heather kept looking. "Considering the location, and the second place that's taped off, I'd say it's almost a sure bet."

Kate jumped when she heard an insistent knock on the door. Heather lowered the binoculars. "Don't answer. I need to see who it is first."

Heather peered through the peephole. A fisheye view of Steve and Jack had a hall-of-mirrors quality to it, but caused Heather to release a tense breath. She unhooked the chain, twisted the handle of the deadbolt, and opened the door.

"I'll take the recliner," said Steve. He spoke as he walked with sure steps, his cane leading the way. "This apartment should have a better view than ours. What can you see?"

"Two crime scenes," said Heather. "One in the parking lot and one off the boardwalk in the dunes. There's a body."

"Man or woman?"

"I can't tell."

"Details." Steve made a steeple of his fingers.

Heather recounted the basics, picked up the binoculars, and said, "Come with me. I'll tell you everything I see."

All four went on the patio. Steve and Kate sat on padded patio chairs while Heather stood beside Jack at the rail. Once again, Heather gazed at the more distant scene. "The body is dressed in black or navy and is fully clothed. He or she has black hair. The face is away from us."

"Can you tell how long the hair is?"

"Not sure, but it's definitely black."

"That eliminates one possible victim," said Steve.

"Who's that?" asked Kate.

"Connie. When I heard all the sirens this morning, I thought it might be her past catching up with her."

Heather handed the binoculars to Jack and turned to see how Kate would react. Her brows were pinched together and she was dry washing her hands. "What past are you talking about?"

"It's best you don't know at this point," said Steve. He must have realized his words could have been kinder. "I counted the number of sirens. The first arrived an hour ago and continued in a steady stream. I quit counting at fifteen. Put that with a body dressed in all black inside crime scene tape and you're looking at a homicide. If so, the police will question everyone who might know something or have suspicions. I did some background checks on Connie for Heather. What I found out could have a bearing if it's a homicide on the property. The police will want to interview everyone. I don't want to tell you yet, because what you don't know, you can't tell."

"Steve's right," said Jack. "Cops can be heavy-handed if they suspect you're holding back. They won't suspect deception if you really don't know anything."

Jack put the binoculars to his eyes. "Forensics is here. They're taking photos of the body in situ."

"Once they get enough photos," said Steve, "they'll go through the pockets and try to find something to identify the victim."

Jack handed the binoculars to Heather. She stared for several seconds. "Uh-oh. They're bagging the hands."

"Does that mean what I think it does?" asked Kate.

"Standard procedure for a homicide," said Steve. "A lot of crimes are solved by what they dig out from under fingernails."

"They're bagging what looks like a wallet," said Heather.

"That could be a good break," said Steve. "It makes a positive ID easier if there's a driver's license. Anything else?"

"There's a couple of cops at the end of the boardwalk. They seem interested in an ATV parked there."

Jack tapped Heather's shoulder. "Take a look at the other crime scene. Whoever drove up has the attention of the officers standing around."

Heather pivoted and found the person Jack referred to. "Looks like a middle-age woman."

"It must be Gloria," said Steve.

"Who?" asked Kate.

"Gloria Giles, the chief of police."

Heather chuckled. "I don't know what she said, but the officers are scattering like someone set off a stink bomb."

Steve rose from his chair. "This is when things slow down. Let's have breakfast while we're waiting."

"Waiting for what?" asked Kate.

"Gloria and one of her officers. They should be here in about an hour." The certainty of Steve's words no longer came as a surprise to Heather. When murder was in the air, Steve changed into a different man, one who rarely made mistakes.

"I'll start a fresh pot of coffee," said Kate, as she bustled to the kitchen.

Heather walked to the glass door and slid it shut to prevent any accidental eavesdropping. "Spill it, Steve. Who's the dead person in the sand?"

His words came back with force. "How should I know?"

Heather took a step toward him. "I may be half-asleep, but I'm not hard of hearing. That song and dance you did for Kate about how it would be better if she didn't know about Connie had the ring of counterfeit money to it. You snapped at her out of fear. What are you afraid of?"

Steve pulled off his sunglasses and rubbed his sightless eyes. "I may be wrong, but if that's not Connie wearing a black wig down in the sand, I think it's Kate's ex-husband, Ricardo."

Heather's stomach tightened.

"Kate's ex?" asked Jack, before he let out a low whistle. "That means Kate will be suspect number one with the cops."

"Like I said, I could be wrong. It's a good thing you were with her all night," said Steve.

"Well," said Heather. "Not exactly all night."

7

Heather traded glances with Jack. She wondered if a tinge of residual adolescent guilt was niggling him as well.

Steve took in a deep breath and allowed it to ease out. "It's your turn to confess. Were you with Kate all night or not?"

Jack played the gentleman and answered. "Heather said we needed to relieve you, so we came in at nine-fifteen. We hadn't finished our conversation, so we sort of sneaked out after you went to bed."

Steve shook his head in disbelief. "I'd better sit down to hear the rest of this. What time did you two leave and when did you return?"

Heather answered in a meek voice, "Eleven fifteen. But we never left the parking lot. The rain finally slacked off about two."

"What could you talk about for almost three hours?" Steve raised his hand to block a response. "Don't answer that. I'm not so old I can't remember late night *talks* with Maggie." He tapped the handle of his cane with a finger. "Did you see anyone coming or going?"

Jack answered in a soft voice. "I had a beautiful woman distracting me."

"Not to mention the foggy windows," said Steve, half under

his breath. He regrouped. "Did you notice any cars come into the parking lot between eleven-fifteen and two?"

"A couple, but between the rain and the people sprinting to the building, I can't give you a description."

"That means Kate doesn't have any of us to vouch for her whereabouts for almost three hours."

Steve's words chafed Heather. "You sound like the police already have a case against Kate. We don't even know if it's her lousy ex-husband on the beach or someone else. Besides, Jack and I are well past the age of consent. If we want to make out in the parking lot, that's our business."

A deep chuckle came from Steve. "That's quite a mental image. Your late-night activities don't bother me, it's the timing. For months you've been up to your eyes with work. When you finally take a half-day to have fun, look what happens."

Jack pulled a hand down his cheek and directed his next question to Steve. "How do you want to handle this?"

"Let's account for Kate's whereabouts last night before the cops get here." He stood. "It's unlikely she left the apartment in the middle of that storm, so let's not get ahead of ourselves."

Heather put a hand on Steve's arm. "Please don't get mad at me, but I'm thinking of the worst-case scenario. What if Kate went out last night?"

"That's not the worst scenario," said Steve. "Have you considered she might have killed Ricardo?"

Was it the words or the lack of emotion in Steve's voice that caused Heather to take a step back? Either way, he was in full detective mode, looking at things from every conceivable angle. He'd said on multiple occasions that it was foolish to eliminate a suspect until you were certain of their innocence.

The sound of Steve sliding the door open brought Heather's focus back. Once inside, she and Jack went to help with breakfast while Steve found the recliner, raised his feet, and sat motionless. She could only imagine what was running through his mind.

Jack suggested a light breakfast, which set the tone for everyone. Toast, coffee, fruit, and yogurt would suffice.

Once they settled at the table, Jack filled in most of the blank spots of conversation by recounting yesterday's adventures on the water and the meal at the restaurant. Their server, Zeke, received a special mention from Heather.

"Do you know Zeke?" asked Heather as she took a bowl of blueberries from Kate.

Kate shook her head. "It's the curse of creative people to be introverts. I moved in a month ago, and my interactions with neighbors have been cordial, but shallow. About all I know is he lives in this complex and he's an artist." Kate picked up her coffee. "I've been meaning to go by and look at his paintings. I think they're some kind of beach scenes."

"Beach sunrise scenes in oils on canvas," said Jack.

Steve kept the conversation going between bites. His ability to know where everyone sat made it possible for him to turn his head in each person's direction, which kept him from calling out a name or causing confusion about whom he addressed. His first comments went to Kate. "Thanks again for helping me yesterday with the short story. I think I'm finally understanding the importance of having an outline."

"Your story is coming along well." Her next words came out in short, jerky sentences. "I've given it little thought. That is, I haven't decided yet what you should work on next."

Steve leaned back and broke the somber mood with a laugh that sounded like relief from a burden. "That's the best news I've heard all day. Why don't we do something fun today instead of writing? Isn't there a big wildlife preserve up the island?"

The tiniest hint of a smile came to Kate. "It's next to Sea Turtle, Inc., a facility dedicated to rescuing and rehabilitating injured sea turtles. I haven't been to either yet, but they're on my to-do list."

"Let's go today," said Steve. "It could be a good place to pick up a fresh idea or two for a short story. What do you think, Kate?"

"Always look for the unusual. Readers tire of the same settings." Her voice trailed off as indecision infiltrated her words. "It might be best if I stayed here today." She moved the yogurt and berries around in her bowl, but didn't lift the spoon to her mouth.

"Sure. That might be best," said Steve. "I may need a nap or two myself. The sirens interrupted my beauty sleep." He made sure he faced Kate. "Did all the noise wake you, or were you still awake?"

"When Heather came in at nine-thirty, I went to bed and listened to an audio book. The pills the doctor gave me the night before worked too well. I slept through the preceding night and all yesterday morning. I didn't awaken until noon and was wide awake last night. Then came the storm. There's nothing like a violent thunderstorm to spark my imagination. The patio was my first choice, but the wind made it impossible to sit there or even have the patio door open. That's when I remembered the covered area by the pool. I dressed, grabbed my notebook, put on a hooded rain jacket and went in search of fresh inspiration."

"Did you find any?"

"I made a few notes of random thoughts for a historical thriller."

"Read them," said Steve. "I remember you telling me to make notes as ideas came to me. I'd like to hear if yours are as rambling as mine."

"I'm sure it would bore Jack and Heather."

"No," said Heather and Jack at the same time. They both apologized for stepping on each other's protest, and Jack said, "I do the same thing when I'm preparing opening statements and closing arguments for a jury."

Kate retrieved a brown leather notebook from an end-table in the living room. She opened the nine-inch by six-inch book and flipped through the pages on her way back to the table.

"This won't take long," she said as she sat. "Long shadows. Jagged fingers maul a black cloth. A cold, wet garment rends amid screams of pain. Contrast heat of lightning with cold rain-soaked sky. Slanted, unmerciful rain. A knife? No. A shot, covered by the crack of thunder. No one saw. No one can tell. Find suspects with motive, means, and opportunity. A mortal wound? Yes, but not instant. Staggering into the dark. Longer shadows, far from light. Life swallowed by the night. Murder or justice?"

Kate looked up. "See? Nothing special, just random thoughts."

Heather tried to stop it, but a shiver ran down her back and into her legs.

"I have so much to learn," said Steve. "How long did it take you to write that?"

"Not long to write, but an hour before my writing muse showed herself."

Heather did the math in her head. Kate might have been somewhere else when the person in the dunes breathed their last. She chided herself for thinking the worst of Kate. There was so much they didn't know. It might be a suicide or an accidental death or simply someone who died of natural causes. Steve's theory of it being Ricardo might be wrong.

Steve's next question to Kate brought Heather's thoughts into focus. "Did you see anyone while you were by the pool watching the storm?"

"I was the only person foolish enough to be there."

The knock on the door caused Kate to jump.

Heather rose to answer the three-tap summons. Her thoughts were still on Ricardo. Steve might be right. The answer was probably knocking on the door.

A GOLD BADGE SAT OPPOSITE A POLICE IDENTIFICATION CARD in a bi-fold leather case. Heather looked at it as the woman said, "Chief Gloria Giles and Detective Ramos. You must be Ms. McBlythe. Can we come in?"

"How 'bout some coffee, Gloria?" shouted Steve, as Heather stood aside.

"I was hoping you'd ask."

The chief of police looked to be in her early forties, with round cheeks and a turned-up nose that reminded Heather of a pug. Gloria had blond hair that didn't fare well in the wind and residual mist. Locks hung like skinny ropes to her collar while wet bangs were pasted to her forehead. She wore a slicker top, fully buttoned, and jogging suit bottoms. She turned to the detective. "Let's take off our shoes. We don't want to track sand on Ms. Bridges' floor, do we?" She kept talking to whoever wanted to listen. "Darn sand. No matter how many times you sweep and mop, it multiplies."

Steve took care of introductions and suggested everyone move to the living room while Heather and Kate provided coffee. Heather watched from the kitchen as the detective chose to stand and Gloria moved to the patio door. She said, "I see you've been watching the show."

"Not me," said Steve.

A sheepish look of embarrassment crossed the detective's face until Steve slapped his knee and laughed. "Sorry, Gloria. Making blind jokes was something I picked up when I learned to read Braille. I promise to behave." He paused only long enough to get a breath to ask, "Is that Ricardo Alvarez in the dunes?"

Kate dropped a ceramic mug, sending shards of broken pottery across the kitchen's tile floor. Her face turned an ashen color.

The detective took a step toward Steve. His voice came with both an accent and a hint of accusation. "What do you know about Ricardo?"

Gloria shifted her gaze from Kate back to her detective and

spoke with a tone of authority. "Settle down, Carlos. I warned you that Mr. Smiley was the top homicide detective in Houston. He didn't get that reputation by accident. By the way, he just tricked you into giving him the identity of the victim."

Kate's hand went to her throat. Tears filled her eyes. She tried to talk, but couldn't. She ran down the hall, leaving Heather alone in the kitchen.

Heather motioned to Jack. "There's a broom and dustpan in the laundry closet. Would you mind cleaning up this mess while I check on Kate?"

Heather tapped on the door to Kate's bedroom and walked in to find her sitting on the bed with her knees drawn up to her chest. Instead of offering sympathy, Heather spoke in her attorney's voice. "I know you've had a shock, but I want you to pull yourself together. That chief of police and the detective aren't making a social call. They suspect you have something to do with Ricardo's death."

Kate's head jerked up. "But—"

Heather didn't allow her to finish. "I'm going to ask you one simple question. Do you have any knowledge of how Ricardo died?"

"Of course not."

"Good. I know Steve already asked you, but did you see anyone last night from the time you left this apartment and you returned?"

"Not a soul."

"Are you absolutely sure? Think hard."

"It was raining so hard. I couldn't see very far into the parking lot or hear anything but rain."

Heather placed a hand on Kate's shoulder. "Dry your tears, put on some fresh makeup, and come back into the living room. Steve, Jack, and I will do the talking. I don't think it will come to it this time around, but Jack will be your attorney if you need him."

"What are you talking about? Why do I need a lawyer?"

"You may not. It all depends on when Ricardo died." Heather walked to the door, but turned back. "We'll explain everything to you after the police leave. When you're ready, come back out and have a cup of coffee. Keep it in your hand. If they ask you a direct question, take a sip. That will give us time to answer it for you."

Heather walked into the living room and said, "Kate will be out in a few minutes. It's been difficult for her."

"Difficult isn't the word," said Steve. "It's been horrible. First, she had a dead teen wrap around her legs in the surf. Next, she's assaulted by an abusive ex-husband that believed he had full title and rights to her. Then today, she learns someone stabbed her deranged ex outside her complex."

Heather noted the corner of the detective's mouth turn up. Steve had set another trap, and he'd walked into it again.

"I bet someone shot Ricardo," she said.

"You're right," said Steve. "With all the lightning and thunder last night, it would have covered the sound."

Gloria came back into the conversation. "It's still early in the investigation, but we're gathering all the information we can before memories fade. You three know the drill on homicides better than I do. Instead of me trying to drag information out of you, why don't you each tell me your movements last night."

Steve chuckled. "That might prove to be an interesting answer from Heather and Jack."

"Why'?" asked Detective Ramos.

Jack cleared his throat. "Ms. McBlythe and I had a long discussion in the parking lot between eleven-fifteen and two this morning."

"What did you talk about?"

"That's not only an indelicate question, but attorney-client privilege protects our discussion."

The muscles in Ramos' jaw flexed. Gloria spoke before Ramos had a chance to. "Pull your neck in, Carlos. What would you be talking about if you were in a car with a beautiful woman on a rainy night?" She made eye contact with Jack. "When you weren't *talking*, did you see anyone in the parking lot?"

He answered with a shake of his head. Heather spoke up. "I vaguely remember seeing a few cars arrive, but that's all. It was coming down in sheets and our discussion became rather... heated."

"I bet it was," said Steve in a loud whisper.

"Could you back up earlier in the day and give me a time line?" asked Gloria.

"Glad to," said Heather. "Steve and Kate worked on writing while Jack and I had a full afternoon parasailing and riding Jet Skis. We went to dinner and arrived back at the complex right when the rain hit. We waited in the SUV until nine-fifteen. Then, I came here and Jack went to the apartment he and Steve are sharing."

Jack picked up where she left off. "Heather and I continued our conversation in the SUV at eleven-fifteen. We stayed there until two this morning."

Gloria had a follow-up question. "Was Kate in this apartment both times when you arrived last night?"

"She and Steve were both here at nine-thirty," said Heather. "As you have probably figured out, Jack and I were very quiet when we left at eleven-fifteen. Kate's door was closed. She told us this morning she listened to an audio book after she went to bed. When I returned at two her door was still closed."

Everyone's focus shifted to Kate when she returned. She looked at Heather. "The coffee's ready. Who'd like a cup?"

Heather rose and said, "Sit down, Kate. I'm not much of a hostess, but I can get coffee."

Ramos moved to the bar and sat overlooking the dining and living room.

Heather returned with a tray of coffee mugs, cream, and sweeteners.

Gloria took a mug and settled into a chair. Then she got back down to business. "I hate to do this, but the elephant in the room is, we have a dead man in the sand dunes not more than a hundred yards from here. I can't tell you much other than I'll bet a gold retirement watch that the justice of the peace rules the death a homicide."

Gloria took a sip of coffee while her eyes shifted from Heather to Jack. "I have a police report on my desk that says Kate threatened Ricardo two nights ago. Because of that threat, I'll need to make this next part formal. Which of you will be representing Kate?"

Steve spoke while Heather was looking at Jack. "Technically, both of them, but I may need Heather working with me. Jack, you're on the clock as of now."

Heather looked at Jack with eyebrows raised. "Is that all right with you?"

"Defending innocent people is my business." He shifted his gaze to Kate. "Gloria is going to read you your rights. This includes the right to remain silent. That's exactly what I want you to do unless I tell you otherwise."

Jack turned to Gloria. "Is it your intention to arrest my client?"

"It depends on how she answers two questions." Gloria pulled out a card and read the standard Miranda warning word-for-word. She then moved to the edge of her chair. "Kate, did you shoot Ricardo Alvarez?"

Jack stood. "Let me have a few minutes alone with my client."

It only took a few minutes before Kate and Jack returned. "Go ahead, Chief Giles, repeat your question."

Gloria did so and Kate issued a firm, "No."

"Were you, in any way, connected to the death of Ricardo Alvarez?"

Kate looked at Jack. He shifted his gaze to Heather. She nodded, telling him non-verbally that it was all right for Kate to answer.

"Answer the question," said Jack.

Kate shook her head as she said, "I have no knowledge of the death of my ex-husband."

"Good," said Gloria. "That means I can have a second cup of coffee. I don't know why mine never tastes this good."

Steve took over and soon had the room distracted with a story of searching under a mobile home for a fugitive, only to discover a mama skunk and a litter of six babies. Even the dour-faced Ramos had to laugh. In fact, everyone did but Heather. Kate wasn't out of the woods yet. She had motive and opportunity. Did she have a gun or access to one? If she didn't kill Ricardo, who did? One thing she was sure of. Steve wouldn't stop until he had answers. He might laugh now, but it was all a show. By noon, they'd be looking for people with reasons for killing Ricardo Alvarez.

8

By mid-afternoon a high-pressure ridge blew away all remnants of the storm and transformed the beach back to a playground. Ambulance attendants removed Ricardo's body, and the forensic team packed their van. Heather summed up her thoughts by whispering, "Like nothing ever happened."

"What was that?" asked Jack.

She shook her head. "Nothing important." Looking up at him, she cupped his chin and cheek in her right hand. "Are you sure you won't come with me and Steve?"

"You have your job, and mine is here with my client. I wouldn't put it past Detective Ramos to come back and pump Kate for information. If he finds out she was out of the apartment in the middle of the night, things will get complicated." He took her hand from his cheek and kissed her palm. "Besides, I have plenty to do with three trials on the docket when I get home."

A text from Steve signaled an end to the conversation. Heather looked at it and let out a sigh. "The bloodhound is anxious to get on the trail. I'll see you later."

After a brief parting kiss, Heather met Steve in the hall as he summoned the elevator. Once inside, he spoke in a low tone. "I called the place that books the sunset cruise we went on and spoke with Sarah Childs. She's the deckhand that kept bringing us food and drinks until I was stuffed."

"She's a busy girl if she takes care of reservations and then works on the boat in the evenings."

The elevator door opened and conversation ceased until they were in the SUV. Once there, Heather added a bit of information Steve might not have picked up on. "I think Sarah and Miguel are a couple. No rings, but there was chemistry between them."

"Miguel? Oh, yeah. The captain's assistant."

"He took the helm halfway through the cruise and brought the boat into dock." Heather cast her gaze to her right. "What are you wanting to accomplish today?"

Steve remained silent so long she wasn't sure if he'd answer her question. Then the words flowed in a steady stream. "We need to find out what kind of man Ricardo was. Was he honest in business? Was he into drugs or alcohol? Did he have any enemies? What was he like to work for? Was he a hot-head? Did anyone besides Kate recently threaten him?"

"In other words, all the usual stuff."

"One question will lead to another, and little by little we'll learn about Kate's ex-husband."

"What about other suspects to take some of the heat off Kate?"

Steve shrugged. "I took an oath a long time ago to enforce the laws of the state and nation. It served me well to follow the evidence and not make assumptions. And speaking of, I need you to find out if Kate has experience with firearms."

Heather spoke with intended sarcasm lacing her words. "No problem. I'll walk up to her and say, 'By the way, Kate, do you happen to have a pistol under your pillow?'"

"That might work, but it wouldn't be my first choice."

"Then how would you do it?" She should have known better than to expect a straight answer.

"You have your pistol with you, right?" asked Steve.

"I always carry unless I'm traveling out of state."

"Have you cleaned it since we've been here?"

"I see where you're going. Clean my pistol in front of her and see how she reacts."

The corner of Steve's mouth quirked. But only for a second. That would be all the answers or conversation she'd receive until they arrived at the dockside restaurant.

A noon crowd of about forty customers occupied the space that could easily hold four times as many. Heather looked to the dock but didn't see Sarah. After scanning the bar and bandstand, she spotted a tiny shed-like building with a sign identifying it as the booking office for the sunset dinner cruises. She described the meager business office to Steve, and they made their way to it. A sliding window allowed transactions to be completed without customers having to come inside.

A tap on the window brought Sarah to the counter. The petite blond greeted them with a wide smile. "I didn't think I'd see you back after what happened the other night. Ready to go on another cruise?"

Heather asked, "Has anyone from the police department contacted you today?"

Sarah's countenance changed from sunny to confused as she answered with a drawn out, "Noo." She folded her arms over her chest. "What's wrong?"

Steve took over. "Could we come in and talk to you for a few minutes? I forgot my hat, and this sun is vicious."

She hesitated. "There's not much room."

"That's no problem," said Heather as she took two steps to her right and turned the knob on an unlocked door.

The office contained a four-drawer file cabinet, a makeshift desk fashioned from wood planks, one secretarial chair, two metal folding chairs, and, mercifully, a small air conditioner. Heather spoke in an even, businesslike tone as she settled Steve in a chair. "My name is Heather McBlythe, and this is my business partner, Steve Smiley. What we have to tell you isn't for everyone to know. At least not yet."

Fear laced Sarah's next words. "Has something happened to Miguel?"

Steve held up his hands. "This doesn't pertain to Miguel. It has to do with Ricardo. His body was discovered very early this morning. Someone shot him."

Sarah fell more than sat in the secretarial chair and whispered, "Thank God."

"You look relieved," said Heather.

"I'm sorry about Ricardo, but relieved it wasn't bad news about Miguel."

Steve pressed on. "Heather and I are private investigators. We're helping a friend. She's the lady Ricardo attacked on the boat the night before last. Her name is Kate and she's Ricardo's ex-wife. She wants his killer brought to justice."

Sarah's gaze went from Steve to Heather and back again. "Is she going to sue the business?"

"Why would you think that?" asked Heather.

"Ricardo promised to sell the business to Miguel." She paused to reform her statement. "I guess a better way of saying it is, Ricardo promised to sell the business to both of us. We're to get married as soon as..."

"As soon as you've saved enough?" asked Heather.

"That's only part of it. Miguel wants to wait until he has his own boat. His father captains a shrimp boat out of Port Isabel. He's a hard man and made it clear to Miguel that until he was the captain of his own boat, he'd treat Miguel like a deckhand."

"I see," said Heather.

Sarah raked her hair back with both hands and sighed. "What are we going to do now? We have our hearts set on buying this boat." She paused. "We have a cruise scheduled for tonight. Do I need to refund all the money? Is it legal for us to keep taking the boat out?"

Before Sarah spiraled down any farther, Heather raised a

hand. "I'm an attorney. Perhaps I can help. Who has access to the company checking account?"

"I keep the books, pay the bills, and make payroll."

"Do you know if Ricardo has a will?"

"He said he did. It's in a fireproof safe in the bottom drawer of the file cabinet."

"Can you open it?"

"Ricardo was forgetful with numbers so he bought a safe that you open with a key. One of them is on his key ring and the other's taped to the bottom of the desk."

Heather took in a deep breath. "Give me a dollar and I'll give it back to you. That way you'll hire me as your attorney and whatever you tell me will be confidential and so will the advice I give you."

With the transaction completed, Heather said, "Get the key, open the safe, and let me read the will."

It didn't take long before Heather had her head down, poring over the document.

"While Heather's doing that, let me ask you a few questions," said Steve. "How would you describe Ricardo as an employer?"

Heather glanced up in time to see Sarah look down at the floor. "He could be good."

"Or bad?" asked Steve.

"He had a temper, but he had a good side, too. I guess you understand about the temper after what he did the other night."

"Did he fire many deckhands?"

"Deckhands, cooks, and singers. Miguel and I are the only ones that stuck it out long enough to know he burned white-hot, but his anger didn't last long. I think it had something to do with him being from Cuba. He rarely talked about where he was from and anyone that did wasn't around long."

"Can you name any of the former employees that received especially harsh treatment?"

By this time, Heather had gleaned what she wanted to know

from the will, but pretended to keep reading, looking up long enough to see Sarah's expressions. Brown eyebrows pushed together as Sarah considered Steve's question.

"Two people come to mind. One guy left because of scheduling and the second was a woman who said Ricardo promised her a partnership in the company. She claimed he swindled her out of a lot of money."

"Do you know their names?"

"The woman's first name is Joy. I don't know her last name, but she runs the novelty boat business about a mile north of here. Look for the overgrown bathtub toys."

"And the man?"

"Zeke."

Heather's head shot up. "The same Zeke that works in the restaurant with the delicious cheese cake?"

"Yeah. Doesn't surprise me that you know him. He's hard to forget."

Heather folded the will, put it back in its envelope and handed it across the desk. She lifted her gaze to meet Sarah's. "You're in good shape. Continue to run the business like you have been until the court tells you otherwise."

"Who'll get the boat and the business?"

"I can't tell you why, but it's important that you don't know the details of the will right now. Put the will back in the safe and the key back where you found it. The police will probably come by today. You have to answer their questions truthfully, but you don't have to give them answers to questions they don't ask."

"Like what?"

Heather knew she was walking a tightrope on this one, so she took her time and hoped Sarah could read between the lines. "A while ago I asked if Ricardo had a will. You responded by saying, 'He said he did. It's in a fireproof safe in the bottom drawer of the file cabinet.' You could have stopped after the first sentence."

By the nod of Sarah's head, Heather knew the young woman

was a quick study. She put the small safe as far back in the bottom drawer as it would go.

Heather stood and passed a business card to Sarah. "Call me if you have any questions or if you can remember anything else that comes to mind about former employees." She placed her hand on Steve's shoulder. "We need to go."

He thanked Sarah for her time and said they'd check back with her in the near future. He didn't say anything else until he was in the car. While reaching for his seat belt, he asked, "What's in the will?"

"Ricardo left the boat and business to Mrs. Mary Elaine Alvarez."

Steve moaned. "AKA Kate Bridges. That will give the police one more reason to suspect Kate once they discover she changed her name." He waved his hand in a forward motion, a signal to leave. "Now I know why we had to leave so fast. Let's stay ahead of Detective Ramos as long as we can. Do you know where the lady with the bathtub boats is located?"

"A mile or so to the north. It won't be hard to find."

9

The trip to find Joy Day was short and quiet, which came as no surprise to Heather. Steve practiced a true economy of words in the early and late stages of an investigation. Like a computer program, he didn't function well until he had sufficient data to process. Heather pulled into a parking lot, some distance away from a sign directing customers to the novelty boat rentals. Steve had already unbuckled his seat belt and opened his door when she placed her hand on his arm. "Wait. There's an unmarked police car coming."

Steve closed his door. "Is it Ramos?"

"I can't tell. Whoever it is, they parked in a fire lane close to the dock." She kept looking. "It might be Ramos, but I need to get closer."

"Try not to let him recognize you."

Heather huffed. "This isn't my first time to play this game." She reached in the back seat, grabbed a silk shawl from her purse and draped it over her head. She topped it with a floppy straw hat, slipped on sunglasses, and eased out of the rental. A palm tree offered cover as she crossed an otherwise open lot covered with grass where a pair of children kicked a soccer ball to each other.

A picnic table in front of a food truck proved to be the perfect place to loiter. She purchased a glass of iced tea and sat where she could see the dock. With an unobstructed view, she was able to identify Detective Ramos, even though she was too far away to hear what he was saying. With the weather cleared from the previous night's storm, customers were taking advantage of the sunny skies and calm waters. The last boat, one that looked like a race car, eased from the dock and puttered its way into Laguna Madre, where it joined five others, including two whose bows were fashioned into toy ducks.

Ramos stood in profile to Heather, as did the woman she assumed was Joy. The distance made it impossible to get much detail of the woman other than her hair was so blond it looked white. She wore a pink sleeveless top. As far as age or other details, Heather couldn't tell.

Indistinct words came from the two, but the increase in volume and the waving of the woman's arms left the distinct impression she wasn't happy to see Ramos.

Ramos' body blocked some of what happened next. The woman returned from a table on the dock with a white, letter-sized envelope. She extended it to Ramos, plopped down with arms crossed, and looked across the bay. Ramos took quick strides toward his vehicle, bypassed it, and headed straight for her. Heather gave herself a silent chastisement. She should have been paying better attention instead of watching that cute little boat pass by. There were only two options—stay and risk him recognizing her, or go and draw attention to herself. She hoped the disguise would be sufficient and took her chances by staying seated. It wasn't long before Ramos' footsteps approached, and then slipped past her. The footfalls stopped behind her at the food truck and she heard a window slide open. "The taco plate special and a Coke."

Heather rose and walked toward the water, veered off, and charted a circuitous path back to Steve. She had to walk a couple of blocks out of the way, but it ensured she escaped discovery by Ramos.

When she arrived, Steve wasn't in a great mood. "Were you trying to bake me like a potato?"

Heather took off her hat and scarf. "You should have reminded me to leave the car running. Sorry."

"Did Ramos see you?"

"He saw me, but didn't recognize me."

"Are you sure?"

"He was too interested in getting a white envelope from the woman I assume is Joy. He also had his mind on a plate of tacos at a food truck."

"Is he still here?"

"Yeah. He must have gone for seconds."

"Lunch sounds good. Let's go to the restaurant you and Jack went to. We can talk to the waiter that lives in Kate's complex. Who knows, he may have seen or heard something last night."

Heather gave Steve a sideways glance. "Not much chance of that, and you can't fool me. You want a good meal."

"Guilty. Breakfast didn't qualify as a meal." He fastened his seat belt. "Is it far?"

"Only a couple of blocks." She maneuvered the SUV out of the parking lot while Ramos sat alone, eating tacos.

By the time Heather and Steve arrived at the restaurant, she'd filled him in on her impression of a terse conversation between Joy Day and Ramos, as well as the exchange of an envelope. As usual, Steve didn't react other than to acknowledge he'd heard her.

A purple-haired greeter with a string of metal studs pierced through her right ear took Steve and Heather to a table. "Is Zeke here today?" asked Heather.

"He called in."

"Sick?" asked Heather.

The greeter chuckled. "People who work on the island don't

call in sick, they just call in. Things are pretty loose around here, especially when the waves are righteous."

"That's a shame," said Steve. "I was looking forward to meeting him. Does he call in often?"

The greeter pulled a chair out for Steve. "First time since I've been here. But that's only been five months."

"No matter," said Steve. "If the food here is half as good as Heather says it is, we'll be coming back."

A server came and took drink orders. Heather described the decor as Steve tapped his fingers in beat with an old Beach Boys tune. When the song ended, he took a trip down memory lane. "Maggie and I used to listen to the Beach Boys every time we went to the beach."

It was this type of out-of-the-blue memory that made Heather wonder if Kate had a chance to break through Steve's memories. An abusive ex-husband had made her leery of opening her heart and seemingly put a padlock on his. It seemed that Ricardo's murder had served to leave Kate emotionally weak and Steve in a guarded mood. Heather wasn't sure if Kate would have the staying power needed to help Steve move beyond Maggie into a new relationship.

As quick as Steve's thoughts went to his former wife, he changed the subject. "Let's go see Zeke after we eat. It seems odd that a man who never misses work took the afternoon and evening off after Ricardo was murdered."

All it took was a phone call to Connie and Heather had Zeke's apartment number. "Okay," said Heather as she guided Steve. "He lives on the floor below Kate and two apartments closer to the beach. That means he should have a view of the parking lot, the wooden walkway, and the dunes where Ricardo breathed his last." Her knock on Zeke's door earned a fast, discourteous response. "Go away."

Steve stood with his hands on top of his cane. "I thought you said this guy was friendly."

"He was when a large tip was on the line."

"Try again."

The next four knocks Heather gave with more urgency. The door flew open. "What do you want?"

"Hello, Zeke," said Heather. "Do you remember me? You served me and my boyfriend before the storm blew in."

Instead of words, Zeke squinted and cast a long gaze at Heather's face. It took longer than necessary for Zeke to process the memory. He finally said, "I remember now. You and your date shared pie for dessert." He paused. "I told you I'm an extrovert at work and an introvert at home. What do you want?"

The hostility in his voice took Heather aback. Steve broke in with a voice of authority. "Heather told me you're an artist. She'd like to see some of your works with an eye to perhaps making a purchase."

This seemed to get Zeke's attention, but not enough to get him to back away from the door. "I don't sell from home to strangers."

"I'm not a stranger," said Heather. "We met at the restaurant and I'm staying on the next floor up with Kate Bridges."

"Who?"

"The lady you helped move in a couple of months ago."

The light of recognition shown in his eyes, but he still didn't budge.

Steve went another direction, still attempting to gain entrance. "Have you ever heard of Maggie Smiley?"

Another light of recognition glimmered. "I've heard of her, but I don't remember from where."

"A few of her paintings are on display in Houston galleries. Her medium of choice was water colors, but she painted in oils, too."

"Yeah, Maggie Smiley." It was almost as if his mind slipped

into the right gear. "A real talent. She did beaches from Galveston to Surfside."

"She was my wife," said Steve. "Heather has one of her works. Even though I have over a hundred more she could choose from in storage, it seems she'd like diversity in her collection."

The reluctant tenant took a step back. Steve mentioning his former wife was like punching in the right password. "Excuse the mess. Except for the cops today, I haven't let anyone in since I moved here." He looked around. "I don't like interruptions to my work when I'm at home."

Heather took stock of the living room. An easel stood in the perfect spot so Zeke could see the beach and catch the light from the sliding glass doors at the same time. The area he painted in was void of furniture save a lone barstool in front of the easel. Canvas painter's cloths started where the kitchen met what should have been the dining room and extended until they ran into the bank of windows and the glass door. Wicker baskets on a makeshift table held an ample supply of unopened tubes of paint. Used tubes filled and spilled over an engorged trash can next to the easel. Along the walls were stacked rows of unblemished canvases in wooden frames. On the opposite wall stood what appeared to be an equal number of either completed, or partially completed, works.

"You have good light to paint by," said Heather.

Zeke looked to the sliding door that opened onto the patio. "It's especially good in the mornings. I move to the patio and paint before the bulk of the people are on the beach."

She pointed to the easel. "Is this your most recent work?"

He took long steps to the easel, grabbed the canvas, and turned it away from her. "Don't look at it." He walked to what she assumed was a bedroom off the living room and closed the door behind him. He returned empty-handed.

"I'm sorry, Zeke. I hope I didn't upset you."

He lifted his chin. "I'm a serious artist and I don't like people judging my work until I can deliver the finished product."

Steve came back into the conversation. "Maggie was the same way. She'd run me out of her studio if I said anything about one of her projects before she was ready to show it."

Heather moved to the wall with what she believed were rows of completed paintings. "Do you mind if I look at these?"

Zeke nodded his permission.

Steve took over the questioning as Heather took her time examining the paintings. "That was quite a storm. Did it keep you awake, Zeke?"

"Yeah."

"And then early this morning it sounded like somebody turned on every siren in the state. I didn't know there were so many emergency vehicles on the island. That put an end to my sleep. What about you?"

"Yeah. No sleep last night."

Steve plowed on like he couldn't quit talking. "Heather says the police talked to everyone in the complex. What time did they come by here?"

Heather glanced at Zeke in time to see him run a hand down his face. "I need you to leave."

"Sure," said Steve. "I know how out of sorts I am when I don't get enough sleep. How 'bout we come back some other day to let Heather look through your paintings?"

"Yeah."

With Steve's hand on Heather's arm, she led him to the elevator. Once the metal doors came together and they were alone, she said. "Zeke's a strange guy. Like two people in the same skin."

Sometimes Heather thought Steve didn't hear her, even though she knew he did. This was one of those times. He simply said, "Let's spend the afternoon doing background checks on the five people we need to know more about."

"Five?" Heather counted fingers as she rattled off names.

"There's Zeke, Sarah the cute blond, her boyfriend, Miguel, and Joy Day, the woman with the fleet of tiny boats. Who am I missing?"

The door opened and Steve walked out of the elevator with Heather a half step behind. He stopped in the hallway. "Is anyone within sight?"

"Not a soul."

"You take Sarah, Miguel and Zeke. I'll check out Joy and Detective Ramos. Of course, everything is subject to change."

"Aah. I should have known that envelope he took from Joy Day bothered you."

"Can you think of any legitimate reason why a detective involved in a homicide investigation would be taking an envelope from a business owner?"

"It doesn't pass the smell test. Where to now?" asked Heather.

"Back to Kate's. I'll work from there. You and Jack can use the other apartment. We'll meet later and compare notes."

10

Kate opened the patio door, and Steve rose from the recliner. "Coming out with me?" she asked.

"Yeah." The door slid shut behind him. He'd gone from air-conditioned comfort to the heat and humidity of a seaside afternoon. The sounds of distant waves rolling to shore, children frolicking in the pool below, music, and an occasional squawk from a seagull assaulted him almost as much as the temperature.

"It's surrealistic," said Kate. "I still can't believe someone killed Ricardo."

"It takes a while to come to grips with death, especially a sudden death."

The scrape of the legs of a patio chair against concrete reached Steve. He heard Kate let out a soft groan as the material of whatever she was wearing slid against the cloth cushion of a chair. He felt his way around the table and chose the one remaining chair that took him out of direct sunshine and into partial shade. "I need to warn you, the police will be back," said Steve.

Kate didn't respond, so he waited.

After long seconds, Steve lowered his voice. "Did you hear me?"

"I'm worried."

"Worry's a waste of time, but you need to be prepared."

"I should never have come here. It was foolish of me to think I needed a change of scenery to spark my creativity. Now I'm suspected of killing my ex-husband."

Steve needed to bolster her hope. "You're not the only suspect. It only took Heather and me a couple of stops this afternoon to find other people with motives for killing Ricardo. Believe me, the cops are asking a lot of people hard questions."

"But I had the most reason for wanting him dead."

"You don't know that."

"Come on," she snapped. "Quit trying to paint this picture with rainbows and sunshine. I hated him. The police will have no problem finding a dozen witnesses from my past who will tell them I wished Ricardo dead."

Steve countered with, "Did you kill him?"

"No!"

"Then stop acting like you did and start trying to help me get you out of this mess."

The cushion behind Kate's back made a rustling sound. The sounds of children's laughter rising from the pool below made an incongruent background as Kate remained quiet for at least fifteen seconds. "What can I do?"

"Tell me every detail of going to the pool last night."

He heard her draw in a deep breath. "Heather tried to be quiet, but I heard her leave."

"Did that surprise you?"

For the first time since Ricardo's murder, he heard Kate issue a soft chuckle. "I've written so many sneak-out-at-night scenes in romance novels. Her leaving was a new twist on a familiar trope, and more grist for the mill. My mind started working overtime to give me a fresh perspective on a familiar plot point. I never had my protagonist run away with her lover in the middle of a violent thunderstorm. The only way I could get a grasp on the emotion of the moment was to experience it and write details."

"Details is what I need to hear." Steve leaned forward. "You can leave out the part about it being a dark and stormy night."

This brought about a genuine laugh followed by, "Touché on the cliché."

"You're in the hall," said Steve. "Did you see anyone?"

"No."

"Now you're in the elevator. Anyone there?"

"I didn't take the elevator. I took the stairs to the ground floor."

"Why?"

"Stairs in the middle of the night are scary. My lead character was afraid she'd get caught by a stalker who lived in the same apartment building, so I wanted to experience genuine fear too."

"Keep going," said Steve.

"There are two stairwells in this building, one at each end."

"Explain."

"One is near the street, and the other on the beach side. The parking lot wraps around the building on both sides, but stops short on our side which leaves room for the pool and a walkway to the beach."

Steve nodded. "Which stairway did you take down?"

"The one closest to the street."

"Why?"

"It's longer. Long hallways in the middle of a stormy night are scary, too."

"Ah. Keep going."

"I walked the length of the building through the hallway on the bottom floor."

"Did you see anyone?"

"No. But someone might have seen me. I heard an outside door open behind me so I picked up the pace."

"What were you wearing?"

"Yoga pants, tennis shoes, and a navy-blue hooded raincoat over a pink sweatshirt."

"Were your hands in your pockets?"

"Now that you mention it, I don't recall. Is it important?"

"Don't worry about it now. You said your raincoat had a hood. Was it covering your hair?"

"Uh-huh."

"Did you ever turn around so they could see your face or a piece of your profile?"

"I kept in character and walked fast with my head down."

This was going better than Steve hoped. Once Kate assumed the persona of her protagonist, she could take herself out of the retelling of her actions. He'd used this technique before on witnesses, but with mixed results.

"Tell me what your heroine did next. It might help if you closed your eyes."

"Her heart is pounding. She's standing at the doors leading to the pool. Lightning is tearing the sky and rain is coming down like it must have poured on Noah. I hear another noise behind me. Is it the closing of the door, or is someone after me? The fear of what's behind me is greater than the storm. I push open the door and sprint through the rain to the covered area. I put a concrete pillar between me and the door and peek around the corner. No one follows."

"Look around," said Steve. "Do you see anyone through the rain?"

"No." Kate's voice took on a different tone. "The muse left me. I'm myself sitting under the shelter's cover, watching rain through diffused lights and wicked streaks of lightning. I wait for what seems like a long time and jot down the notes I read to you this morning."

"Are your eyes still closed?"

"No."

"Close them and relax." He paused as she took in another breath. "Without opening them, using only your mind, look around and tell me if you see anyone or anything."

"Nothing by the pool and nothing on the balconies or on the

walkway to the beach. I'm standing to leave and glance in the parking lot." She stops talking. "Wait. What was that?"

"What is it?"

"I heard something. It was loud and sharp. Lightning and something else. Not the same, but similar."

"What do you do next?"

"I pick up my journal and go back upstairs." She took in a breath and blew it out through her mouth. "Was that a gunshot I heard?"

Steve rose from his chair. "It very well could have been." He heard her rise. "Do you know the exact time you got back?"

"Not exactly, but around twelve-twenty."

"Let's go down to the pool. We'll start where you were standing last night and take the exact route back to your apartment. If you heard a shot, we'll narrow down the time of the shooting to about fifteen minutes."

"Why is that so important?"

"To eliminate suspects. People with motive and means can't be in two places at the same time. We're looking for someone with motive, means and opportunity."

Steve pulled up short of the door. "I almost forgot. Do you own a gun?"

"I did, but not anymore. Someone broke into my place in Florida three winters ago. Like an idiot I had it in my nightstand drawer."

"Was it ever recovered?"

"The police never called." Kate was nobody's fool. She let out a groan. "One more strike against me."

"Maybe not. What caliber was it?"

"A .38 with a two-inch barrel and pink grips."

Steve didn't respond other than to say, "Let's go to the shelter by the pool."

After establishing a likely time of the attack on Ricardo, Steve went to his apartment to retrieve his computer. He needed it and his phone to do background checks on Joy Day and Detective Ramos. He was entering dangerous waters by investigating a cop, but something wasn't right about Ramos, and he needed to find out what it was. To cover his bases, he placed a call to Police Chief Gloria Giles.

She answered the call on the second ring. "I didn't expect to hear from you so soon. Have you solved the case already?"

"Not quite. But Heather and I found a witness that might have heard the shot at twelve-twenty, give or take fifteen minutes."

"That's within the window of time we're looking at. Who's this witness?"

"Before I give you the name, I want to tell you something Heather witnessed this afternoon. I'd like for this to stay between you and me for the time being."

"I'm listening, but I can't make any promises until I hear what it is."

Steve thought himself to be an excellent judge of character, so he took a chance. "We heard a rumor that Joy Day had a grudge against Ricardo, so we went to talk to her."

"The lady that runs the novelty boat business?"

"Yeah."

"Hold on, Steve. Are you snooping on your own or do you have a client?"

"Given the circumstances, Jack is Kate's lawyer, and Heather and I are kicking the bushes to see who might have a motive for killing Ricardo."

"This may be the strangest phone conversation I've ever had. My experiences with private eyes and attorneys have been adversarial. Are you trying to play me?"

Instead of answering her question directly, Steve said. "You've already checked me out. Make some more phone calls. I don't play games when it comes to murder."

"Then why are you opening up with information that might incriminate your client?"

"Because she didn't do it."

"Are you sure?"

"Ninety-nine percent."

Steve heard Gloria tapping either a pencil or pen on her desk. "Let's get back to the boat lady. What did she say?"

"Nothing to us. We went to talk to her, but Detective Ramos beat us there."

"Ramos? Are you sure?"

Gloria's voice had a different tone to it, an intensity that wasn't there before she heard Ramos' name. Steve answered her question. "Heather covered her head with a scarf and floppy hat. She wore big sunglasses and hid in plain sight at a picnic table. Joy handed Ramos a white envelope after a heated discussion."

Silence followed the sound of Gloria swallowing. "Are you sure?"

Heather pretended to take pictures of pelicans, but filmed the encounter on her phone.

The long exhale of a breath came next. "I need to meet with you and Heather. How about later tonight?"

"What time?"

"Nine-thirty. At your apartment."

"We'll be waiting."

Back at Kate's, Steve moved to the recliner while Jack reported no visitors carrying badges had showed up.

"It's only a matter of time," said Steve. "Jack, when you get back to our digs, would you tell Heather I need to talk to her?"

"Sure."

Kate rose from the couch. She may not have intended it, but she closed a book with too much force and it made the sound of a sharp whack. "I tried reading, but my mind is a jumble. Do you need to meet with Heather in private?"

"We can go on the patio."

"No need. I'll be outlining a story from the notes I took last night. Bang on my door if you need anything. I wear ear buds when I work, so make sure you knock loud."

When Heather arrived, Steve gave her a full rundown of his phone call with Gloria.

"What were you thinking?" asked Heather. "That violates every rule of confidentiality for us, not to mention Jack. He'll blow a gasket when he finds out. Why did you do it?"

Steve knew Heather was right about confidentiality according to normal practices, but this wasn't normal. It involved Kate. He searched for words and hoped for the best. "There's something twisted about Ramos and Gloria knows it. I heard it in her voice today. Think about it. Why else would she be playing cloak and dagger by coming here late tonight?"

"Nine-thirty doesn't sound late."

"I'll bet she parks along the strip and walks the rest of the way wearing some sort of disguise."

"Ten bucks?"

Steve couldn't help but smile. "Five, and don't cheat me again by giving me another one dollar bill. You know I can't tell the difference."

Heather's voice didn't sound so caustic, but she made sure he understood she didn't appreciate his breach of protocol. "I still don't understand why you told Gloria that Kate went to the pool area last night. That puts her within fifty yards of where someone shot Ricardo."

"I didn't tell Gloria it was Kate. She probably assumed—"

"Probably? You all but said her name. Two direct questions and the police will have Kate at the scene at the right time. You did everything but put the gun in her hand."

"Exactly," said Steve. "They already have enough to take her in for questioning. The best chance we have of keeping Kate out of jail is to go on the offense. That means showing most of our cards to Gloria. If we try to hide anything, she'll come with handcuffs at the ready."

"What about Jack? You all but guaranteed him coming unglued when he finds out you blabbed to Gloria."

"About that," said Steve, with a hint of devilment in his voice.

"Now wait a minute," said Heather. "Are you kidding? You want to tell the chief of police everything we know, but you don't want to tell Kate's attorney?"

"I know it sounds backward, but Jack might tell us to find another attorney. We need him. I'm not telling Kate, either."

"I'm surprised you told me," whispered Heather. "Is there anything else you'd like to tell me?"

The sound of Heather scooting to the edge of the couch caught Steve's attention. It was time to change the conversation. "How're the background checks coming?"

"One down and two to go. What about you?"

"I haven't started yet."

Heather's voice came from a higher angle. "Can I trust you to do background checks and not call the local paper with what you find?"

"Newspapers are old school. I post the juicy stuff on social media."

Footsteps away from him preceded the closing of the door to the hallway. Steve grabbed the wooden handle on the side of the chair and lifted his feet. "Time to think." The afternoon passed without incident. Jack and Heather made their appearance back at Kate's a little after six. No one felt like cooking, so Jack made a large salad while Heather called out for pizza.

With the meal completed, the next set of bangs on the door came as a surprise. Steve was the first to speak. "Jack, Detective Ramos knocked four times this morning, as has our current visitor. Let's get Kate to her room. I want to see how far he'll try to press us to talk to her."

Heather said, "Come on, Kate."

"No. I spent most of my adult life running from a man. I'm through with living in fear."

Steve admired her courage, but wondered if she was still in the heroine's mind. "Suit yourself, Kate."

The voice of Detective Ramos spilled into the apartment as soon as Jack opened the door. "I need to speak to Ms. Bridges alone."

"That will not happen," said Jack. "I'm her attorney and I'm giving you notice you may not speak to my client unless I'm with her."

"Move aside. You're interfering with an official police investigation."

Heather's voice came next. "I'm also an attorney representing Ms. Bridges. I'm going to stand beside Mr. Blackstock to block your path. If you so much as touch either of us, we'll file charges on you for official misconduct, illegal search and seizure, and assault. We told you and Chief Giles this morning that we fully intend to cooperate with the police, but we draw the line if you question our client without legal representation."

The officer standing behind Ramos asked, "Do you want me to call for backup?"

"Shut up, Juan."

By this time, Steve had made his way to the confrontation. "Let's everyone settle down. You're welcome to come in and ask anything you want. The only condition is they're going to be present to protect their client." He issued a fake smile. "We can make coffee and have a nice peaceful chat if you'd like?"

"No, thanks," said Ramos. "I'll be going for now."

The door slammed shut, and Steve didn't think it was Jack or Heather who was responsible.

Kate's shaky voice betrayed her fear. "I don't understand. Why was he so mean? He wasn't like that this morning."

As Heather and Jack returned to their seats, Steve explained. "He was with his boss this morning. The fact that he showed up here tonight gave me a read on his true personality. I'm afraid he's much like your ex-husband. That's why either Heather or

Jack will be near you as long as it takes for us to find who killed Ricardo."

"I feel like I'm already a prisoner."

"Look at the bright side. If Ramos had his way, you'd be sleeping on a hard bunk instead of in your nice soft bed tonight." Steve relaxed in the recliner. "One more visitor tonight and we can all get some sleep."

11

Nine-thirty came and went. At ten minutes after ten, there was still no sign of Gloria Giles. "Are you sure she said tonight?" asked Heather.

"It's my eyes that don't work, not my ears," said Steve in a huff. "Why don't you go back to Kate's and spend time with Jack? I'll send you a text when she shows up."

Heather squared her shoulders. "Not a bad idea. I feel like a heel being away from him when we're supposed to be on vacation."

A soft knock on the door put Heather's plans to be with Jack on hold again. She opened the door and in walked the chief of police, disheveled and red-faced. "Sorry. I was surrounded and ambushed on my way here."

"What do you mean, ambushed?" asked Steve, his voice laced with concern.

Gloria passed Steve and kept walking until the closed patio door stopped her forward progress. Her words came out fast and hard. "Someone was following me. Headlights stayed far enough behind that I couldn't get a make or model of the car." She turned and began to pace from the patio door to the kitchen counter. "I went into a store on the drag and pretended to shop while I looked out the store's windows. I didn't see anything suspicious but as I prepared to leave, a group of three teens showed up."

"How old were they?" asked Steve.

"Juveniles. Between thirteen and sixteen. All on bicycles. It wasn't long before four more rolled up. They came in together, talking loud, and cussing up a storm. They blocked me in one of the store's aisles."

"Sounds like a small flash mob," said Heather.

"Did they threaten you?" asked Steve.

"Not directly, but five of them had me pinned in while two filmed with their cell phones."

"Did you call for back-up?" asked Steve.

Gloria shook her head as she answered. "That's the mistake I made last time." She continued to pace back and forth across the living room. Steve interrupted her flow of words. "You're going to wear a path in the floor. Please sit down. Heather will get us all something to drink and you can tell us the rest of the story."

"All I need is a tall glass of cold water."

The tension in the room abated as Gloria cooled her throat and stilled her emotions. She excused herself, went to the bathroom and returned with hair brushed, looking much more put-together. "Sorry to barge in with my tongue wagging."

"No need to apologize," said Steve. "You were in a tight situation. It sounds like someone's trying to get your job and they're playing dirty. Do you know who it is?"

Gloria gave Steve a sideways glance. "Did you know someone was after my job before tonight?"

"I had my suspicions."

Heather tried not to act surprised, but couldn't help but ask, "Steve, how did you know?"

"During my research this afternoon, I found several newspaper articles that caught my eye. Gloria wasn't a unanimous choice to be chief of police."

"He's right." Gloria took another long drink of water.

"There's a vocal minority on South Padre Island that would like to see a change. I'm guessing they want someone who will look the other way when it comes to activities that benefit the cartel."

"I was wondering how much clout the cartel has on the island," said Steve.

"More than tourists realize. That's why the city leaders brought me in from outside. I don't look the other way." She tilted her body toward Steve. "What else did you discover in your research?"

"A little over a year ago, well-funded attorneys filed a civil rights case against you. The charges went nowhere, but it made a splash in the newspaper and the local television stations picked it up. Were the kids in the restaurant you were dining in Mexican nationals?"

Gloria placed her glass on a coffee table and leaned back with arms crossed. "They claimed to be from a private school in Matamoras, here to study sea turtles. I just happened to be enjoying a quiet dinner at a local restaurant when they showed up. They sat down, and immediately started causing a ruckus. The manager knew me and said he was receiving complaints. I talked to the adult in the group and told him they'd have to leave if he couldn't control the students. He cussed me out in Spanish. I called for back-up and things got loud. The video the television stations played was carefully edited. Luckily, there were other customers who filmed everything, as well as the officers' body cameras."

Steve asked, "Where does Detective Ramos fit into this?"

Gloria took in a deep breath and let it out in a huff. "I'm not sure. He may be in cahoots with the cartel or he may be an opportunist, waiting to make his move if I get canned. Now you know why I'm interested to hear the full story of him receiving an envelope from Joy Day."

Heather took over. "Before I show you the video, how did you get away from the kids who boxed you in tonight?"

"I knew they wanted me to react, so I ignored them and read the labels on T-shirts. I carry ear buds in my purse so I put on some old tunes and sang along. They gave up after twenty-five minutes of listening to my off-key attempt at singing."

"Did they ever touch you or threaten you?" asked Heather.

"Now and then, one would walk by and bump me. They'd always apologize and walk on."

"Did you say anything to them?"

"I made a point of telling them not to worry about it in English with a country drawl. I spoke that way so they wouldn't suspect I speak fluent Spanish. I learned quite a bit about them while they were talking on their phones to their handler. Poor street kids brought in for the night. Only three of them had phones."

"Two to record and one to communicate with the guy who was following you?" asked Steve.

Gloria nodded. "That's the theory I'm working with. The kid taking orders put his phone on speaker so the others could hear. I knew what they were going to do. They had instructions to provoke and bump into me, but not to take it any farther."

With the encounter relayed, Gloria seemed to right her emotional ship. She scooted forward on the couch with a new spark in her eyes. "So much for me. Let's have a look at what you recorded today."

Heather grabbed her phone off the counter, went to the couch, and sat beside Gloria. "The audio is horrible. Nothing but street sounds, seagulls, and people walking by."

After viewing the video, Gloria turned to Heather. "What do you two make of it?"

Steve answered before Heather formed her words. "It's suspicious, but it might not be as bad as it looks."

"Then again," said Heather, "it looks like some sort of payoff."

Steve jumped back in. "Gloria, you haven't asked us what we were doing at the novelty boats."

"That was one of the questions on my list. Enlighten me."

"I'll need to tell you about our first stop yesterday for this to make sense. After you and Ramos spoke to us, Heather and I decided we'd do a little research on our own."

Gloria countered with, "To find other suspects. Right?"

"Kate didn't kill Ricardo, but we know there's a nice pile of circumstantial evidence against her. I wasn't sure if Ramos would be open to looking at other people. I'm still not. Do you know if he went to Ricardo's business and talked to either Miguel Sosa or a deckhand named Sarah Childs?"

Gloria stood and walked to the window. Heather knew she would have trouble discussing the shortcomings of one of her more senior officers. It went against an unwritten code of police conduct that said cops protect each other. Steve sat mute and emotionless as a sphinx. After an uncomfortable wait, Gloria turned. "I spoke to Ramos before he left at six this evening. He said he spent the afternoon putting together a case file and doing research on Kate. He made no mention of conducting any interviews other than people in this building."

"Ah," said Steve. "Then you don't know about him and a uniform coming to Kate's this evening and trying to bully his way past Jack and Heather."

Gloria groaned. "You two had a busy day. Why don't you start with your trip to the sunset cruise office and go from there?"

Steve relayed the account of their first stop and their conversation with Sarah. Heather noticed he intentionally left out the discovery of a will.

Gloria summarized. "What you're telling me is while my detective shuffled papers and did background on Kate, you found two suspects with a motive for wanting to harm Ricardo."

"Possibly three," said Steve. "That's why we went to Joy Day at the novelty boat business. We'll try to talk to her tomorrow."

Gloria massaged her temples as she asked, "What's this about Ramos trying to get to Kate?"

"I hate to throw him under the bus," said Steve. "But he tried to bluster his way past Jack and Heather earlier this evening. He threatened them with obstruction after they told him Kate wasn't to answer any questions without one of them present."

Gloria let out a long moan and continued to rub her temples. Steve kept talking. "Heather's already mad at me for telling you so much about Kate, but there's more."

"Steve," said Heather, her voiced pitched on purpose. "We need to talk. Now."

HEATHER'S COMMAND FOR A PRIVATE, CLOSED-DOOR discussion reminded Steve of a trip he took to the principal's office when he was in the sixth grade. That experience wasn't pleasant, and he didn't expect this one to be either.

"Have you lost your mind?" asked Heather as soon as the bedroom door closed. "I looked the other way when you blabbed to Gloria earlier today, but not this time. We've always maintained strict confidentiality and now you're unilaterally changing the rules without so much as consulting me. This has to stop."

Steve sat on the bed while Heather lectured. He waited for her to stop talking before he spoke. "Anything else?"

"Yeah. If you and Kate had some sort of falling out and you're trying to ditch her, there are ways that don't involve her going to prison."

"Now are you finished?"

"You're worse than my father," whispered Heather through clenched teeth.

Steve sat another twenty seconds before the silence got to Heather. "Don't just sit there, say something."

Steve stood and spoke in a low, commanding tone. "You had your turn, now it's mine. Sit down and listen without interrupting. This isn't a courtroom, but the stakes are just as high."

The bed squeaked as Heather traded places with him. "First of all, I'm only going to tell Gloria about Kate owning a pistol that was stolen three years ago in Florida. She could find that out tonight if she started digging. I'm also going to tell her it was a .38. There's a better than even chance Ricardo was shot with something else. That will help eliminate Kate as a suspect."

"And it might not," said Heather.

Steve knew before he told her not to interrupt that he was wasting his breath. Something about being raised in Boston made her predisposed to argue.

"Look at the big picture," said Steve, with his hands outstretched. "The cops already have enough to arrest Kate, but Gloria won't if I keep trading information with her. I'll spoon out a little nugget about Kate here and there, and Gloria will reciprocate with some things we don't know."

"But what about my oath as an attorney? I have to protect Kate and do everything within my power to use the law on her behalf. That means I keep my mouth shut."

"That's why we need to split up. You and Jack will do the leg work and search for more suspects. Start tomorrow with Joy. Follow up with Zeke at the restaurant."

"What about you?"

Steve pulled a hand down his face. "When we spoke this afternoon, I told Kate it's best if Gloria knows about the pistol that was stolen. I also told her I may have to tell Gloria about the late-night visit to the pool and the gunshot. I'm going to hold that card up my sleeve and not play it unless it's absolutely necessary."

"I still don't understand why you'd tell all that."

"There's a chance Ramos already knows or will find out that someone was seen in the ground-floor hall not long before the murder. If he gets to question Kate, it will look like she withheld information and she'll be charged for sure. If I tell Gloria about it before Ramos can get to Kate, it looks completely different."

"I see your logic, but I still don't like it."

"That's why you and Jack aren't going to be a party to my game of hide and seek with Gloria. By splitting up, you two will maintain your professional integrity as officers of the court. I'm under no such obligation and can trade information with Gloria. Besides, you know as well as I do that defense attorneys and cops seldom play well together."

"I can't argue with that. What about the division of labor? It seems a little one-sided."

"I need to have a chat with Connie Diaz. I find it interesting that she was married to an attorney known for his dealings with the cartel. Now a murder has been committed on this property."

"I forgot all about her. The reason I came to this sand box was to see if this complex might be worth buying."

Heather stood but didn't step to the door. "How do you want me to play this next scene with Gloria?"

"Act like you're mad at me."

She placed a hand on his arm, squeezed, and leaned in to whisper. "It won't be much of an act."

Back in the living room, Heather issued a curt goodnight to Gloria and left without a word to Steve. He proceeded to tell Gloria about the .38 Kate claimed was stolen from her in Florida three years past. In return, Gloria told him no shell casing had been recovered from the parking lot. As for retrieving the bullet, it had been found and sent off to to the crime lab. From Gloria's description, the bullet was mangled and she doubted forensics would get anything useful from it. That was not the report he hoped to get. Kate remained suspect #1, and they both knew it.

Gloria yawned, and Steve matched hers with one of his own. It was as if enough information and emotion had been expended for one day. Steve rose and led the way to the door. "Be careful. Someone sent kids to do their bidding tonight. They may send adults next time."

"My head's on a swivel," said Gloria. "Let me know the next time you want to trade baseball cards."

Steve chuckled. "I'll be out with my nose to the ground tomorrow. Call when you get the lab reports. All I need is something that will take Kate off your radar."

The door closed and Steve went into his bedroom. He pulled out his phone and instructed it to call Mike Moreno. The Texas Ranger answered and asked what Steve had to report. "Gloria Giles is in danger and I'm not sure if it's from the cartel or her own department."

"It didn't take you long to sniff that out. Is it related to the murder of Ricardo Alvarez?"

"Possibly. Are you recording?"

"I turned it on as soon I saw who was calling."

"Good. Here's what I know so far."

12

Steve and Jack traipsed down the hall to Kate's at 9:00 a.m. "What's the weather today?" asked Steve.

"Bright and sunny. A perfect day to be at the beach, go fishing, or anything else normal people do when they come to the coast. Did you know they have the world's largest sandcastle here? I wonder if Heather would like to go see it. They even have sandcastle building classes."

"You've been studying the local hot spots," said Steve in a way that he hoped wouldn't encourage Jack too much. He knew Heather would be more interested in buying real castles than building ones out of wet sand.

Kate opened the door and bid them a good morning. Her voice sounded neutral, and she smelled freshly showered. Both were good signs. Steve walked through a pleasant plume of her perfume as his cane searched the area in front of him. Once he knew the furniture hadn't been shifted, he wouldn't need it.

Heather's voice came from the kitchen. "We decided to have a good breakfast this morning."

"Define good," said Steve.

"A fruit cup, yogurt, whole wheat bagels, and a poached egg."

Jack replied that it sounded perfect while Steve issued a tepid, "Wonderful."

Heather's next comments seemed to be directed to Kate. "Don't pay attention to his grumbling. He has clogged arteries in his brain from excessive consumption of biscuits and gravy."

Two pots of coffee later, the slow-paced breakfast ended. It took some doing, but Jack talked Heather into taking a couple of hours off to visit a nature preserve on the north end of civilization. After they left, Steve worked with Kate as he wrote seven hundred words of a short story. Kate's critique and his rewrite reduced his work to three-hundred seventy usable words. In between her pearls of wisdom, Kate cranked out two chapters of her next novel.

"It takes time and practice," said Kate with encouragement in her voice.

"Time I have. Practice I can do. It's the brains I seem to be lacking." Steve closed his laptop. "Let's go swimming. You said you do laps almost every day." He tried to sound upbeat. Kate hadn't left the apartment since Ricardo's murder, and he knew she needed sunshine and exercise.

He had to admit, if even to himself, his desire to go swimming wasn't entirely altruistic. He hoped Connie was by the pool so he could bring her into a conversation about her dealings with the cartel. He also wanted to know where she was at the time of the murder.

Kate made up a lame excuse about not going, which came as no surprise.

"Suit yourself," said Steve. "How do I get to the pool?"

She started to give him directions, but stopped with a sigh. "Go change. I'll come and get you."

The smell of sunscreen filled the elevator on the way to the ground floor. Kate's sandals made a scooting sound on the carpet in the long hallway while Steve's flip-flops popped with each step. Kate pushed open a door and Steve stepped into the incongruous world of heat from the sun's rays but no light. With his hand on her arm, Kate led him toward the pool.

"Do you see Connie Diaz?"

"She's in a lounge chair, looking like a goddess dipped in olive oil."

"Let's say hello."

Kate didn't take a step forward. "You should have told me you're on the clock."

"Huh?"

"Don't play dumb. You're investigating Ricardo's murder, and you wanted an excuse to talk to Connie."

She'd discovered his plan. "You're half right. We both could use some vitamin D and exercise. But you're right. I need to find out what I can from Connie. Watch how she reacts to my questions and make mental notes of her reactions."

A spark of excitement came in to Kate's voice. "Does this mean I'm a partner in your detective firm? When do I get a badge?"

"Let's just say you're an underpaid contract worker. Don't be afraid to talk to her. It will seem more natural since you know her better than I do."

"I'll pretend it's dialogue for a screenplay."

Steve wondered how much of her life Kate lived through the minds of her characters. "Let's go before she leaves."

The smell of chlorine permeated the air. Noise rose to the level of a school gym at a close basketball game. When Kate stopped, Steve caught a whiff of coconut oil mixed with a sweet perfume. He remembered the same scents from when he and Jack first talked with the widow.

"Connie," said Kate. "You look more lovely every time I see you."

The sultry words of thanks sounded well-practiced. "Ah. Steve. Where is Señor Jack?"

"Hot date. He and Heather went to the wildlife preserve to look at alligators, birds, and butterflies."

"Ah, yes. The mysterious Heather McBlythe. She's very lovely. Please sit, and let's talk."

The sound of a chair scooting across concrete preceded Kate instructing him to take a step back. He found the arms of the chair and lowered himself. "Much better. I even have some shade. Must be an umbrella."

"Sí," said Connie. "You tell me Steve, does Ms. McBlythe really want to buy this property?"

Steve rubbed his chin. "She was very excited when she came back from talking to you, but..."

"But what?"

Steve wiggled his hand in a way that he hoped would communicate that he wasn't sure of his next words. "She did mention that the property might be stigmatized because of the murder."

Kate spoke next. "By Connie's expression, she doesn't know what that means. To be truthful, I don't either."

"Sorry," said Steve. "Stigmatized is a real estate term. It refers to how a traumatic event can adversely affect the value of a property."

"I still don't understand," said Connie.

"The murder in the parking lot might affect the value of the property. Heather's doing additional research on it."

"That's not right. Ricardo die in the dunes."

Steve noted that when Connie's emotions flared, her English became more cryptic.

Kate's voice held a strong suspicious note. "How do you know where Ricardo died?"

"You use his name like you knew him," said Connie with a tone of accusation.

Steve needed to calm Connie down, so he answered for Kate. "They knew each other a long time ago."

"Where?"

"I don't think that's relevant," said Kate. "What about you? Did you know him?"

Steve thought he heard a hint of accusation in Kate's questions. Or, was it jealousy? He intervened again. "The four of us went on Ricardo's sunset cruise earlier this week. All was perfect until we docked. That was a bit bumpy."

The air sparked with tension. If either, or both, of the women shut down, he'd miss an opportunity to glean information. "Did you ever go on the sunset cruise, Connie?"

"Not the one you went on. My late husband hired Ricardo for moonlight private cruise."

"What fun, and how romantic," said Kate. "I'll need to be sure to use that as a setting in a future book." Kate rambled on about writing romance novels. The two finally found common ground.

"Did your husband often take you on private cruises?" asked Kate.

"Only once. From then on he invited others."

Steve needed to pull the conversation in a different direction. "The police asked us if we knew why Ricardo was in the parking lot the night before last."

It wasn't exactly truthful that the police had asked that specific question, but Connie's answer might lead to additional information. "Did they ask you the same question?"

"It didn't surprise me. Ricardo was not a young man, but he and I became friends after my husband died."

"Ah," said Steve. "An exciting Cuban boat captain. My imagination is running wild."

Kate cleared her throat, making it clear he didn't need to pursue the mental images any further.

Steve ignored her and pressed on. "How long had you been seeing Ricardo?"

"Ricardo never lasted long with any woman. I was one of many *friends*."

Time again to change the subject. "The police were rather rude to us yesterday evening," said Steve. "How did they treat you?"

"Paco came to talk to me. He's always nice."

"Paco?" asked Kate.

"Detective Ramos. I call him Paco."

Steve sensed they'd stayed as long as they could without raising suspicions that would shut off the flow of information. He rose from his chair. "Kate, are you ready to cool off?"

She stuttered out an unsure, "I guess."

He wanted the last thing for Connie to think about was the sale of her complex. Not Ricardo, or Detective Ramos. "Have you given Heather an asking price for all this?" His arms stretched out wide.

"Not yet."

"I don't know much about this sort of thing, but I believe negotiations start with the seller setting a price. After that, the buyer makes an offer. I'm sure she's crunching the numbers to see if it's a good investment."

"Tell Heather I make a good deal for her."

Steve closed with, "Kate, take me to the pool before I melt into the concrete." This wasn't far from the truth, as sweat dripped from his nose.

"Leave your shirt and shoes here."

She led him on a circuitous route and released him. The next thing he felt was a firm shove to his chest. He flew backward with arms flailing. Instead of landing on hot, hard concrete, he sank into cool water. Stunned, and not knowing how deep the water was, or which direction to go, he panicked. Then Kate's arm wrapped around his chest and pulled him to the surface. It was the first time since Maggie died that he'd felt a woman press against his back. Guilt and pleasure played tug-of-war with his emotions. Was he really ready for this?

"That felt good," said Kate.

Steve pushed his hair from his face. "What felt good?"

"Pushing you in the water. I think I took out some pent-up frustrations on you."

"Glad to be of service, but I hope you don't get the urge to repeat pushing me when we're on your balcony."

Kate's laugh had a nice tone to it, genuine and sincere, perhaps because she didn't overuse it. Her voice lowered. "Two cops just came through the gate. They're walking toward Connie."

"They must be in uniform. I hear leather squeaking and keys jingling. Go back to the chairs and see if you can eavesdrop on their conversation. I'll hang on to the side of the pool."

Between the music and the noise created by the teens and children, Steve couldn't hear anything that transpired between Connie and the officers. It was only a few minutes before Kate returned. "They're gone. Connie too."

By this time, Steve had located the ladder. "Let's go upstairs. You can tell me what they said in private."

They shared the elevator with three teens, so the update had to wait. Back in her apartment, Kate was able to give her report. "The cops received a noise complaint from Zeke. Connie did a lot of smiling and flirting while the cops took their time admiring the scenery. They told her they had to check out the complaint, but, in the end, they determined the noise wasn't excessive."

"Zeke," said Steve. "Heather and Jack are supposed to interview him again. It's odd that he keeps popping up. He was working at the restaurant the night Ricardo died. I wonder what time he got off?"

The knock on the door preceded Heather's voice. "We're back." Footsteps went into the kitchen. The refrigerator door opened, followed by the clicking sound of bottle screw tops being opened.

"You two must be parched," said Steve.

"It was horrible," said Heather.

"It wasn't that bad," said Jack in a voice that lacked conviction. "Very hot and not the most pleasant-smelling place I've ever been."

"Says the king of understatement."

Things became quiet again, except for the sounds of bottles being drained.

"A hot day must not be the ideal time to go to the nature preserve," said Kate.

"The wooden boardwalk seemed like it was ten miles long," said Heather. "I was sweating before we made it twenty yards. I should have turned around at the pond that held the juvenile alligators. It gave me the willies. There were at least a hundred of them in and around a muddy pond. They were laying on each other like soggy matchsticks. As far as other wildlife, there wasn't much to look at. We saw some interesting birds, but most of them had better sense than to fly in the heat of the day."

Jack countered with, "It's quite a facility. I wish we'd gone early in the morning or late in the afternoon."

"To top it all off," said Heather, "they built a sewage treatment plant next door. The smell was atrocious."

The lid to Kate's recycling container squeaked open and the sound of a plastic bottle hitting the bottom was soon followed by a second.

"I see you two displayed better judgment and kept cool in the pool," said Heather.

"Kate tried to drown me," said Steve, which earned him a playful sock in the arm.

Steve went into a thorough accounting of their poolside visit with Connie and the appearance of the local police. Kate wasn't bashful about joining in when she could add a detail.

Heather recounted the things that stood out to her in their narrative. "The widow of the former attorney to the cartel is on a first name basis with the detective investigating Ricardo's murder. That's worth noting. So is Connie's willingness to make a quick deal on this complex."

"You can pay me a commission for getting the price down by telling her the property is stigmatized," said Steve.

"That was a nice touch," said Jack. "Any word from Ramos or Gloria I need to know about?"

"All quiet so far," said Steve. "Are you and Heather going to pay Miguel and Sarah a visit this afternoon?"

"We were," said Heather. "But when I checked the cruise schedule today, they'd added an afternoon cruise. We'll need to catch them between the time they get back and their sundown cruise."

Steve didn't say anything, but the news of an afternoon cruise took him by surprise. It didn't take Miguel and Sarah long to make changes.

13

A band unloaded instruments and sound equipment as Heather and Jack arrived at the restaurant and bar to speak with Miguel and Sarah. Only a handful of patrons sat on stools drinking, and a few tourists were at tables eating either a very late lunch or an early dinner. The catamaran for the sunset cruise nestled against the dock, resting between voyages.

"I didn't notice the office when we were here last," said Jack.

Heather kept walking. "It's easy to miss. Let's hope Miguel and Sarah are both here."

As before, Heather went to the sliding glass window of the structure that was nothing more than a ten-foot by twelve-foot storage shed changed into a makeshift office. The smiling face of the young man appeared behind the glass and slid the barrier open. "Good afternoon. I hope your schedule is flexible; this evening's cruise is full."

Heather pulled out a business card and handed it to the man. "Remember us, Miguel?"

"Yeah, you were on the boat a couple of days ago when Ricardo attacked the woman with the blind man."

"I'm Heather McBlythe. Did Sarah tell you my partner and I came by and spoke with her?"

His head dipped as he studied the card. "Come in where it's cool."

Jack opened the door for Heather and followed her in. "Aah. Much better. The best thing about one of these sheds is, once you insulate them, a small window unit can cool them with no trouble," said Jack as a way of making small talk.

Jack stuck out his hand. "I'm Jack Blackstock, here on vacation with Heather and Steve. He's the blind guy."

"Are you a private investigator, too?"

"Attorney. I'm representing the lady Ricardo attacked a few evenings ago."

Heather took over. "We're trying to get a read on what kind of man Ricardo was. How he treated his customers and his employees. Also, what kind of businessman was he?"

Miguel extended an open palm to two chairs. "Sarah said something about you told her not to worry about us being able to run the business. What did you mean?"

"I can't give you a full explanation," said Heather, "but keep doing as many cruises as you can. Pay yourself what Ricardo paid you per hour, and everything will work out for you and Sarah." She didn't wait for him to formulate a response or an objection. "What kind of boss was Ricardo?"

Heather took stock of the young man while Miguel formulated an answer. He looked to be in his mid-twenties, but the sun may have added a year or two to his clean-shaven face. His hands gave evidence that he wasn't afraid of work.

Miguel shrugged his shoulders. "Not as bad as some."

"That's not much of an endorsement."

"Look," said Miguel. "I don't know who you are. The only reason I'm talking to you now is Sarah said I could trust you. Ask me what you really want to know and I'll give you a straight answer."

Heather gave her head a firm nod. "Did you kill Ricardo?"

"No." The quick reply came without emotion.

"Did you want Ricardo dead?"

"You can probably find people who said I did."

"Who?"

"Just people."

"Did other people want him dead?"

This question slowed Miguel as he searched the floor for an answer. After his eyes stopped moving back and forth, he nodded. "Sarah already gave you a couple of names. There are probably more that he had bad business dealings with, but I don't feel comfortable saying any names."

Heather didn't want to press him too hard, so she gave him a softball question to slow him down. "Why do you want to own this boat?"

Miguel cut his eyes in the catamaran's direction. "It's perfect, and I can triple the income. That would give me all I want in life."

"Like what?"

"I'd be more than my father ever said I'd be, and I could marry Sarah."

Heather knew she was getting to the heart of what made Miguel tick. She pressed on. "Your father sounds like mine. Good was never enough."

His eyes locked on hers. "He's the captain of a shrimp boat. I worked for him growing up, and he said I'll never be anything but a deckhand." His gaze became even more intense. "You may not understand this, but I have to be a captain of my own boat and earn more money than he does."

Heather swallowed as she thought of her father and the desire to prove herself worthy in business. Her voice cracked. "I understand." She gathered her wits. "What other reasons?"

"To prove to myself that I can support a wife and family."

"Did you think Ricardo was going to cheat you?"

"He promised to sell the boat to me at a good price." Miguel looked away. "He put nothing in writing, but he promised. Then I heard rumors he was talking with other people about them buying the boat."

"Do you know who?"

"Only rumors."

"You already said that. Who was interested in buying the boat?"

"I can't give you a name." Miguel stood and looked out the window. By now the band was doing mic checks. As soon as they began to play, it would be much harder to communicate. He sat back down. "You have to understand how things work down here."

Jack interrupted. "What do you mean, 'down here'?"

"In the Lower Rio Grande Valley, but I'm also talking about on the island. We're technically in the USA, but it's the closest thing to living in Mexico you can get without crossing the river. Sometimes, legitimate businesses find it best to sell, even if they don't want to."

Heather issued a nod to show she understood what Miguel was saying between the lines. "Was the cartel siphoning money off this business?"

Miguel's black hair shifted when he shook his head. "Sarah keeps the books. There's nothing shady going on, but this is the type of business they would be interested in. It doesn't bring in but a fraction of the money it could, especially on charter cruises."

She remembered hearing about the charter cruises Connie went on with her deceased husband. Did Ricardo enter into some sort of agreement with the cartel? She considered it and partially rejected the idea. Then she thought again. Could Ricardo's death be attributed to his turning down an offer from people who didn't like to be told no?

"Any more questions?" asked Miguel.

Heather came out of her thoughts. "Do you still do moonlight cruises?"

"Ricardo stopped about six months ago."

"What went on during those special charters?"

"It depended on the clients. If they didn't ask for anything special, we'd run them like the sunset cruises, with a full meal and stay close to shore. Ricardo made an exception for one client in particular. He was a hot-shot lawyer and had a movie star wife. Those cruises went out in Laguna Madre, away from prying eyes. It's a good thing, too. I didn't have a good feeling about them, and I wouldn't let Sarah go. Ricardo wasn't happy, but later told me I'd done the right thing."

Miguel stood again. "Sarah will be back soon with groceries for the evening cruise." He paused. "I know little about the law or wills, but I read the one in the file cabinet. It says that everything Ricardo owns goes to a woman named Mary Elaine Alvarez. It doesn't take a genius to figure out Ricardo named the boat after his ex-wife. I don't know why you're telling us we have nothing to worry about. As soon as the will is settled, I'll be back on a shrimp boat and Sarah will have to get a job in a gift shop selling T-shirts and flip-flops."

Heather ignored the accusation. "One more question before we go. Have any police officers been by to talk to you since Ricardo was killed?"

His head tilted. "Not yet."

"Expect a visit soon," said Jack.

"Should I worry?"

"Do you know and trust a local attorney?"

"Why would I need one?"

Jack answered for her. "Innocent people sometimes get convicted of crimes they didn't commit. The main reason is because they tell the police things that can be misconstrued." He gave Miguel a hard look. "Cops don't always play fair."

"Can I wait until tomorrow?"

Heather's next question caused Miguel's eyes to widen. "Where were you the night Ricardo was killed?"

"At home. We had to cancel the cruise because of the thunderstorm."

"Were you alone?"

"Sarah was with me until ten-thirty. She shares a tiny apartment with a girl she went to high school with."

Heather issued a huff. "It goes against my better judgment, but I'm going to give you some free legal advice. Call an attorney as soon as we leave. Don't let a receptionist put you off. Explain what's going on and do exactly what the attorney says."

Heather had her hand on the doorknob when she turned. "Both you and Sarah need to be completely honest about where you were when Ricardo was killed when you talk to the attorney."

"What do you mean?"

"Your attorney will explain," said Jack.

The band cranked out a long instrumental opening number. Heather and Jack wove their way around tables, past the bar, and into the parking lot. They didn't speak until Heather brought the SUV to life. "Why did you have to caution Miguel to tell the truth?" asked Jack.

"That wasn't for him. Sarah's trying to protect him. She told me and Steve she was with Miguel all night."

Jack groaned. "That one mistake could have landed both Sarah and Miguel in jail."

"Love can make liars out of honest people."

"That's fine, but I thought we were trying to protect Kate."

"We are. That's why I stressed so hard to Miguel that he needed to talk to an attorney today. The attorney will tell him not to talk to the cops. That will make Ramos doubly suspicious and it will take some heat off Kate."

"And give you and Steve more time to discover the actual killer." He glanced out the window and turned back to her, holding up three fingers. "Miguel had motive and opportunity." He wiggled the index finger. "That only leaves means."

Heather put the vehicle in gear and maneuvered onto the street. "It would be nice if we had a forensics report on the gun used."

"They may never find the murder weapon," countered Jack.

"If they can place Miguel or Sarah at the scene that might move them to the head of the list of suspects."

Jack scratched his head. "If Ramos comes after Kate, and they haven't talked to Miguel and Sarah, I may have to use them to help spread suspicion around."

Heather understood the legal maneuvering and the contingency plans. "It would be better if we had a couple more possible suspects with motive."

"Aren't Steve and Kate going to talk to the boat lady?"

"They should be there now. Let's go back to the apartment. I need to type up my notes while the interview is fresh on my mind."

"What about tonight?"

Heather looked away from Jack's inquiring eyes. "Tonight?"

"What do you want to do?"

"I'm waiting on phone calls from CPAs and people doing title research on the complex. Between what Steve and I have to talk about concerning the murder investigation and doing due diligence, I'll be burning the midnight oil."

Jack ground his teeth but said nothing else.

14

Seagulls squawked overhead. Kate's perfume competed with the smells of salt water, somewhat diluted by recent heavy rains. The fragrance Kate used was pleasant, strengthened because she sat pressed against Steve's shoulder in the tiny boat. The overall sensation was one he could get used to with little effort. "Do you have the controls on this thing figured out?" he asked.

"Not yet. Joy said she'll give me a crash-course as soon as she gets the boat that looks like a 1930s roadster out of the way."

"Crash-course may be an awful choice of words. How seaworthy is this overgrown bathtub toy?"

"We'll not search for Moby Dick in it, but there's no leaks and the water is smooth as glass."

Steve stretched out his legs. "There's plenty of room, lengthwise."

"Not that much," said Kate. "The boat can hold four passengers, with the seats facing each other. If we had company, our feet would all be tangled together in the middle. It's comfy with just the two of us."

"Hi, folks." The voice came from the direction of the dock.

It had a snappy, cheery sound to it. Mature, but not cracked with age. "Ready to shove off?"

"Show the captain how to operate it and hand me a life jacket," said Steve.

The woman laughed like she wasn't a stranger to doing so, one of those perpetually cheerful laughs. "There's one on the seat in front of you. Most people prefer to leave them off. Haven't lost but two people so far this week." The laugh made a repeat performance.

"Is this the forward and reverse lever?" asked Kate.

"Up is forward, all the way down puts it in reverse, and neutral is in between."

"How do you control the speed?"

A laugh came back, followed by an explanation. "The only speed is slow, either forward or backing up. To slow down, put it in neutral. To slow down faster, put it in reverse. That little trick will come in handy when your hour is up and you come back to the dock. Be sure you coast in. I'll be here to catch you and tell you when to take it out of gear."

"Is that all there is to it?" asked Steve.

"It steers like a car, except the wheel is mounted between you and comes up from the deck. We had to put it there to keep lovebirds like you separated. Otherwise, we'd have to change our name to The Love Boats." Her laugh erupted one more time.

The jovial owner gave the boat a gentle push and instructed Kate to lift the control to the forward position. A hum from the electric motor came on, and the little boat gurgled its way forward.

After they'd putted along about thirty seconds, Steve asked for an update.

"We're about twenty-five yards from shore. I'm turning to starboard."

"You're going nautical on me. I hope you don't expect me to swab the deck."

Kate patted his arm. "You don't live in Miami every winter

and not pick up on a few terms. I set several of my novels there and yachts played an important role in two of them."

"Tell me what Joy looks like."

"Sun-baked."

"That's a good start. A little more if you don't mind."

"I'd say late thirties. Her hair is so sun-beached it's white. She's wearing a sleeveless pink top that reached down to the bottom of stretchy black shorts."

"Height? Weight? Facial features?"

Kate took in a breath and rattled off information in a monotone voice. "5' 2", 135 pounds, round face, bright teeth, no jewelry, no wedding band, no visible scars or tattoos." She took in a breath and changed her tone to something that didn't sound like a memorized speech. "Police reports wouldn't be so dull if you put something more in them."

"Like what?"

"Like... Her sparse lashes were mere slits, hiding all but a sliver of cornflower-blue eyes guarding a nose that reminded me of a Pomeranian pup I once owned named Buster."

Steve let out a guffaw. "Do you have any idea what the other detectives would have done to me if I'd turned in a report like that?"

"That may be, but answer me this: Could you picture her with my description?"

"It made me want to know Buster."

"That's because it evoked an emotion."

Steve enjoyed these teaching moments with Kate. She'd been generous with her time, but he still wondered if he had a future in writing.

"How fast are we going?"

"Put your hand in the water. You should be able to tell."

Steve hesitated.

"Don't worry. I can swim faster than this poor duck can."

"See any dorsal fins? I'd hate for Jaws to be waiting for an afternoon snack."

"That reminds me," said Kate. "I think chapter four of your short story could use some humor to help break up the intensity. You need to give the reader a chance to breathe now and then."

Steve wasn't convinced. "Do you really think discussing an autopsy is a good place for a joke?"

"Not there," said Kate in the same tone his tenth-grade English teacher used. "At the beginning, and not with your protagonist. Come up with a quirky minor character. Use satire, irony, or gross exaggeration."

"Gross exaggeration, with gross anatomy, in a gross setting? That's gross to the third power."

Kate chuckled. "Not a terrible line for your story. Put it coming from the mouth of a neat-freak to introduce irony and you've got it."

The boat puttered along, slow, but sure. "Did the wind shift or did we change directions?"

"A slight course correction. There's a pelican in the water to our port. I want to see how close I can get to it."

"First you're trying to feed me to the sharks and now you want a pelican to finish me off."

"Oh, my goodness. He has a switch-blade knife in his wing and he's spotted you. He's coming this way. Look out!"

Kate poked him in the ribs. He grabbed her hand before she could pull it away. She didn't ask for it back or make any move to release his grip until she said, "Steve."

"Yeah."

"Do you remember what Joy said about the steering wheel?"

"Uh-huh."

"We're going in a circle around the pelican and he's giving me a funny look. You have my steering hand."

"Oh. Sorry." He released it. "I guess we need to go back and stay close to the dock. We'll wait until there aren't any boats coming back. I need some time to talk to Joy."

The trip back to the area around the dock was quieter than the trip away from it. Steve meditated on what was becoming a recurring theme with Kate. All was great until something that smacked of intimacy came into play. Then, like two magnets turned the wrong way, they pushed each other away.

When they reached the place of the boat rental, Kate told him there were several boats lined up, coming in to dock.

"Keep going," he said. "We still have plenty of time on the clock."

After ten minutes, Kate announced. "No other boats in sight. I'll turn around and bring it in."

"By the way," said Steve. "Did you say we're in the duck boat?"

"The one with the big yellow ducky on the bow."

"When we get to the dock, ask Joy to take a photo of us on your phone. You need a souvenir."

Kate's voice lowered. "I hope that's the only photo that's taken of me."

There was something about her statement that didn't sit right. "What do you mean?"

"An orange jumpsuit with a number under my chin isn't a look I want."

"You have a team to make sure that doesn't happen."

The little boat puttered and sloshed its way to the dock, pulling in without a bump.

Joy's happy voice came from above and to Steve's left. "Great job. You piloted Mr. Ducky like a pro."

"Thanks," said Kate. "It must be a trolling motor that propels it."

"A battery and a one-speed motor," said Joy. "Did you have a good time?"

"Awesome," said Steve. "I loved the canopy. It kept my noggin from frying." He turned to Kate. "Give her your camera so you'll have something to remember the moment."

The boat tilted a little when Kate stood, but despite its small size, it was surprisingly stable.

"Lean into each other and smile... got it. What a cute couple you make."

"Now the fun part," said Steve. "Getting out without taking a salt-water bath."

"I'll pull," said Joy. "You tell him how high to step and make sure he ducks his head."

It was awkward, but Steve made it out of the fiberglass boat onto the dock without incident. From there, he could feel with his cane.

"I'd like to ask you a few questions," said Steve.

"Sure," said Joy.

"It's about a man you used to work for. Ricardo Alvarez."

Like biting down on a cherry pit with a sensitive tooth, Joy's bubbly speech pattern changed. "That bum." She all but spit out the name.

"Did you know he was murdered?"

"I heard, and good riddance." She continued after a short breath. "You're not a cop, and neither is she. Why the questions?"

"I used to be a homicide detective. I'm a private investigator now and I'm trying to help out a friend who, like you, may be a suspect in his murder."

"Me? I didn't kill him, even though I thought about it plenty of times. All the promises he made. All the years I wasted with him. Yeah, I had plenty of reasons, but I didn't, so that's that."

"Do you have an airtight alibi for midnight until two in the morning?"

"If I'd known I needed one, I would have planned better." She paused. "Who's this friend of yours that the cops are interested in?"

Kate spoke before he could stop her. "That would be me. I'm his ex-wife."

Steve took a step back. The proverbial cat was out of the bag, which might prove beneficial. The interaction of the two women might glean some nuggets of information.

Joy didn't waste time. "So *you're* Mary Elaine. I heard your name plenty of times when he'd get mad. How many broken bones?"

"Four ribs and a wrist," said Kate. "What about you?"

"Only two ribs, but this nose is the after picture, as in before and after."

"I get it," said Kate. "How long were you with him?"

"Six years. How'd you get him to put a ring on your finger?"

"We were young. I was rebelling against my parents. He was looking for a wife with a birth certificate from the USA." Kate took a breath and asked, "Did he go nuts if you ever bought anything for yourself?"

Joy huffed before she answered. "That's what happened to the nose. I bought a new pair of cross-trainers without asking permission."

Steve noticed the longer the two women talked, the more they calmed down. He felt like the third on a date. No, not exactly, but this was definitely a conversation you waited to be invited to join.

"We have a lot in common," said Joy.

"Yeah. We're both suspects."

The next thing out of Joy's mouth took Steve by complete surprise. "The cops haven't talked to me yet." Joy's voice changed again. "I may have spoken too soon. Here comes Detective Ramos, and he's not smiling."

"How far away is he?" asked Steve as he pulled out his phone and said, "Call Heather."

"He's almost here. There's another cop car pulling up to join him."

"I need you now," said Steve into the phone. "We're at the toy boat dock."

A hand snatched the phone from his grasp.

15

The dock creaked under the weight of additional people. The first voice Steve heard after Ramos took his phone came from Joy. Her tone didn't match her name. "Give it back to him."

"Stay out of this."

Steve controlled his breathing and spoke in a quiet, firm voice. "That wasn't the brightest thing to do, detective. Even a blind man can tell there are multiple witnesses watching you now. Look around. There's a police body camera recording. If you give me back my phone, I might not press charges."

"Give it back, you overpaid errand boy," shouted Joy.

"One more word from you and you're going to jail."

Steve expected what Ramos' next words would be, and he didn't disappoint. "Kate Bridges, you're under arrest for the murder of Ricardo Alvarez. Put your hands behind your back."

The sound of handcuffs ratcheting shut was accompanied by the standard warning police give at every arrest. Ramos followed this with, "Officer Blake will take you to her car and pat you down. If you have anything illegal on you, you'd better tell her now."

"Wait a minute," said Steve, trying to keep the worry out of his voice.

"Take her," said Ramos.

"Don't tell them anything except your name," said Steve.

Kate's fears of wearing an orange jumpsuit were coming to pass. Steve needed to act, but without his phone, he could do nothing.

"My phone," said Steve in a much harsher tone.

"It's evidence."

"Without a warrant? What crime do you suspect I've committed?"

Steve knew he was on solid legal ground and Ramos was making one mistake after the next. He had to know better, so Steve changed his tactics. "I tell you what, detective. You take me with you to the station and I'll let you look at whatever you want to on my phone."

"This isn't a game, Smiley."

"Use your brain, Ramos. Have you considered what kind of grief those two attorneys I came with can bring down on you?"

"Are you threatening a police officer?"

Steve responded with a sarcastic laugh. "A blind guy threatening a young stud like you? I only asked a question. How you interpret it is up to you." He paused. "Or, it might be up to a judge to interpret it. Do you want to bet your job how that ruling will go?"

Steve had not only moved to block Ramos' path off the dock, but backed him up to where Joy stood at the end of the dock. He also had used his cane to find the locations of the toy boats. Steve's plan was to give Heather and Jack time to get to him.

"Out of my way, Smiley."

Steve shook his head. "First, my phone."

"No way. Move or go to jail."

The next thing Steve heard was a splash. Joy's laugh preceded the change of her voice to a somber tone. "I'm so sorry, Detective Ramos. My flip-flop got caught on a board. I didn't mean to bump into you."

While Ramos thrashed in the water, making accusations and threats, a hand found Steve's. He felt a thin, rectangular object being passed to him.

Joy whispered, "Don't tell anyone, but I dated a guy who taught me how to lift wallets. It works for cell phones, too."

"Thanks."

Tires squealed. "Steve," shouted Heather.

"On the dock."

Joy took Steve by the arm and brought him to dry land. "I'd better make sure Ramos doesn't drown."

"He'll probably arrest you."

"Won't be my first. This time it was worth it."

"I'll be in touch," said Steve. He motioned to Heather. "They took Kate."

Heather took his hand and placed it on her arm. "I dropped Jack at the police station. We saw the officer arrive with her."

When he wanted to Steve could relay vast amounts of detailed information in a short time. Heather concluded he didn't want to when he issued a one sentence explanation. "Ramos showed up mad and arrested Kate."

"Why now?"

Steve didn't reply.

She swung the SUV into a parking spot and hurried around the vehicle to get Steve. He mumbled, "This is twice in one week to be here. Demand to speak to Chief Giles when we get inside."

Jack met them in the lobby. "They're booking her in. I can't see her until they finish the preliminaries."

Heather took Steve to a window that separated them from an officer and a couple of employees dressed in business casual. As Heather approached, the window slid open.

"Can I help you?" The officer looked to be pushing retirement with tired eyes and a substantial paunch.

"Would you tell Chief Giles that Heather McBlythe and Steve Smiley are here to see her?"

"Not possible."

He tried to close the window. Heather stuck her arm in it. He responded with an impatient scowl and a terse, "Take your arm out. She's not here."

Steve had heard enough. "Call her on her radio. She'll want to talk to us."

"Not possible." The man pointed to Jack. "Are you with him?"

Heather nodded. "I'm also an attorney."

The officer pointed to a row of chairs. "Take a seat. As soon as we're through with photographs and fingerprints, you can see your client."

"Come on, Heather. I have an idea. Take me outside."

Heather motioned for Jack to follow them. She led them to a spot in the shade, away from prying eyes and listening ears. "No one can hear us."

Steve had his phone in hand. "Call Mike Moreno."

The Ranger didn't mince words. "Yeah, Steve. I guess you heard."

"Heard what?"

"Someone ran Gloria Giles off the road on her way to Brownsville this morning."

"That's news to me. Was she injured?"

"The last I heard she's going for X-rays and a CT scan."

Steve let out a sigh. "That explains why Detective Ramos arrested Kate Bridges."

"He did? When?"

"Less than fifteen minutes ago. He's trying to pin the murder charge on her. Gloria's had him on a short leash, but that's all changed now that she's out of the way."

The next words from the Ranger came out sounding like an

apology. "Are you sure she had nothing to do with killing her ex?"

"I'll stake my pension on it," said Steve, without hesitation. "But." He let the word hang in the air. "There's a lot of circumstantial evidence against her."

"That's not good. I doubt there's anything I can do to keep her out of county jail."

"I wouldn't ask you to. Where will they take her?"

"On a murder charge, they'll transport her to Brownsville, the county seat for Cameron County. Anything else?"

"Yeah. This whole thing smells like rotten fish. Without trying, I've been able to find four other people with a grudge against Ricardo Alvarez. The police haven't spoken to any of them."

"That might help Kate's attorney get her out on bond."

Heather and Jack traded glances and head nods.

Mike Moreno spoke up. "Have they searched Kate's apartment yet?"

"I was thinking the same thing," said Steve. "I need to go."

"I'll call later and give an update on Gloria."

Steve wasted no time. "Heather, you and I need to get to the complex. I wouldn't put it past someone to have planted something in Kate's apartment."

Jack's raised eyebrows spoke of disappointment. "I'll drop you two off and come back to speak with Kate. Since it's late Friday afternoon, they'll likely leave Kate here overnight and take her to Brownsville tomorrow morning."

"What about a bond hearing?" asked Steve as he opened the door to the back seat.

Jack spoke in a matter-of-fact tone. "She'll have to appear before a magistrate within forty-eight hours, but there are ways they can stretch it out to seventy-two hours before they set or deny bail."

"What a lousy way to spend a weekend," said Heather. She glanced in the rear-view mirror and saw Steve take off his sunglasses and rub his sightless eyes. It would be a long weekend for him, too.

He put his sunglasses back on. In a firm voice he announced, "I don't care how you do it, but Kate is to be out of jail by Sunday night. On Monday night I'm putting Ricardo's killer behind bars."

She'd never heard him give a deadline like this. Looking at Jack, he shook his head in a way that told her he didn't believe it would happen. She turned her head back to the road and lifted her chin. "Sunday for Kate. Monday for the killer. I'm all in."

16

Instead of rushing back to the city jail, Jack climbed out of the SUV when they reached the parking lot. Heather met him at the front of the vehicle and grabbed his arm. "Where are you going?"

He looked down at her hand. "If it's all right with you, I'll get my briefcase and put on something that makes me look a little more professional."

"Oh. Sorry. I'm a little on edge."

"Heather," said Steve. "We don't have time for this."

She spun away from Jack and went to get Steve.

They made it to the elevator, only to find Zeke waiting for a ride up. He stood erect, with hands held loosely behind his back, as he whistled a catchy melody. "Hey, my favorite customers. When are you going to come back to the restaurant?"

"Hello, again," said Steve. "Heather was saying how impressed she was with your studio. Do you think you might have time tomorrow to show her your collection?"

Heather wasn't sure what Steve was up to, but she knew she needed to play along. "I saw some in your place the other day that caught my eye. I haven't been able to stop thinking about them."

"Sure," said Zeke with teeth in full view. "Just don't come until after lunch. I reserve mornings for painting."

"Do you work tomorrow?" asked Steve.

"I have the late shift, so I won't leave until around three in the afternoon."

The elevator chimed, and the metal doors parted. "I'll be there between one and two with my checkbook."

Heather turned to face Steve as soon as the doors closed. "Do you think he knows something about the shooting?"

Steve rubbed the back of his neck. "Possible. His apartment is closer to where the shooting took place."

"Seems unlikely," said Jack.

"Probably," said Steve. "Investigations are usually a lot of wasted time and effort looking for that one thing that seals the deal."

Another chime from the elevator and soon Steve and Heather were inside Kate's apartment while Jack jogged down the hall to their rental and a quick change of clothes.

"We need to leave everything belonging to Kate as is," said Heather.

Steve nodded. "Get everything of yours pertaining to the investigation and take it to my place. I'll grab my laptop."

"That's going to look suspicious if I take my tablet and computer. I'll put them in my room. If they come to search, I'll claim attorney-client privilege."

"No." The word came in a rush. "All Ramos has to do is get you alone. He could say you gave him permission to take your devices. You weren't there to see it, but he didn't hesitate to snatch my phone, and that was in front of witnesses."

Heather took a step forward. "He took your phone?"

"I got it back, thanks to Joy. He doesn't know I have it and that's what I want him to think."

Heather's next words dripped with sarcasm. "This sounds like a delightful story. Care to fill me in?"

"Later. For now, grab everything you need to carry on our

investigation without interruption. Let's get as much out of here as we can and still be on the right side of the law."

Heather moved to her bedroom and made quick work of stuffing everything electronic in her computer bag. By the time she reached the living room, Steve was waiting for her with laptop in hand. They passed Jack in the hall. He had his attorney's face on and didn't speak.

After Steve and Heather made it inside, she went to Jack's room and deposited her bag under a spare blanket in the closet. She went back in the living room where Steve was plugging in his computer. "Check the parking lot," he said.

She pulled open the door and stepped into balmy heat. Retreating into air-conditioned comfort, she gave her report. "Nothing so far."

"Good. Let's go back to Kate's and wait for them."

Once back at Kate's, Heather asked, "Are you hungry?"

Steve shook his head. "More mad than hungry."

"Ramos?"

"Mostly mad at myself. I should have seen this coming. Ramos was waiting for a chance to arrest her. I spoke to Joy long enough to find out no one from the police have talked to her about Ricardo's murder."

Heather went to the kitchen. Steve might say he wasn't hungry, but he'd snack on crackers and cheese and drink iced tea if she put it in front of him. While she busied herself, she asked, "What's the full story on your phone?"

Steve told her about Ramos jerking it out of his hand and telling him it was evidence.

She interrupted. "What did he mean by that?"

"No idea." Steve chuckled. "Joy pretended to trip and sent him into Laguna Madre." His laugh became more pronounced. "But not before she picked his pocket."

The corners of Heather's mouth pulled up. It was good to see him laughing.

"And he doesn't know you have it?"

"I want him to think he owes me a new phone." Steve took in a deep breath and let it out. Already in the recliner, he raised his feet. "Send Jack a text to make sure Ramos didn't arrest Joy for putting him in the drink."

"Did she do it on purpose?"

"All I heard was her saying she tripped. I guess it will be his word against hers."

Heather spent the next thirty seconds speed typing on her phone. Next, she fixed two plates of crackers, cheeses, celery sticks, and carrot wedges. Pounding on the door interrupted their late afternoon snack.

"Police! Open the door."

Heather opened the door and encountered an officer with a battering ram poised to force entry. She planted her hands on her hips and looked around him to give Ramos a narrow-eyed gaze. "A bit of overkill, don't you think, detective?"

He ignored her and pushed past the officer. "Stand back. I have a warrant."

"Then you'd better let me see it, read it, and make sure it's in order before you touch anything."

He hesitated. "What are you two doing here?"

"I'm staying here, and I'm acting as Ms. Bridges' co-counsel. Mr. Smiley is currently working for Kate. The real question is, what are you doing here?"

"It's in the warrant."

Steve hollered from the living room. "You owe me a phone, Ramos."

"It's Detective Ramos, and tell Joy Day your problems." He walked to the living room.

"She tripped. I saw her."

"She didn't trip. It was a deliberate push."

"It will be our word against yours when this goes to court."

Heather had to cover her mouth with the warrant to keep from laughing, but Steve kept on. "First an illegal seizure of personal property without probable cause, followed by an illegal arrest of Joy Day. Then, you went swimming while on duty. This hasn't been a good day for you, Ramos."

The officer with Ramos spoke up. "You didn't arrest Joy."

"Shut up. Go to the bedrooms, and start searching," said Ramos.

"What am I looking for?"

"Anything to do with a murder. Laptops, phones, anything else electronic."

"You might try looking for a pistol or a rifle," said Steve. "Of course, we already did, so if you come up with one, we'll know you planted it. I made sure we recorded our search."

Heather knew it was a lie, but Steve could get by with it. They could argue that Steve filming a search of a house was nothing more than a hyperbolic joke. How could a blind man know for sure what was or wasn't recorded?

A light of revelation came into Ramos' eyes. He tilted his head back and looked at the ceiling. "You may think this is a joke, Smiley, but you won't think so after a night in jail."

It was Heather's turn to goad Ramos. "Smile, Detective. You're being recorded. I also need to tell you that threatening a citizen with incarceration without justification is very much illegal. The only thing Mr. Smiley's guilty of today is not putting his iced tea on a trivet. You, on the other hand, have racked up enough charges to get you fired five times over."

He went to a desk and picked up a laptop.

"Gloves," said Heather. "You're contaminating evidence."

"Hey," said Steve. "Whose team are you on?"

"Sorry. Old habits are hard to break."

Steve changed tactics. "Look, Detective Ramos, there's no reason you and I can't get along. I know what happened to Chief Giles today and—"

Ramos cut him off. "How did you hear about that?"

Instead of answering, Steve lifted his chin and spoke so Heather had no trouble hearing him. "Could you fix Detective

Ramos and the officer a glass of iced tea? I'm sure they could use something cold on a hot, stressful day like this."

"Sure."

Ramos shot a glance to Steve, Heather, and back to Steve. "What's your angle, Smiley?"

"No angle. We're after the same thing, the person who shot Ricardo Alvarez."

"I know who did it and she's in jail."

Steve leaned back. "You might be right. But then again, what about the other suspects?"

"There are no other suspects."

"Why not?"

Heather delivered a tall glass to Ramos, who took it without acknowledgment. He delayed his response by taking a long drink.

Steve leaned forward in his chair. "I'll tell you why there are no other suspects. It's because you haven't looked for any."

"You don't know that." Ramos' words sounded a little too defensive, and he looked at the floor after he made the protest.

Heather chimed in. "Yes, he does. The question Steve's asking himself now is why you're fixated on Kate Bridges?"

Ramos put his glass on the table. "I don't have time to play these games."

He moved to Kate's desk and pulled files from a drawer. After a few minutes of scanning, a crooked smile came across his face. "If this Bridges woman is so innocent, why is she confessing to the murder?"

Heather went to the desk. It only took a second for her to realize what Ramos had stumbled onto. "I hate to disappoint you, but that's a copy of Steve's short story. He patterned it after a murder/suicide case he worked in Houston. If you keep reading, you'll see there's an interesting twist at the end."

"Hey," said Steve. "Don't give away the ending."

The officer came back into the living room. "The only electronic device I found was an e-Reader."

"Bag it and search the bathrooms. I'll start in the kitchen."

For the next hour, the two officers searched almost every inch of the thirteen-hundred-square-foot apartment. Based on the limited number of evidence bags they carried out and the expression of frustration on Ramos' face, he didn't find what he hoped to.

As for Steve, he brought the recliner to its full laid-back position, folded his hands on his stomach and issued soft snores after only a few moments. He didn't stir until the door closed behind the two officers.

When Heather returned to the living room, Steve was on his feet. "Get me a plastic bag of some sort," he said with urgency in his voice.

"There are plenty of plastic grocery bags."

"Bring a couple."

Heather arrived back in the living room with what he required. "Now what?"

Steve pointed to the chair. "Use one bag as a glove and gently slide your hand between the arm of the chair and the cushion."

"Which side?"

"It was on my right side when I was sitting."

She covered her hand and slipped it between the chair's arm and seat cushion. She gasped and withdrew her hand. "There may be contaminants on these grocery bags. I think Kate keeps zip-locks under the sink. They'll be less contaminated."

Heather scurried to the kitchen, found the quart-sized bags, used one to grasp the pistol, examined it, and slid it into the second bag. "It's a Ruger nine-millimeter." She looked at Steve. "How long have you been sitting on it?"

Steve ignored the question. He already had his phone in his hand and instructed it to call Mike Moreno. It went to voice mail. Steve huffed and spoke after the prompt. "Mike. Steve Smiley. If Ricardo Alvarez was shot with a nine-mil, I have the murder weapon. I can't give it to the locals. Call me as soon as you get this."

Steve went back to the recliner and plopped down. "I thought Ramos would never leave."

"You were sitting on it the whole time and didn't tell me?"

"I didn't know it was there until I leaned the chair all the way back. I figured my best chance of them not searching the chair was if I was asleep."

"Asleep, or playing like you were?"

"It was only a brief nap. I needed it to appear realistic."

Sometimes all Heather could do was shake her head in disbelief. Working with Steve had taught her not to be surprised by any of his antics. His command over his body and emotions was a source of wonder.

"What do you want me to do with the pistol?"

"Take it to my room and put it in my suitcase. The chances of me being searched before you turn it over to Mike are slim."

Steve's phone announced an incoming call from Mike Moreno. The Ranger spoke as soon as Steve answered. "I'm on my way. There's an HEB grocery store in Port Isabel. Meet me there in an hour."

"We'll be there."

Steve reached down for his cane. "Never mind about hiding the pistol in my room. Call a cab. We're going to Port Isabel."

17

Heather slipped the pistol into her purse. The weight of two weapons combined with her other necessities put a strain on the purse's strap. She looped it over her neck, making it possible to keep both hands free. Steve tapped his way to his apartment on the now familiar path.

Once inside, Heather kept the purse pressed against her side, just in case Ramos wanted to make a surprise visit.

"How long will it take to get to Port Isabel?" asked Steve.

"Fifteen minutes tops. It's on the other side of the causeway."

"That gives us some time. What was your impression of Ramos?"

Heather didn't hesitate. "He's a jerk."

"Get your emotions out of the way and try again."

This wasn't the first time Steve cautioned her to leave feelings out when evaluating people. He was right, of course, even if he didn't always practice what he preached. She took in a deep cleansing breath to release stress as she reconsidered his question. "Ramos isn't the sharpest detective I've ever met. He didn't pick up on you telling him you saw Joy trip, and the crack about you filming went right over his head."

"I'm glad you picked up on that. Joy called him an errand boy, which is an accurate description. A good detective would have made me get out of the chair."

Steve paused. "The question is, did someone send him to search or did he do it on his own initiative? Check the search warrant."

Heather did, and Ramos' name was on it. She reported her findings to Steve. He waved a hand. "That doesn't mean he wasn't told to get it. We already know he had ample evidence."

Steve made his way to a barstool and settled on it. "We need to find Joy when we get back from delivering the pistol."

"We may not find her if it's after dark."

Steve brought his chin down and flipped open the lid of his laptop. He instructed his computer to search for novelty boat rentals on South Padre Island. A mechanical voice responded with the name of the business, and he instructed the computer to place the call. An effervescent voice answered after four rings, giving the hours of operation and asking for a call back number.

The lid to the computer came down with more force than necessary. Steve spoke as he slid off the barstool. "Let's go. She still may be there."

"The cab said they'd be here in twenty minutes."

Steve stomped to the patio door, slid it open, and walked to the iron railing. Even from a distance, she could see his rounded shoulders. Frustration wasn't a garment Steve wore often or well.

She joined him as dusk chased the sun. It was the in-between time on the island. Vacationers would put on their evening attire of loose-fitting, lightweight clothes and prepare to find a restaurant with cold drinks and fresh seafood. Some wouldn't return to their rooms until they'd danced the last dance the band played. Heather thought of Jack for a moment and how he was giving up his time, doing a favor for her and Steve.

Heather's phone rang. After the briefest of conversations, she took Steve's arm. "The taxi's here early."

It took mere minutes for the taxi to cover the distance to the other side of the island and deposit them in front of the dock, where Joy's boats bobbed in the water. Heather told the driver to wait. This fare, and the tip she received, would probably make her night.

Steve had his hand on her arm as they climbed down some steps. The last boat puttered its way to the dock. A teen couple climbed out and apologized for bringing in the boat late. The apology didn't sound sincere.

"Joy's securing the last boat," she whispered.

"Take me to her."

"Hello, Joy," said Steve in a friendly voice. "Glad to see you didn't get thrown in jail."

She continued tying the rope, straightened up when she'd finished, and issued a toothy grin. "Ramos wouldn't dare. It would cost someone money if I couldn't rent the boats."

"What do you mean?"

"I don't own them. I lease the dock and the boats."

"Who owns them?"

"Some corporation I never heard of. It could be a real sweet gig if they didn't keep raising the rent."

Steve changed the subject. "This is my business partner, Heather McBlythe."

Joy laughed. "And here I thought you were some sort of Casanova with one girlfriend for days and another for nights."

It was Steve's turn to chuckle. "Actually, we're private investigators, and we're trying to get Kate out of trouble. She's the woman Ramos arrested today."

Heather shook her hand. "Unfortunately, we don't have time to talk to you right now. Can we take you to dinner in an hour or two?"

"Make it tomorrow," said Joy. She wiggled her blond eyebrows up and down. "I have an engagement tonight with the man of my dreams. He's sixty-eight, a lonely widower with a heart condition, and a five-bedroom home on the canal."

"Ah," said Steve. "But can he dance?"

"Probably not as good as you."

Heather didn't mean to, but a snort of a laugh came out her nose.

Steve put his hand over his heart like she stabbed him. "Pardon Heather's boorish manners. Can we take you to breakfast tomorrow?"

"Brunch," said Joy. "Remember, you're on island time."

"Ten-thirty?" asked Heather.

"Sounds good. I'll put the name and address of where to meet on a business card."

She returned from a small table and held out a card to Heather. "Here you go."

Steve held out his right hand toward Joy. "Thanks for delaying Ramos today."

"That was my pleasure."

Heather led Steve up the steps and to the taxi. She wished they had more time with Joy to extract additional information on the boat rentals.

They drove south a mile or two and swung to the west. A sign warned drivers to watch for pelicans on the causeway. She used the time to process the conversation with Joy and to make a mental checklist of questions to ask her at tomorrow's brunch.

Shrimp boats lined the docks as the causeway spit them out on mainland Texas and into the small city of Port Isabel. The grocery store sat a mile or two down the main road, on the left. She told the driver to make a pass through the lot and prepare to wait as they met with a business associate.

As they finished their second loop through the store's busy parking lot, Heather caught sight of an unmarked black SUV pulling off the main road. She pointed. "There he is. Pull up next to that SUV."

"Can I go in for a pit stop?" asked the young woman.

"Sure. We need to pick up some groceries while we're here. Why don't you wait inside where it's cool."

The Ranger rolled down his window and Heather slipped the

plastic-enclosed pistol to him. She walked Steve around the SUV and placed him in the front while she took the back. With the air conditioner running, they sat in relative comfort.

"I'll put a rush on getting the lab to process this." The Ranger shifted in his seat. "They released Chief Giles this afternoon. No serious injuries. A sprained wrist and some bruises."

"Were they trying to kill her or just scare her?"

"She said a late model truck with a push bar on the front did a pit maneuver on her and sent her off the road and into a telephone pole. She was lucky. It happened on a sandy stretch of highway without a steep ditch."

Steve responded with a nod. "If they meant to kill her, they would have. It sounds like a warning."

"It doesn't fit," said Mike. "We're used to the cartels trying to bribe or blackmail cops, but to go after a chief of police is something new. That sort of thing brings down more heat than they want to deal with."

"I have a favor to ask," said Steve.

Mike looked at Heather, his head tilted. "Ask," he said, while turning back to Steve.

"Kate's in jail, and the police on the island aren't looking for anyone else to pin the murder on. The list of people with grudges against Ricardo is growing every time Heather and I talk to someone who knew him. That doesn't count the cartel. We know Ricardo rented his boat out to Connie Diaz's husband for special charters. We found out a few minutes ago that it's possible the cartel also has their hooks in another boat rental business. It could be that Ricardo wouldn't play ball with them and he paid the price."

Mike was nodding the entire time Steve was talking. "That's a very likely scenario." He leaned toward Steve. "You haven't asked for a favor yet."

"I think Kate is being used as a scapegoat to get pressure off the local cops. They waited until the start of the weekend to arrest her and I was told by these two lawyers that came with me they can keep Kate locked up for three days without a bond hearing. I want her in front of a magistrate ASAP and a bond hearing by Sunday morning."

Mike pulled a hand down his face. "When you ask for a favor, you don't mess around. Let me talk to my captain and see what we can do." He opened his mouth to speak, but Steve cut him off.

"To sweeten the pot, I'll send you reports twice a day on the progress we're making. We won't hold anything back, even if it might incriminate Kate."

"When will I receive the first report?"

"Put your phone on record. Heather and I will tell you everything we have so far and the appointments we set up for tomorrow."

Step by step, Steve gave a chronological history of the investigation from the time he awakened to the sound of sirens to the last meeting with Joy. Mike only needed clarification on a couple of items. Heather gave her accounts and opinions to the parts that Steve wasn't present to hear.

A tap on Steve's window took Heather by surprise. Mike pushed a button on his armrest, and the window rolled down.

"Sorry to interrupt," said the cab driver. "Dispatch is calling me, making sure I don't get stiffed on the fare." The driver's eyes shifted to the computer and to Mike with the badge pinned to his shirt.

Heather opened her purse and withdrew a platinum credit card and a hundred-dollar bill. She handed both to the driver. "We're almost finished."

"Sorry to bother you."

Mike and Steve shook hands, and the Ranger left after committing to do all he could to get Kate in front of a magistrate as soon as possible. Night had fallen while they were talking with Moreno and all manner of insects flitted around the bright parking lot lights. Steve spoke as they headed for the grocery store front door. "Get me brain food. Steak, potatoes, and something green."

"You won't be able to sleep eating heavy late at night."

"I don't plan on sleeping."

THE CLOCK ON THE MICROWAVE READ 10:22 P.M. WHEN THE scrape of a key in the door caused Heather to walk out of the kitchen and Steve to raise his head. Jack came in with a bounce in his step. "You may be in the presence of the greatest defense attorney in the world."

"So much for humility," said Heather as she gave him a peck on the cheek. "What has you walking on sunshine?"

"I caused enough of a commotion at the police station until someone finally listened and got a judge to conduct a teleconference and Kate's formally arraigned."

"Ah," said Steve. "Well done. What about a bond hearing?"

"No word on that yet. They'll transfer her to Brownsville in the morning. They tried to do it tonight, but something stopped them. I never found out what."

Heather didn't have the heart to tell Jack about Steve and her working behind the scenes to bring about the quick arraignment. She changed subjects. "Were you able to get something to eat?"

"I grabbed a burger."

"Oh." She tried to keep disappointment out of her voice.

"You didn't cook for me, did you?"

"It was nothing. You can have it for lunch tomorrow."

"Afraid not. I need to go to Brownsville and make sure someone doesn't drop the ball on the bond hearing."

Steve stayed in his chair. "What was it like at the jail tonight?"

"What do you mean?"

"Did it seem like they were in a hurry to process Kate?"

"At first it did. Detective Ramos came in, mad as a wet cat.

He tried to tell me I couldn't speak with Kate or be with her when he questioned her. I let him know how wrong he was. By the time I stopped quoting case law, civil rights violations, and their punishments, he changed his mind."

"Strange," said Steve. "Even a rookie cop knows better than that."

"It's strange and stupid," said Heather. "Denying an attorney the right to see their client is crazy."

Steve stood. "I'm going to Kate's. You two need some time alone so Heather can tell you about the pistol we found."

"What?" Jack's eyes widened as his chin jutted forward. "When? How? Where did you find it?"

"Don't worry," said Heather. "We bagged it and turned it over to a Texas Ranger."

Steve took Heather's key and excused himself.

"He seems worried," said Jack after Steve and his sensitive ears made it out of range.

"Not so much worried as intense. He does it every time he has a hard knot to untie. He'll make a pot of coffee and stay up most of the night thinking. About five in the morning, he'll nod off for an hour. After that, he'll get his computer and go over every scrap of information we've gathered."

"Does it always work?"

"Only if he has enough information. I don't think he has enough yet, but he will."

Jack gave her a look that telegraphed a desire for more than solving a mystery. She placed both hands on his chest. "We've both had a full day and we need to be at the top of our game tomorrow. I'm going to put your steak, baked potato, and grilled asparagus in the refrigerator. After that, I'm going to Kate's, wash my face, and go to bed. I suggest you not stay up late."

"Not before you tell me about the gun and the Ranger."

The clock on the microwave read twelve thirty-seven when Heather finally put Jack's meal away. The telling of their night's activities had taken only half an hour. She gave him one last kiss goodnight and padded her way to Kate's, shoes in hand.

The smell of coffee and Steve's voice greeted her when she arrived. "Did you read Jack a bedtime story?"

"Not exactly. I'm not sure this one will have a happy ending."

"Ah."

A deep yawn half escaped before she covered her mouth. "Put on a fresh pot at six-thirty if you're still awake."

"You always get up at five-thirty."

"I'm adjusting to island time."

"Get to bed. We have a busy day tomorrow. Brunch with Joy at ten-thirty and looking at paintings with Zeke in the early afternoon. Call Connie in the morning and see if you can get her to come here to discuss selling the complex to you."

"You have my day all planned out."

Steve leaned back and put his feet up. His voice took on the all-business tone it did when he was hot on the trail. "Can't be helped. Someone's desperate and they don't mind killing to get what they want."

18

The hand on Heather's shoulder took her so much by surprise that she lashed out at it.

"Whoa," said Jack. "That's no way to start your day, sweetheart."

She looked at him through crusty eyelashes. "What are you doing in my bedroom?"

"Trying to wish you a good morning."

She sat up straight, then realized the camisole she had on left little to the imagination. Out of instinct, she pulled the covers up to her chin. "You should have knocked."

Jack took a step back and held out his palms. "Sorry. I thought we'd made it past some of your middle school shyness. Who's this new woman that moved into your skin during the night?"

Heather closed her eyes. She'd never done early mornings well, and didn't want to start today. She held out a hand and flipped her wrist. "Go talk to Steve. I'll be out in ten minutes."

"Steve's not here. He went for a walk on the beach."

"You let him go by himself?"

"Why not? He's a grown man who can find his way around as well as most sighted people."

If it was one thing she didn't want when she first woke up, it was to have a debate with another attorney. "Out. If there's no coffee, make yourself useful." She knew the words came out too prickly, but she wasn't in the habit of talking to anyone before she brushed her teeth.

She emerged from her sanctum ten minutes later, wearing a running outfit. The constricting sportswear felt like a straitjacket. Jack's idea of early morning courting derailed her plan on wearing skimpy silk until she'd downed at least one mug of stimulant.

Jack tried to apologize again, but she waved it off. "It's not you. I'm always this way if I don't sleep well."

"You looked like you were sleeping good to me."

"If you haven't figured it out, I'm an absolute witch before coffee."

He didn't contradict her, which rankled her all the more. She pulled a thumb and index finger down on the corners of her mouth to make sure she'd removed any residual toothpaste. For the first time this morning she took a good look at Jack. "You packed a sports coat and slacks."

"I wanted to be prepared for any eventuality. I thought there might be a romantic candlelight dinner."

"You must have been a Boy Scout."

He held up three fingers. "Be prepared."

Heather settled on a barstool and sipped from her mug. "Did you make this?"

"Steve was making it when I came in. He gave me a rundown of the day. If there's not much for me to do in Brownsville, I'll be looking for a way to entertain myself until you and Steve get through playing Holmes and Watson."

A tingle of anger shot through her. "What do you mean by that crack?"

"It means I'm wondering if you'll be able to fit me into your schedule."

Heather bit her tongue. The conversation about her priorities was overdue, but she didn't want to have it now. She wasn't awake enough and had too many things on her plate. Her cup made a slight clink when she lowered it to the granite counter. "Now is not the time or place for us to have this conversation."

"A typical lawyer tactic. Delay when you have a weak case."

They traded stares until Jack threw up his hands, turned, and walked away. The last thing she heard was the door click shut. She placed her elbows on the counter and put her chin in her palms. "He didn't even slam it. What kind of guy doesn't slam doors when he's treated so badly? What's wrong with me?"

The question haunted her through her second cup of coffee. The cobwebs of sleep melted away, and the realization of how many mixed messages she'd sent to Jack since they arrived on the island became apparent. She wondered if a genealogy trace would reveal witches in her bloodline. Something wasn't right about her, but she couldn't put her finger on it.

She moved to the patio and looked out over the dunes to the beach. This should be the perfect place to fall in love. Her gaze shifted in from the surf to the spot in the dunes where Ricardo had breathed his last. Like a child playing with a light switch, her mind shifted between her desire for being with Jack and a compulsion to solve the crime. Was it right to send Jack to twist arms for a bail hearing? Why didn't she insist they go together to do it?

The ringing of her phone put introspection on hold. The call was from Steve.

"I need help."

"Same here." Then, she considered the tone of his voice. "What's wrong?"

"I'm hurt. It feels like someone poured gasoline on my foot and set it ablaze."

She was off her chair before he finished the sentence. "Where are you?"

"About a mile south."

"Have you called EMS?"

"No. Don't call them. Just come help me get back."

"Stay still. I'm on the way."

Heather grabbed keys and made for the door. She defied Steve and spoke to the 911 operator on her way down the hall. With only scant information to give, the conversation ended by the time she reached the door on the bottom floor. She carried keys in one hand and phone in the other as she sprinted to the boardwalk. It didn't take long to realize she'd never make the mile if she didn't slow her pace. Sand seeped into her shoes when she left the boardwalk and ventured onto the last of the dunes before they gave way to the beach.

Running along the edge of the incoming waves, she made good time. The bad news was, distances were hard to measure, and she soon had to slow her pace even more. An ambulance appeared in the distance, coming toward her with emergency lights pulsating. Because of the early hour, only a few beachcombers were out. Sweat rolled down her face, stinging her eyes. She wiped them and strained to see what looked like a football huddle of people. One of the EMT's stood in the surf with Steve.

With eyes smarting and lungs about to explode, Heather pressed the pace even more. By the time she arrived, she was gasping for air and both paramedics were standing in knee deep water with Steve.

Through labored breathing she said, "I'm... his... partner."

A voice from the gathering on shore quipped, "Lucky guy."

She ignored the comment and tried to get her breath. That's when she saw his foot in shallow water. What looked like a series of red strings had left bright lines on his foot and ankle.

"What is it?" she asked the paramedic.

"He got into a Portuguese man o' war. Some people call them blue-bottle jelly fish. The sting is like someone put a dozen lit cigarettes on your skin. The best first aid is to let it soak a while in salt water. We'll get him in the ambulance and check him out."

The EMTs helped Steve into the back of the ambulance and

made way for Heather to join them. They checked vitals and hooked up a heart monitor. After what seemed like an inordinate number of questions related to medical history and demographics, the woman conveyed their findings via radio. The lead paramedic, a woman with short hair and broad shoulders, looked to Heather and then Steve. "It's your call, Steve. We can treat you here or take you to the hospital in Port Isabel."

"Here," said Steve.

Heather expected the answer, but wanted to make sure he didn't need more advanced care. "What's the best treatment option?"

"The sting from the man o' war is rarely fatal. He's not showing any signs of anaphylactic shock. That's the primary concern. After that, the stingers need to be removed. Then we'll irrigate the area with saline. We can do all that here. When you get back to where you're staying, soak the foot in hot salt water for another twenty minutes. After that, apply an ice pack."

"Can we stop talking and start pulling off those stingers?" asked Steve. "I have an appointment this morning I can't miss."

The EMT looked at Heather, and she nodded. There was no way he would miss the interviews they'd set up, no matter how much pain he had to endure.

"Trade places with me," said the EMT. Heather maneuvered around Steve and scrunched into a seat near his head as the woman tore open a bag containing a sterilized pair of tweezers. She grabbed an IV bag but made no move to find a vein. Instead, she used some of the contents to irrigate the bright red welts. Next, she went to work removing the red string-like stingers. All the while, Steve held a white-knuckled grip on the sheet-covered mattress.

"That does it." The announcement came from the EMT, followed by, "Remember, twenty minutes of hot salt water. Ice packs after that, but only for twenty minutes at a time. Do that as long as it brings relief. Also, use an over-the-counter pain reliever, but not to excess."

"That's it?" asked Heather.

"It's always good to have Benadryl on hand. It's the go-to for stings and bites that might cause an adverse reaction. Also, it could help if it itches." She took a breath. "You might pack tweezers with you when you come to the beach. The cheapest first aid treatment for these stings is salt water and to get the stingers off the skin."

The EMT patted his leg. "You'll be feeling better soon. How 'bout we take you back to where you're staying. You'll need to call the number on the bill my partner is going to give you to make payment." She looked at Heather. "Steve gets an air-conditioned ride, but we're not allowed to carry anyone but patients."

The back door to the ambulance opened and Heather found herself face to face with Detective Ramos. "Need a ride?"

19

The door to the aging Ford Crown Victoria creaked when Heather opened it. Heather kicked a McDonald's sandwich wrapper and an empty coffee cup out of the way and took a seat in the unmarked car. She turned to her left as she put on the seat belt. "What's with the Crown Vic? The only department vehicles I've seen since we got here are SUVs and pickup trucks."

Detective Ramos shook his head and frowned. "The chief took mine until hers is out of the shop. This is the only other unmarked unit in the fleet."

"It looks like it should have gone to auction two years ago."

Ramos looked straight ahead. She couldn't tell if he was frowning or pouting.

"When did Gloria get that shiny new Explorer from you?"

"Last night."

He put the car in gear, accelerated too fast, and dug a hole in the sand. A muffled string of words in Spanish littered the air. It took a few tries, but he alternated between reverse and forward until the tires found adequate traction and they were on their way. Ramos mumbled in English about hating to drive a car in the sand. He made it down the beach, gained speed, cut the wheels, and plowed through dry sand until he reached blacktop on one of the many cut-throughs between the dunes.

Once on solid ground, he turned to her. "How long are you and your friends planning on staying?"

The abruptness of the question took Heather by surprise. "Why do you ask?"

He stuttered, but, like the car, found traction and moved forward with his words. "Just curious. The case against the Bridges woman is solid. It seems odd that you three would want to stay here."

"The case may not be as strong as you think. Who says she'll be in jail much longer?"

He responded with a scoffing laugh. "She murdered her ex-husband. He was a decent guy and a respected business owner."

"Ever heard of a bond hearing?"

"She won't make bond."

Heather wondered why Ramos was so sure. Were things so different in this part of the state that Kate wouldn't get a fair hearing? She needed to press harder, but they were already pulling into the parking lot. She only had time for one or two more questions, but she didn't want to sound desperate. "You must have found the murder weapon."

He didn't respond with words, but bit his lip and refused to return her gaze.

The ambulance doors were open. Steve was already out and moving to the entrance.

Ramos had to give his door an extra hard push to get it open. It was in worse shape than the one on the passenger's side. A slam put an exclamation mark on his unspoken expression of disgust.

Heather cleared the car and jogged to intercept Steve. The second ambulance attendant cut her off and handed her several sheets of paperwork.

By the time she made it to Steve, Ramos was by his side.

"Since you're here," said Steve, "why don't you come up and have a cup of coffee."

"We need to get hot water on that foot," said Heather. "Are you sure you're up to having company?"

"Positive," said Steve.

Once in the apartment, Steve made a bee-line for the recliner. Heather went to the sink and turned on the hot water. "I'll get you something for pain."

"No need. They gave me happy pills in the ambulance. They're already kicking in." His grin spread. "Whatever they gave me is working."

A roasting pan with deep sides was extracted from the back of a kitchen cabinet. Heather dumped salt in it and filled it halfway with steaming water. She set it in front of Steve and he gingerly lowered his foot.

By this time, Ramos had taken a seat on the couch, close to Steve. His eyes shifted around the room, giving the impression that he was looking for something.

"What do you take in your coffee?" asked Heather.

"Huh? Oh. Cream and sugar."

"All we have is half-and-half."

"Yeah. That's good enough."

Heather took steps toward the kitchen, speaking for Steve's benefit. "Detective Ramos got stuck with a geriatric Crown Vic. Gloria pulled rank on him and took his Explorer."

Steve picked up on the hint to explore deeper. "How is Gloria?"

"She's a little banged up. How did you know?"

Steve shifted in his chair and gave a slight grimace. "You can't do anything these days without it showing up on the Internet. I guess they'll total her Explorer?"

"It's not bad. I went to see it yesterday."

"I assume they took it to a dealership for repairs?"

"Like I said, it wasn't that bad. The wreck occurred just a few miles out of Port Isabel."

"Still," said Heather. "Detective Ramos had to give up his ride and now he's driving a bucket of rust."

Heather delivered the coffee to Ramos and brought Steve a bottle of cold water. Steve received it and said, "Would you look out from the balcony and see if Connie's car is here?"

Heather didn't know what kind of car Connie drove, and Steve certainly didn't. Ramos stuttered. "Wha... why do you want to know if Connie is here?"

It only took a slight movement of Steve's foot to make him yelp. He gripped the arms of the chair and sucked in an extra-large breath of air.

"Perhaps those were defective happy pills." said Heather.

"Remind me not to bump the side of the pan." He turned to Ramos. "Heather's considering buying this complex."

"The whole thing?"

Steve laughed. "I thought you understood that from the first time you were here."

Ramos stood, dry washed his face and paced.

Heather played along. "I'm meeting with Connie today to discuss terms. She told us she's ready to get back into show business."

Steve let out another gasp of pain. "This isn't working. Let's try an ice pack."

Heather put cubes in a plastic bag, wrapped it in a dish towel, and brought it to Steve.

"Thanks. Help me to the couch so I can elevate my foot. Detective Ramos can have my chair so he can enjoy his coffee."

With Steve resituated and the ice pack adjusted, Heather went to the patio and pretended to search the parking lot. She looked down at the pool. "There she is. I guess Connie's getting in her sun early today."

Ramos ran a hand through his hair and plopped down in the chair Steve had claimed as his own. Heather closed the patio door behind her and stood at an angle behind Ramos, watching his hands. In quick succession he thrust his right and then his left hand between the chair's arms and the seat.

Heather circled around to catch a glimpse of his reaction, but was too late. He was already on his feet and headed for the door. Steve said nothing, even though he could hear Ramos' footsteps beating a hasty retreat out of the apartment. As soon as the door slammed, he said, "Look in the parking lot again."

Heather left the patio door open and went to the rail. She stepped back to the doorway and relayed what she saw. "Two marked patrol vehicles." She went back to the rail, took in the scene below and came back for a second report. "Ramos is waving his hands and pointing toward the street. They're leaving."

Heather stepped back onto the balcony. A few minutes later, she made another report. "Ramos made a phone call. He's at the pool having what looks like a heated discussion with Connie. Do you want me to keep watching them?"

"Get me three extra-strength Tylenol."

"I thought you said they gave you happy pills in the ambulance."

"I wanted Ramos to think I was getting loopy, so he'd put his guard down. You were right about him not being too bright. He doesn't have much of a guard to lower."

Heather slid the patio door shut. "How did he make detective?"

"I've been asking myself the same question." Steve pointed toward the hall that led to the bedrooms. "Pain medicine, please. This ice pack isn't cutting it. The hot water was doing better."

When Heather returned, Steve was back in the chair and on the phone with Mike Moreno, giving the Ranger a line-by-line account of the meeting with Ramos. After he gave his version, Heather told Mike of the medical emergency. She then moved on to her brief conversation with Ramos in the car and added that she was positive she saw Ramos search Steve's chair for the pistol.

Mike closed the conversation with, "I'll call the captain right away. This should be enough for him to call the DA and get charges dropped."

"I recommend she stay another night in jail," said Steve. "Kate's in less danger being there tonight than on the island."

"What about an expedited bond hearing?"

"Only if charges aren't dismissed. If the DA doesn't play ball, Jack will have her out on bond tomorrow."

"Someone on the island won't be happy if they lose their lead suspect."

A hint of a smile nudged one corner of Steve's mouth up. "It's time we ruffled some feathers. I'm also counting on Heather to keep Kate safe after she's released."

Heather moved to the couch after Steve hung up. "I need to get a shower and dress for the meeting with Joy."

"Same here. Help me up."

"You're not going."

"Why not?"

She tented her hands on her hips, a wasted gesture when talking to Steve. "For starters, you can't walk without help."

He rose to his feet. "A hot shower, more ice, and I'll be good as new. Besides, I haven't had breakfast."

Heather rubbed the back of her neck. Steve was crossing the line between determination and common sense, but it would be useless to attempt to talk him out of it. Instead of coddling him, she turned and spoke over her shoulder. "Take a shower and put on the shirt that's hanging on the far right-hand side of the closet. The first pair of shorts in the second drawer will match. Rinse the sand off the flip-flops Jack bought you."

Steve was already moving to the door. "I'll be back in thirty minutes."

"No. Meet me downstairs in an hour. I can't stand to be without transportation."

"Do they have a rental car place here on the island?"

"There are rental places all up and down the main drag."
"Are you sure?"
"Trust me."

20

Heather brought the cherry-red four-passenger golf cart to a stop at the door to the complex. It had knobby tires that made it perfect for on-road or off-road travel. Steve stood on the other side of a glass door, scowling.

"You're late," he said as soon as the door opened.

She looked down and noticed he had an ice pack draped over his foot. "Only five minutes. There was a line at the rental place."

She led him to the vehicle and gave a further explanation of how they'd be traveling. "There're no doors, so make sure you buckle your seat belt."

"What is this contraption?"

"A golf cart that's powered by a gasoline engine. They rent these all over town."

"Are they street legal?"

"They are on the island. This one comes with headlights and a canopy that is bordered with colored LED lights that make it look really cool at night."

"How fast will it go?"

"Fast enough to blow your hat off. Climb in. We have six minutes to get to the restaurant."

Heather fired up the engine, double checked that Steve's seatbelt was hooked and said, "Hang on."

"To what?"

Heather glanced over once she'd reached twenty-five miles an hour. Steve's wind-blown brown hair was in complete disarray, and his smile reminded her of a kid riding a roller coaster. It was easy to forget what sensory input meant to him. She considered how much she took having perfect vision for granted. Shaking off a wave of pity, she launched into a loud narrative describing the sights along the route south to the restaurant Joy chose for their meeting.

They passed the turnoff to the causeway and came to the entrance of a large KOA campground. She wheeled the knobby-tired vehicle down a paved road, past motor homes and travel trailers, and parked as close as she could to a pier jutting out into the Laguna Madre. The restaurant sat perched midway out on the pier.

"We have a bit of a hike ahead of us. Are you up to it?"

"Ice has been on my foot for twenty-five minutes. I'll be fine."

A line formed outside. Since they were a couple minutes late, Heather hoped Joy had arrived early and snagged a table. She wove her way through customers waiting and spotted Joy at the front of the line.

"You made it just in time," said Joy. "They don't do reservations and they won't seat anyone if the entire party isn't here." She looked past Heather. "Where's Steve?"

"At the other end of the line. I'll get him."

Once seated, Joy made an astute observation. "Looks like you kicked a man o'war this morning."

Steve gave a nod. "Not my finest moment."

Joy asked for a more complete report while Heather took in the restaurant. It was long and narrow, with multiple additions reaching farther and farther out the pier. The section they occupied had booths on one side and tables for four running down the opposite side. Nautical decor was sparse, mainly because so much of the wall space was glass. The views eclipsed anything a designer could create.

After a server with a pierced eyebrow took their orders, Steve kept the conversation light. "How did your date go last night?"

Joy's eyebrows pinched together. "I'm not sure. The old codger would be a good catch if he was officially on the market."

"Still married?"

"He says they will complete the divorce in the next month or two."

"Are you sure?" asked Heather.

"Sure about what?"

"That he even filed for divorce."

Joy's eyes opened wide. "That would be good information to know. How can I find out?"

"I can do it for you, if you want me to."

"Sure."

"Write his full name and his home address."

"It's in Amarillo is all I know."

"That's plenty as long as you know his full legal name."

Heather pulled the phone from her purse and placed a call to her office in Conroe. After instructing a paralegal to drop everything and call her back with answers, she rested the phone on the table. "I should hear something before we leave."

"Wow. Thanks."

"Legal proceedings are public record. You just need to know how to navigate the system."

"And speaking of legal things," said Steve. "Could you clarify for us why you gave an envelope to Detective Ramos?"

It surprised Heather that Steve asked such a direct question. She wrote it off to him being in pain and worried about Kate. He was also cashing in a big favor while it was fresh.

Joy's smile came back. "Isn't Ramos a trip? If he wasn't so pathetic, I'd get mad at him. I probably shouldn't have called him an errand boy, but that's all he is." She took a drink of water and seemed to collect her thoughts.

"Let me start at the beginning and work my way forward. When I was living with Ricardo, he got chummy with the lawyer that took over the complex you're staying in. He was looking for someone to run the novelty boat business. Ricardo recommended me. I'm not sure what happened to the guy who was running it and I knew better than to ask. This all happened about the time Ricardo lost interest in me."

Heather asked, "Did you keep the books for Ricardo's business?"

"Yeah."

This meshed with Sarah's statement of her keeping the books for the company. Then it occurred to Heather that it was possible that Sarah kept the authentic account and someone else was cooking a second set of books to launder cartel money. It was also possible that Sarah might not be the innocent, perky young woman she appeared to be.

"Who owns the boat that goes on the sunset cruises?" asked Steve.

"Ricardo." She paused. "Well, he did. I'm not sure if he sold it or who will get it now."

"Keep going," said Steve.

"I didn't plan on Ricardo dumping me. That left me charging batteries in toy boats, standing in the tropical sun all day, and giving away a cut of my earnings."

"Why the envelope?"

"I used to send a check to Connie Diaz's husband. Now it's cash that Detective Ramos collects every two weeks."

"Do you get a receipt?"

"Not anymore."

Steve shifted in his seat and grimaced. "Tell us about Connie Diaz."

Joy laughed out loud. "It's women like Connie that give me a good reputation."

The tilt of Steve's head bid Joy to explain.

"I want to be a one-man woman, but I've been extra good at picking losers. I thought Ricardo was my one-and-only, but he fell for Connie the first time he saw her. Of course, he did nothing about it until her husband was dead, except dump me to clear the deck."

Heather's brain worked overtime. Could Ricardo have been the one that put Connie's husband in the canal? Who were her other paramours? Her thoughts were swirling so fast she almost missed Steve's next question.

"What about Detective Ramos? Do you think he killed Connie's husband?"

"It wouldn't surprise me," said Joy. "I hear rumors of him and a few others that know the way to her penthouse."

The arrival of their food put an end to the conversation, which was fine with Heather. Instead of getting closer to discovering who killed Ricardo, the waters seemed murkier than ever. She hoped Steve could make sense of the new information.

Halfway through a mostly silent meal, Heather's phone rang. She picked it up and listened to the report from the paralegal. The news for Joy wasn't good.

"Give it to me straight," said Joy.

Heather hated to spoil breakfast with the news, but Joy was a big girl and could take the report unvarnished. "Your one-and-only hasn't filed for divorce in Potter County."

Joy's fork fell to her plate. "I fell for a stud in high school. He dumped me. Then came two duds. Ricardo was one of them. Now I can't even land a..."

"A fud?" asked Steve.

"Exactly," said Joy. "I can't even find an old fuddy-duddy that won't lie to me."

Heather covered her mouth with her napkin and tried not to laugh. It didn't work, and soon both Steve and Joy joined her. The mirth lasted until people at other tables were smiling, too.

After Joy composed herself, she glanced at her phone. "I have three marine batteries on chargers that I need to take off before I open. Thanks for the breakfast and especially for the information on the fud. If words can burn ears, he'll need to call an ambulance when I get through with him."

"One more thing before you go," said Steve. "Has anyone from the police department talked to you yet about Ricardo's murder?"

"Not a soul."

"No one asked you where you were the night Ricardo was killed?"

"Me and the old fud were watching the storm come across the bay from his living room." She took a breath. "Correction. I was watching, he was snoring in his recliner."

Joy slid out of the booth. "I've got to go and get opened up. Thanks for the breakfast and the info."

She walked down the narrow aisle but didn't get far before she stopped and spoke with a silver-haired gentleman sitting by himself. Heather couldn't hear what they said, but she saw Joy reach in her purse and hand the man a business card. She dragged a hand across his shoulders in a caressing good-bye and retreated with her ultra-blond hair bouncing. The man leaned into the aisle to get a longer look at the retreating figure. Heather was sure she'd never met such an optimist as Joy Day.

When Heather refocused on Steve, he had pushed his half-eaten breakfast to the center of the table. "Is your foot hurting too much for you to finish breakfast?"

"I was thinking about what Joy said about Connie." He pulled the plate back in front of him. "Do we have time to take a long ride in that golf cart?"

"Are you sure? What about your foot?"

"Ask our server to fill the bag with fresh ice. I liked the feeling of wind in my face. It helped me think."

"We still have plenty of time before I'm supposed to meet Connie. We can go north to where the pavement ends on the island and cut over to the beach."

"Let's go."

Heather made the unusual request to the server, paid the bill, and picked up the baggie of ice on the way out. Steve wasn't limping as much on his way to the golf cart. They drove about ten miles and pulled off the blacktop. Unlike the ride to the restaurant, Heather didn't play tour guide. Steve's expression wasn't one that invited conversation. Long periods of quiet usually meant he had gone to a place of deep contemplation.

"We can cut over now and drive on the beach. Do you want to do that or go back and soak your foot?"

He pointed to the sound of waves coming ashore.

"We'll be going through loose sand for a while before we get to the beach."

"Get up speed or you'll bury down to the axles."

She did as instructed and had no problem. "We're going past tall dunes. Much taller than the ones by the complex."

Once they reached the beach, she turned north and followed the waterline, staying about ten yards from the nearest incoming waves. The beach had a distinctly wild feeling this far from civilization. It seemed more feral than the gentrified areas she'd seen up to now. This was much more peaceful. Occasionally they passed other adventurers, either camping or driving, but for the most part they were seeing the barrier island before man came with concrete, surfboards, ice chests, and suntan lotion.

She lost track of time and distance and only came out of her own head when Steve raised a hand and made a circular motion for her to turn around. She turned the wheel and didn't stop until they faced the pounding surf. "It's like I'm in another world. It's been so long since I've been in such a wild, desolate place. Thrilling and scary at the same time. Can you imagine what it's like when a hurricane comes through here?"

Steve spoke while facing the relentless onslaught and retreat of the waves. "Sometimes I wonder who can be the cruelest... man or nature? Since we've been here, they're even at one death each. Let's catch a killer before the body count goes up."

21

Steve took two steps into the entry and stopped. "Someone was in here while we were gone."

Heather slipped the key to Kate's door in her purse and locked it behind her. "Are you sure?"

"The smell is so faint that I can't tell what it is. Take me to Kate's bedroom."

Heather placed Steve's hand on her arm and led him down the hall. He went in by himself and closed the door. It didn't take him long to come out.

"I didn't smell it in the bedroom or bathroom." He shut the door behind him. "Now your room."

Heather pushed open the door and Steve repeated the process.

"It's your hair spray."

"I didn't use any today."

"Or yesterday," said Steve. "Someone helped themselves to it or they use the same brand."

Steve stood holding his cane while Heather slipped into the bathroom and examined the metal can without touching it. "I'll get a large zip lock and bag it for prints."

Steve nodded. "I'm going to get fresh ice for my foot. Did Kate mention anything about a maid?"

"She said she prefers to clean the apartment herself."

Heather looked around her bedroom. "I can't tell if anything is disturbed or missing. I'll need to do a thorough search."

Steve was already turning the corner past her bedroom door. Heather followed him to the kitchen and filled his bag of ice. She located a pair of Playtex gloves under the sink and put them on. "I'll be in my bedroom."

"Be sure to search Kate's while you're at it. Look for something to tie Kate to Ricardo's murder. Someone may still be trying to frame Kate."

"Do you think Ramos paid us another visit?"

Steve sat in his chair and placed the ice pack on his foot. "Bring me a couple more extra-strength Tylenol when you get a chance."

Heather took care of her patient and moved to search Kate's bedroom after she put the travel-size can of hair spray in the plastic bag. The gloves were designed to protect hands from household chemicals and dishwater, so they didn't give her the touch she'd have with the blue gloves she was familiar with. Step by methodical step, she searched every inch of Kate's bedroom and bathroom, but came up blank. She wondered what she might have missed. If Ramos wanted to plant something else to incriminate Kate in Ricardo's murder, surely he'd put it in a room she used exclusively.

She retreated from Kate's place of privacy and went back to the living room to give Steve a preliminary report. "Nothing in Kate's bedroom or bathroom that I could find."

Steve gave the slightest of nods. "I didn't think so."

The knock on the door caught Heather by surprise. She looked at the clock on the microwave and groaned. "I'm supposed to be at Connie's."

"That's her," said Steve. "You must have had your head under the bathroom sink when I called her. I told her about my battle with the man o' war, and I needed you to stay here with me."

Heather stripped off the yellow gloves, tossed them in the kitchen sink and went to welcome their guest.

Connie returned Heather's welcome with a gushy, "I so sorry to hear about Mr. Steve."

"Come in, Connie," said Steve, loud enough to be heard from the far side of the living room.

Connie took quick, choppy steps toward him. She'd have made better time if she hadn't worn high heels and a tight skirt that showed off almost all of her tanned, sculpted legs. When she reached him, she bent over and took his hand. "This is why I swim in a pool and not ocean. Too many things to bite."

"Sit on the couch close to me," said Steve. "You smell great."

"I didn't put on perfume today."

"No?"

Heather cut in. "Thanks for coming, and I apologize for not being able to come to your apartment. I'd love to see it."

"Yes, you must come to the penthouse. I have best view of beach."

"I see you brought a file with you," said Heather. "Are you ready to tell me what you want for the complex?"

Connie swallowed hard. "Make me an offer."

Heather took her time drawing a chair in from the dining room and forming a triangle with Steve and Connie. "That's not the way I play the game. You set the price. If I want to negotiate, then I'll continue conducting due diligence and make a counter-offer. Of course, I'll need to have your books audited, get comps, have the building inspected, do a title search to make sure there're no liens against the property, check insurance rates and a hundred other things."

Connie had the deer in the headlights look. Heather had purposefully spoken fast. She needed to know if Connie was serious about selling or was shopping for a price that she'd use to pit buyers against each other.

"You are very rich. I looked you up on Google. Make a good offer and I sell."

Steve chimed in. "Heather, would you go get that can of hair spray?"

"Sure." She made a quick trip to her bathroom and returned wagging the plastic bag and placed it in Steve's hand.

"We had a break-in today," said Steve.

Heather checked for a reaction. Connie looked toward the patio door, averting her gaze from Steve, even though he couldn't tell if she was looking at him or not.

"We have the can in the plastic bag to give to the police," said Steve. "We think whoever went into Heather's bathroom and used her hair spray left fingerprints on the can. We were about to call the cops when you knocked on the door."

Connie shifted her gaze back to the can.

Steve continued. "Heather says the lock wasn't forced. Whoever came in and used Heather's hair spray must have had a key."

Heather joined in. "The funny thing is, I can't find anything that's missing."

Steve added, "The biggest thing of value in this apartment is the information on Heather's laptop." He shifted his face to Heather. "What were you working on?"

"A valuation of this complex," said Heather. "That reminds me, Connie, who does the books for the complex?

"The couple that runs the office where you checked in. They take care of everything."

"Do you have an accountant check their work?"

"Why would I? They do everything."

Heather knew to not press too hard, and so did Steve. He changed the conversation back to Connie breaking into the apartment. "I'm not saying that you saw us leave this morning and came here to find out what Heather might offer, but—"

Heather didn't let him finish as she gave Connie an icy stare. "The fingerprints will tell the police who it is."

Connie squirmed. Her eyes darted left to right, then began to tear. "I can't go to jail."

It didn't take much to break Connie down, which came as a surprise to Heather.

"I have questions I need you to answer," said Steve. "Tell us the truth, and Heather might take the can of hair spray out of the bag and wipe it off. But if you lie—"

"No jail," said Connie, her hands shaking. "They'll kill me."

Steve fiddled with the ice bag on his foot. "Now that we have an understanding, was Detective Ramos with you the night Ricardo Alvarez was killed?"

She nodded and offered a weak, "Yes."

"All night?"

"Most of night."

Heather noted that Connie's speech became choppy and heavily accented. Was the former actress putting on a show? Was she lying? Perhaps she was embarrassed at getting caught breaking into Kate's apartment.

"When did he leave?" asked Steve.

"Before dawn."

"How long before dawn?"

She shrugged. "An hour. Maybe less."

"Did Ricardo come to see you the night he was killed?"

"Yes, but he no stay long. I sent him away before Ramos came from the bedroom."

"Did you hear a shot?"

"Only big booms from storm."

Steve slipped his foot out from under the ice bag. Most of the red lines were gone, but the skin was pink from the cold. "Let me make sure I understand. Ramos came to your apartment, spent almost all night with you, and left before dawn. During the storm, Ricardo paid you a visit and left. Is that correct?"

"He was very mad when he left."

"Why?"

"Ricardo a jealous man. He didn't like me seeing other men. I told him I see who I want."

Heather had heard enough. Ramos was number one on her list before Steve started the interview with Connie. She had to be covering for him. Heather put a pretend star by his name. If Steve continued to pressure her, she'd admit that Ramos followed Ricardo to the parking lot.

Instead of continuing, Steve pursued another line of questions. "Tell me what you know about Miguel Sosa."

She shrugged. "He's a nice kid, but Ricardo wanted to do him wrong."

"Explain."

"People my husband worked for. They didn't like Miguel, and told Ricardo to get rid of him."

"Why didn't they like Miguel?"

"He complained about drugs and wild parties. Miguel told Ricardo he could make more money by having more cruises."

"Did Miguel know these bad men wanted to get rid of him?"

Connie shrugged.

For Steve's benefit, Heather said, "She doesn't know."

"What about Sarah, Miguel's fiancé? Did she know about the plan to get rid of Miguel?"

"Ricardo said she's a smart girl. That's all I know about her."

Now Heather understood Steve's continued questions. While she was focused on Ramos, Steve hadn't forgotten about others who might have wanted Ricardo dead. Miguel or Sarah could have known about Ricardo's will, leaving the boat and business to Ricardo's ex-wife.

"Tell me about Joy Day," said Steve.

A blank look crossed Connie's face. "Who?"

"She runs the novelty boat business on the other side of the island."

"What is novelty boat?"

"The little boats that look like ducks and toy cars."

"Oh, yes. I don't know her."

"Your husband did," said Steve.

For the first time since Steve started questioning her, Connie straightened her spine. "My husband did many things and knew many people. All he tell me about is this complex."

"And Ricardo's boat?" asked Heather.

Connie's eyes flashed. "My husband say nothing about boat, but I hear things on midnight cruises when men drink tequila and do cocaine."

"What things?"

"Things like many businesses on Island that might change hands."

Connie continued to stare at Heather. "Make offer."

"If I do, it will be for less than half of what you might get from someone else."

Connie bristled, then stood and tugged her skirt down. "I know you're rich. Make offer soon." Her heels clicked a path to the door, and she was gone.

Heather fell on the couch face down and groaned. "I'm more confused now than ever. I knew it was Ramos until you started asking her questions about Miguel and Sarah. Either one or both of them had motive." She sat up. "The only one that I'm sure didn't kill Ricardo is Joy."

"Why are you ruling her out? All you have is her word that she was with the old fud. And even if she was, and she was telling the truth about him snoring in his chair, she could have left long enough to kill Ricardo and return."

"Stop it," said Heather. "My brain will explode if you give me any more suspects."

Steve chuckled. "How much of what Connie told us do you think was lies?"

Heather sat up. "Keep it up and I'll be taking more Tylenol than you."

"Then I guess you need to cancel your appointment with Zeke to look at art. Did you forget that he used to work for Ricardo, and that he's a bit flakey?"

Heather jerked her head to look at Steve straight on. "Good heavens. I forgot. I'll be back as soon as I can."

"Be sure to take your purse and buy me a nice painting. I'll give it to Jack as a memento of the vacation he didn't get to take."

Heather stopped in her tracks. "We've been so busy I forgot to call him and tell him that the Rangers are contacting the DA. Jack's going to be livid."

"You're covered... again. I called him while you were searching Kate's room. He should be here by the time you get back from Zeke's."

"Augh!" shouted Heather. How could she have forgotten to call Jack?

22

Once outside Kate's, Heather told her phone to call Jack. He answered with a terse, "Yeah?" The background noise told her he was driving.

"I'm calling to apologize. Things have been super-busy. The good news is, I think Steve is getting close to wrapping things up."

"Uh-huh."

She stepped in the elevator and waited for Jack to say something else, or at least give her a piece of his mind. The doors slid together and her phone played the mechanical notes that tell the user the call dropped. Once the elevator reached Zeke's floor, she repeated her instructions to call Jack. After eight rings, she concluded he didn't want to talk to her. At least not now.

Heather stuffed the phone back in her purse, stomped her foot, and mumbled a series of self-deprecating declarations. She stopped, leaned against the wall, and tried to compose herself. When was the last time she actually stomped her foot? It must have been as a teen. She'd slept late and missed a French class at her finishing school. That had broken her string of perfect attendance, and it seemed like the world stopped spinning. It hadn't, and, with the wisdom that comes with age and experience, she knew it would go on spinning now, with or without Jack.

She stepped from the wall, squared her shoulders, and walked to Zeke's with the posture she'd perfected at that same school for young ladies. Her firm knock on the door brought a quick result. The painter/restaurant server opened the door, bid her a pleasant afternoon and a hearty welcome to his humble studio.

At first glance, nothing had changed in the apartment. Finished and unfinished works sat in rows stacked against the walls and an easel held a work in progress.

Heather pointed at the easel. "Is that the same painting you were working on the other day?"

"It's still not finished."

Her gaze shifted to the paintings propped against the walls. "If I remember correctly, some paintings are still works in progress. Is that right?"

"You have an excellent memory. I'm not satisfied with those along the right-hand wall. The ones on the left are all for sale."

Now that she knew the house rules, she could move with the assurance that she wouldn't inadvertently offend Zeke again. "Is it all right with you if I pick out five or six of my favorites and select from those?"

"Sure," said Zeke with a lift in his voice. "Look all you want." He took long strides across the living room, pulled the painting down from the easel, and rested it against the right wall with the other works that weren't for sale.

She looked at the first painting, a close-up of a seagull perched on the railing of Zeke's balcony with the dunes and surf appearing fuzzy in the distance. She didn't like the composition of the painting, but it gave her the opening to ask a question. "Is this your balcony?"

Zeke was back to his jovial self, ready to please and provide all the service a customer could hope for. "It is. I took a photo of the gull in late winter. The sky was drab that day and the mood gray. The work isn't for everyone, but someone who's been down and out will identify with it."

"Right now that would fit Kate Bridges, the woman I'm staying with."

"She's a nice lady and a fellow artist of sorts," said Zeke. "Has something happened to her?"

Zeke's voice didn't carry any hint of deception, but Heather knew not to trust her ability to pick up on the subtle nuances of speech. That was Steve's forte. "Kate's in jail for a crime she didn't commit."

"You're kidding. There has to be a mistake."

Not only did Zeke's voice not hint he was lying, his gaze and his tone was one of genuine surprise and disbelief.

"I would have thought you'd heard about it by now."

His gaze shifted to the patio and the landscape beyond. "I live in two worlds. I'm a hundred percent at the restaurant working my best to serve customers or I'm here, pursuing the love of my life. I have all my supplies and groceries delivered."

Heather moved to the second painting and gave it a good look. A shrimp boat trolled off shore, not far past the first breaking wave. The rising sun made a halo around the wheelhouse and cast a hint of a shadow over the blue-green waters. "Where are the seagulls? Don't they follow the boat to pick up scraps?"

"Good eye," said Zeke. "I'm sorry, but that one's not for sale. It's a special commission from a customer who doesn't like seagulls. I can paint one like it with birds included if you want me to."

Heather handed him the painting. "I'm not crazy about seagulls either." She kept going through the stacks. "These are very good." She glanced at the next work. "Did the police ever come back to question you again?"

"Not yet. They caught me in a foul mood the morning that guy was killed. I thought they might come by the restaurant, but they didn't."

"Were you awake that night?"

"Who could sleep? Lightning was striking so close it made my hair stand on end. It was awesome."

"Were you out in the storm?"

"On the patio." He pointed at the next painting. "You didn't take a good look at this one. I think it's one of my best pieces."

Zeke was right. The foreground showed the boardwalk leading to the beach, along with the dunes. It captured the sun appearing as half of a huge orange ball coming over the horizon. The beach was desolate, and the waves were but soft nudges of water to the shore. It spoke of peace, tranquility, and something more. But what was it?

"Does this have a title?"

"*Hope For the Day*. It has a companion piece I painted a few years back when I worked on the sunset cruises. Would you like to see it?"

"Please."

Zeke scurried to the bedroom and came back with a painting and another easel. He set up the tripod next to the one catching light from the patio and placed the paintings side-by-side. Heather stared at the works and found herself lost in their beauty.

"Stand back against the wall and move slowly forward."

Heather did as instructed. The first painting seemed to glow with hope and the promise of what might lie ahead. The second showed the sun setting on Laguna Madre, half resting on the horizon and half reflected on what looked like a sea of glass. It spoke to her of gratitude for the day.

"And this one's title?"

"*Thankful*."

"I'll take them both."

"Don't you want to know how much they are?"

"Name your price."

Heather would have paid double and thought them a bargain.

Jack could choose which one he wanted, and she'd take the other.

After staring at the paintings from all angles, she nodded and allowed her gaze to drift away. It rested on the unfinished painting that Zeke had taken off the easel and turned away from her.

Heather walked over to the canvas. "Do you mind if I look at this one? I know it's not finished, but it intrigues me."

Unlike the other day's violent rebuke, Zeke acted like he didn't care. It might have been because she was bringing him closer to his dream of being a full-time artist. "I still need another day or two to finish some details." He scrutinized it. "I'm not sure if I like it or not."

Heather turned to him. "A while ago you said the lightning made your hair stand on end. You were on the balcony?"

"In and out. I got soaked, but it was worth it. I was so excited after finishing the sketch I didn't sleep at all. I'd never been so close to anything so terrifying."

Heather looked again at the painting. Zeke had captured the exact moment lightning coursed through the sky and struck a palm tree bordering the parking lot below. The only way you could tell it was a night scene was by the black outline of the buildings in the distance. Two figures in rain gear walked across the parking lot, one behind the other, separated by only ten yards or so. Both were moving away from the building. A hood covered the first person's head, but the head of the second person remained unpainted. The outline was there, without a hood, but not the color of the hair. This could well be a painting of the seconds before the commission of a murder.

With heart pounding, Heather knew she couldn't signal the significance of what she was seeing. "I'll pay you for the first two and also this one. I don't want to take them with me today. They're a surprise." She pointed at the painting that caused her mouth to go dry. "Can you finish this one by tomorrow? I'm very interested in it."

"Three more hours and it can be yours. Same price."

Heather couldn't wait to get back and tell Steve. Her thoughts went to Jack. She had some serious groveling to do.

Zeke stared at the check for so long Heather thought she'd made a mistake in filling it out. He finally placed it on the bar. "You don't know what this means to me. I've had my eye on a place up the beach that's perfect because it doesn't have a pool. That means no screaming kids. I'll be able to pay cash and move if I can get Connie to let me out of my lease."

Heather didn't want to promise more than she could deliver, but she had a desire to help Zeke. "Let me talk to Connie. It's possible she won't be your landlord much longer."

He gave her a look that asked for details, but didn't verbalize his thoughts.

"I can't tell you anything more at this point. Finish the painting and I should have news for you in the next few days."

"Get me out of the lease and you can have your pick of anything I have at half price."

Heather extended her hand. "It's a deal, but only if I can get the lease canceled."

When the door closed behind her, Heather wanted to skip down the hall. She had important information to add to the case that might be the puzzle piece Steve needed to bring the picture into focus. She stabbed the up button to call the elevator and waited. When the doors slid open, she stood looking at Jack. He wasn't smiling.

23

Heather's plan to fill Steve in on her meeting with Zeke and then formulate a plan on how to apologize to Jack crumbled at her feet. She issued a contrite smile and waited to see if there was any good will left in Jack at all. From outward appearances, the well had run dry. He punched the symbol to close the elevator's door, kept his gaze on the floor numbers as they changed in front of him, and didn't say a word.

"Would an apology help?" asked Heather.

He didn't respond.

"I'm sorry." She grabbed the sleeve of his shirt. "I'm really sorry."

The doors opened. He tried to step around her, but she blocked his way.

"Would you please move?" he asked.

She stepped into the hall and as soon as she did, he bolted past her, heading to the apartment he shared with Steve. She walked in his footsteps, with him giving no sign she was there. Once at the door, he inserted the key, walked in, and tried to shut it behind him. It reminded her of long-ago days as a cop when she put her shoe in the door to keep it from closing.

He huffed in disgust. Once in the kitchen, he took a pint bottle of amber-colored liquor from the pocket of his sports coat, pulled down a high-ball glass from the cabinet, and retrieved three cubes of ice. After pouring a double-shot into the glass, he stepped to the living room and plopped down in the recliner Steve usually sat in.

Heather copied his ritual of pouring a stiff drink and joined him in the living room. She chose to sit on the middle cushion of the couch, not too near, but close enough to facilitate a conversation. He ignored her, and she mimicked his every move, except he didn't lose his breath when he took the first drink. Her gasp for air did earn a stare that held no compassion.

Their glasses were almost empty when he placed his on a coaster. She followed his lead and sat with hands folded in her lap.

"What do you want from me?" asked Jack.

The abruptness of the question took Heather aback. In six words, he'd managed to pin her to the wall with a question she'd asked herself a thousand times and came up with as many answers. She tried to speak. It might have been the liquor that had scorched her gullet, but more likely it was her own uncertainty that caused her to sound like a nervous teen. "Uh... I don't know."

Jack kept his gaze focused on something on the other side of the room. "That's the problem, isn't it? You don't know what you want when it comes to me." He paused. "The funny thing is, this trip is showing me I'm not sure what I want from you either."

He turned his focus to her, and she wished he hadn't. "Let's make a list of the things that are important to you. Number one: your job." He leaned against an armrest. "I put that as number one, but it only applies if you're not working a murder with Steve. When there's a murder, everything else comes to a halt. That takes care of priorities one and two."

"What are you saying?"

"Isn't it clear?" Jack's voice wasn't raised. He'd made his point, and he'd come alarmingly close to hitting the bull's eye.

Her next question was one she wished she hadn't asked, because they both knew the answer. Still, it wasn't in her not to defend herself. "What about you? What do you want? I didn't ask you to come on vacation with me because I think of you as number three on my priority list."

"Are you sure? It's my bad luck that you and Steve fell into a murder investigation, but your real reason for coming was because you received another hot tip on a business deal. Face it, you invited me to come along so there'd be an even number and I'd be your lap dog when you had time for me. Now you're using me to play lawyer instead of your convenient boyfriend."

The words stung, but like everything Jack had ever told her, it was truth. Perhaps not the full truth, but enough to cause her stomach to churn and her cheeks to warm. She dipped her chin to her chest. "Your right about me using you to help Kate. I took you for granted and I shouldn't have. But you're not right about how I feel about you. I love you."

She didn't know where the words came from. She'd never uttered them before to any boy or man. Did she really mean them?

If she wasn't sure, neither was Jack. "You have a funny way of showing it."

She nodded as her eyes began to burn.

Jack heaved a sigh and scooted forward. His next words came out sounding like a legal argument. "Let's assume what you say is true. You love me. Fine. But the real question is, how much is each of us willing to work to see if whatever this goofy thing we have for each other will last?"

"I'm willing," she said, while a tear slid down her cheek.

"I know you want to, but can you?" He picked up his glass and finished his drink. "Or, can I?"

"I don't understand."

He leaned back in the chair and drummed the arms with his fingers. "Let's see. I work ten-hour days. You work fourteen or more. I play golf most weekends. You promised you'd join me, but that hasn't happened yet. You don't want children. I do. My family is close and we enjoy each other's company. You went ten years without seeing your parents, and now it might be a couple of times a year." He picked up his glass and swirled the nearly melted ice cubes. "I like a good stiff drink once in a while. You prefer wine. I like college football while you'd rather track the S&P 500."

"You're right. Everything you said is true, especially my preference for wine. Scotch tastes like burnt wood." She made a feeble attempt at a smile. "What other issues do we need to work on?"

His voice lowered. "That's the thing. There's too many to mention and new ones keep popping up. Can we communicate enough to work through them? Up to now, you haven't let me into much of your world and I haven't let you into much of mine. Do either of us want to be that vulnerable?"

He raised his hand when she started to speak. "That last question shouldn't be answered in haste. Let's leave it to simmer."

A few long seconds passed before Heather asked, "Where do you suggest we start?"

"Come with me tomorrow to the bond hearing in Brownsville."

She almost told him she needed to stay with Steve and help him with the case. Her mouth hinged open to speak, but she looked at Jack's raised eyebrows and his keen eyes. It was a test that she wanted to pass. "I'll come with you."

A smile pulled up the corners of his mouth.

Heather moved to sit on the arm of his chair. After giving him a kiss, she stood and said, "I guess that was the answer you were looking for."

"I was going to fly home the first thing in the morning if you turned me down."

Heather looked closely to see if he was kidding. He wasn't. She nudged her head toward the door. "Come on. I have big news for Steve and we need to fill you in on all the developments in the case."

"And I need to tell both of you about my wasted day in Brownsville."

With their relationship back on a more stable footing, Heather and Jack strode down the hall in lock-step with her hand around his waist and his across her shoulders. They separated when she opened the door to enter Kate's apartment. As expected, Steve was in the recliner, leaned back with his hands folded over his stomach.

"Been back long?" asked Steve.

Jack moved to the couch and sat on the end closest to Steve. "I thought you were asleep. No, not long."

"Long enough to kiss and make up?"

Jack shot a stare at Heather even though his words were meant for Steve. "Not exactly making up. Something closer to a truce, or, at least, a break in the hostilities. How did you know?"

"Don't ask," she said. "He's omniscient."

"Hardly," said Steve. "I caught a faint whiff of Heather's perfume when Jack sat near me. The last time I spoke with him, he was put-out with both of us. I know I haven't kissed him since he returned, so that left Heather as my chief suspect."

"Guilty as charged," said Jack.

"Did she apologize?"

"She did."

"Good. She needed to. You don't need to be treated like a spare tire."

Heather put her hands akimbo. "What's that supposed to mean?"

"Explain it, Jack."

He couldn't help but chuckle. "It means you don't usually need me, but I come in handy now and then."

Once again, the truth stung, but Heather knew this time it was two men who cared about her that were picking on her. Being a cop for ten years trained her to take the ribbing and dish some back.

"Just for that, we're leaving you alone tomorrow while we get Kate out of jail."

Steve lowered his feet. "That's good. I have a job for you two on your way. Go by the garage where they hauled Gloria's SUV after the wreck. It should be in Port Isabel. Ramos said they were keeping it local."

"What are we looking for?" asked Jack.

"Damage. Take pictures from all angles if you can."

"Anything else?" asked Heather.

"Yeah. Tell me what you found out at Zeke's. How did he act today?"

Heather took a seat next to Jack with her hand resting on his thigh. "Zeke was a new man today. I'm not sure if he has some sort of split personality or if he's a super-intense, obsessive-compulsive type. It's like his brain shifted from artist to salesman."

Steve nodded, but didn't say anything.

"He's almost finished with a painting that I'm supposed to see tomorrow. He was standing on his patio when a bolt of lightning hit a palm tree that borders the parking lot."

"On the night of the murder?" asked Jack.

"Better than that." Her voice rose with excitement. "I think it was very near the exact time the killer fired the shot. It shows two figures walking across the parking lot, one following the other in driving rain."

"What are they wearing?" asked Steve with new urgency in his voice.

"Both are wearing rain gear. The one in the lead has a hood

over his head, but Zeke's not finished with the head of the second."

"You don't know if that person had a hood on or not?"

"The outline didn't look like it, but we'll have to wait until tomorrow to be sure."

Jack, thinking like a defense attorney, had to question what Heather saw. "It was pitch dark, and the rain was coming down in buckets. How could he see to capture images in the parking lot that must have been at least fifty yards away?"

Heather patted Jack's leg. "The lightning acted like a giant flash bulb. It might as well have been full daylight. But you're right, the images are blurred by rain, and the two figures are walking away. He couldn't make a positive ID in court."

"Still," said Steve. "It could corroborate some of the information the police gathered at the scene. There might even be a surprise or two in the painting that could lead to something."

For the next half hour, Steve and Heather caught Jack up on the interviews they'd conducted and answered all the questions they could. He concluded that Ramos should be moved to the top of the list of all the suspects, especially after he looked for the pistol in the recliner.

At the end of the update, Heather asked Steve, "What do you have us doing tonight?"

Steve pulled the lever on the side of his chair and reclined. "I don't know about you two, but I'm ordering a pizza and staying home."

"Are you sure there's nothing you need help with?" asked Jack.

"Now that you mention it, let Heather take you out for a really nice meal. Then have her drive you to the end of the road in that fancy golf cart she rented, and cut over to the beach. Drive another five or ten miles north, gather driftwood and build a fire. Watch the waves and count the stars. That's what I'd do if Maggie was here."

"Sounds good to me," said Jack.

"Me, too," said Heather, matching the excitement in Jacks' voice.

It didn't take Jack long to scurry from the apartment to prepare for their date. As Heather eased the door shut, a lump caught in her throat. Steve had pictured his former wife and not Kate in the motion picture he'd produced in his mind. She doubted Kate had a chance, even if she wanted him.

24

The next morning, Heather was glad she wasn't driving when she and Jack topped the causeway and began the long descent down. The height of the bridge was such that ocean-going vessels could pass under it. That meant the view from the top went on for miles and included Padre Island in the rear-view mirror. The massive bay lay beneath them, and Port Isabel directly ahead. Off to her right, a pair of Jet Skis skimmed over the water, shooting up a rooster tail behind them. A shrimp boat chugged toward the jetties that would guard it on its way to the Gulf of Mexico and waters teeming with bounty.

"This is a special place," said Heather to herself as much as to Jack.

"There's a lot to like about it," he replied while keeping his eyes on the road and a lookout for pelicans. "How far into town is the repair shop?"

"We go past the cutoff to Brownsville. You'll turn off the main road to the left. I'll let you know in plenty of time."

"Why did Steve want us to take photos of the car?"

She watched a long-necked heron make a beak-first dive into the water and come out with a wriggling fish. "Your guess is as good as mine. I'm surprised he told you as much as he did yesterday. The closer he gets to the end of a case, the more secretive he becomes. I think there's a movie director living in him who's dying to get out."

"Or a writer?" asked Jack.

"His stories are getting better. Kate's coaching has made a tremendous difference."

"I'm surprised he lets you read them."

"It's a game we play. I pretend I'm not interested, and he pretends I don't listen when he's dictating or listening to the computer read it back to him."

"Do you miss not living in a big house?"

Heather turned to him. "Where did that question come from?"

"Just asking."

"You know my story. The last time I lived in a big house was when I was growing up, but it never was a true home. Being born to the Boston elite meant special schools at an early age. They were live-in schools, most being out of state. Those gave way to exclusive prep-schools, some in Europe. Then came the Ivy League education."

Jack shook his head. "I still can't believe you rebelled against your father and became a cop in Boston."

"I can't believe he took away my allowance, and I lived in a third-floor walk-up and ate Ramen noodles five days a week."

"Is that why you're so intent on making money?"

So that was the reason for the questions. Jack wanted to know if she had any desire to live in what he considered a normal home.

She shrugged and pulled her phone from her purse. "You'll turn after three more blocks." After she gathered her thoughts, she said, "One thing I learned while going through the police academy and being a cop is that I enjoy having money more than not having it."

Jack shot her a glance. "That's something we agree on. At least up to a point."

She was about to launch into a monologue of what a rush it was to make a deal that would be worth seven or eight figures when she stopped herself. That might lead to a long philosophical debate involving what things in life are of true value. "Next street. Turn left."

They traveled a block and came to a building made of corrugated, rust-dappled tin. "Go around the side. There should be a gate."

The side she pointed to was all chain-link fences, so they made the block and came from the opposite direction. A double gate stood open with no one around.

Jack pointed. "That looks like an unmarked SUV close to the fence on the other side of the lot. Do you want me to pull in?"

"Park on the street. I'll go alone. Honk if you see someone coming out of the building."

Heather exited and slipped the strap of her purse over her head. She dug out her cell phone and prepared to take photos. According to the signs on the fence, she had no right to come on the property. Concluding that some signs are best ignored, she walked across the lot with no one taking notice of her. The reason might be the loud music and a noisy air compressor kicking on from within the building. It wasn't long before she had photos of the right side, the crumpled hood, and the left side. She was moving to get photos of the rear of the vehicle when a horn honked. Her head jerked up, and she saw a burly man wearing a sleeveless shirt barreling toward her. His words were rough, seasoned with a thick Spanish accent.

"Hey! What are you doing back here?"

Heather snapped two more photos and approached the man with her right hand extended. "Good morning. My name is Sally Greenberg. I'm a reporter doing a follow-up story on the attack of Chief Giles." She pointed. "That's her SUV, isn't it?"

The man pointed to the gate. "No customers allowed back here."

Heather walked to the man who stared at her through

narrow slits for eyes. "Sorry. I didn't see a sign. Do you mind if I ask you a few questions?"

"There's no trespassing signs in English and Spanish."

She spoke in a pleading voice. "I only have a few questions."

"Get lost."

Not wanting to press her luck, Heather made for the car. She knew she'd accomplished her mission without incident when she buckled the seat belt and they were driving past the building.

"Was that guy giving you trouble?" asked Jack.

She thought about the man, his clothes, and his manner. "He would have if I'd stayed any longer. The grip of a pistol was sticking out of his waistband."

Jack cut his eyes to look at her. "I didn't know they fixed cars with pistols these days."

"It makes you wonder, doesn't it?"

"Any more stops before we go to Brownsville?"

Heather pointed to the right. "You know the way. Let's get Kate out of jail and back to the island. I'm sure she's ready for a shower and a decent meal."

STEVE WAS ON HIS WAY TO THE FRONT DOOR BEFORE THE third knock sounded. Despite being alone, he opened the door and invited the caller to come in and have a seat.

"You're a trusting man." The voice belonged to Gloria Giles.

"The odds of a bad guy making a house call at ten in the morning are pretty slim." Steve walked past the kitchen and pointed in the coffeepot's direction. "There's an extra mug on the counter and the coffee should still be hot."

"Thanks. I'll take you up on it."

He heard the scrape of the pot as Gloria slid it from the warming plate. The trickle of liquid into a mug followed. "What brings you out on a Sunday morning? I thought you'd be in bed recovering from your injuries."

The chief of police settled on the couch to the left of his chair while the aromas of coffee and lavender bath soap drifted his way.

"No injuries except a sprained wrist and stiffness. They put me in a padded neck brace that does nothing but make it hard for me to see my feet."

"Sorry to hear about the accident, but I'm glad it wasn't more serious."

"Accident? Is that what they're calling it?"

"I heard it both ways. I guess it depends on who's reporting and what their agenda is. Tell me what happened."

"I had business in Brownsville and wasn't but a few miles out of Port Isabel when a truck came from behind and did a pit maneuver on my brand-new ride. He put me in the ditch and I smacked a telephone pole. Luckily, it was close enough to the coast that there was a lot of sand in a shallow ditch. It slowed me down and probably saved my life. I think it was the air bag deploying that did the damage to my neck."

Steve nodded at the appropriate times. "I guess it all happened so fast you didn't have time to see the license plate or get a description of the driver."

"No plate on the front of the truck. It was plain white. There must be a thousand of those in the area."

He heard her take a sip from the mug and resettle it on a stone coaster.

"I guess you're wondering why I'm here."

"Let me guess. You came for a good cup of coffee and stimulating conversation."

Gloria chuckled. "Those are bonuses, but not the real reason. I heard the DA is dropping the charges on Kate and I wanted to see if she was back yet."

"Heather and Jack are on their way to pick her up." Steve didn't keep the anger out of his voice. "Whose idea was it to lock her up in the first place?"

"That's what I need to talk to you about. I have a dirty cop and I'd like advice on how to handle this."

"Ramos?"

"How did you know?"

"Simple. He considered no other suspects. Heather and I found three other people with a reason for killing Ricardo in half a day. The way I have it figured, as soon as Ramos found out Kate was available to pin a murder rap on, he lured Ricardo to the complex." Steve allowed Gloria to draw her own conclusion to what happened next.

Gloria took another sip of coffee. "Any ideas on where the murder weapon might be?"

He considered telling her that Ranger Mike Moreno had it, but decided not to. Heather accused him of being dramatic when a case was winding down. He didn't want to disappoint her, so he made up a plausible explanation.

"There's plenty of salt water around here. If it were me, I'd have given it a burial at sea."

"You're probably right."

"I wouldn't worry too much about not finding it. You have plenty to put Ramos away."

"Are you sure?"

Steve nodded. "Tell me what you have so far and I'll add to your list."

Gloria stood and went to the patio door. "You made a good point earlier when you said he didn't look for other suspects. In fact, he sat around the office for two days putting together a case file instead of doing any real investigating."

"What else?"

"He waited until I was in the hospital before he arrested Kate."

"You had to be out of the way. It all fits. He had someone take you out of the picture and he made his move."

Gloria moved from the door to stand in front of Steve.

"What I don't have yet is a motive for Ramos wanting to kill Ricardo."

Once again, Steve didn't want to show all his cards, so he made up another plausible but incomplete answer. "When in doubt, look for a woman."

"What's that supposed to mean?"

"Both Ramos and Ricardo were friendly with Connie Diaz. Ramos still is."

"Are you sure?"

"One reason we came here is Heather heard Connie wants to sell this complex and go back to acting. Those two are banging out a deal and trading notes on their love lives. Ramos was with Connie the night of the storm—well, almost all night."

He heard Gloria take in a big breath and slowly let it out. "I don't want to make any mistakes on this. Are you saying Connie told Heather that Ramos was here at this complex when Ricardo Alvarez was shot?"

"Yep."

"And Heather can swear under oath that Connie said that?"

"Better than that. Heather and I can both testify to what Connie said."

Gloria stood and paced. "Almost perfect. The only thing better would be an eyewitness."

Steve chuckled. "I can't help you there."

A quick stutter preceded a rushed apology.

Steve waved it off. "I was a fan of dark humor before the lights went out for me." He paused. "What's your next move?"

She didn't hesitate. "Get a warrant for Ramos' arrest."

"That sounds like a good idea. Kate will sleep better tonight knowing he's behind bars." Steve stood. "One more thing. Why don't I round up everyone Heather and I talked to and bring them here tomorrow morning? This would be a much more comfortable place for you to interview them than down at the police station. There's no telling what else you might learn about Ramos."

Gloria hesitated, so Steve kept talking. "Think about it, Gloria. It's Sunday. That means you're going to have to hunt down a judge, assemble a team, and make a clean take-down of Ramos with no one getting hurt. Then, you'll want press coverage to put the community at rest because you've cracked the case. After that, you can sit back, drink coffee, have some snacks, and take statements in comfort.

Gloria was almost convinced. "That does sound like a good plan, but I pictured the press in front of the police department."

Do you really want to sit for hours on a hard chair in an interview room?"

"You'd be good at selling cars. I like your idea of having everyone meet here for statements, but not until tomorrow afternoon. I'll wait until early tomorrow morning to serve the warrant on Ramos, then hold the press conference with the police department as a backdrop. After that, I can come here and take statements from the others."

"We can make it a celebration party," said Steve. "After all, you deserve it."

Steve walked her to the door and let out a sigh after she left. He went back to his chair, picked up his phone from where he'd placed it on an end table, and told it to call Mike Moreno.

After two sentences of small talk, Steve got to the point. "I need a few state troopers to prevent a murder tonight."

25

With a population of under seven thousand residents, Port Isabel had a down-in-the-heels vibe about it, as did many blue-collar towns. It didn't take long before Jack and Heather left the city limit sign behind them, and entered a surrealistic world of massive windmills dotting the coastal plains. Mile after mile of the three-bladed, one-legged giants rose from the salt-grass to crank out energy. The prevailing breezes off the Gulf of Mexico made this one of the most sought-after areas in the state for producing the holy grail of the twenty-first century: clean, renewable energy.

While Heather tried in vain to count the massive metal structures, Jack opened a conversation. "Thanks again for last night. I saw a side of you I didn't know existed."

"What side is that?" Heather turned in her seat to look at him.

"A woman who enjoys being outside, collecting firewood, and isn't afraid to lie on her back and look up at the stars."

"I couldn't help it. There were no lights, and the clouds cooperated by staying away. Between that and the sound of the rolling waves, it was like the beach transported me to a world where time had no meaning." She paused. "The company wasn't bad, either."

Jack moaned and put a hand over his heart. "It's good to know I've moved up to a rating of tolerable."

"Most of the time," said Heather in a teasing way.

"Let's have a repeat tonight."

She brought her gaze to the road that stretched ahead of them. "I can't commit until I see what Steve needs me to do."

Jack let out a tiny murmur of frustration.

Heather placed a hand on his arm. "It's almost over." She brought her right hand up and moved her thumb and index finger to within a fraction of an inch from touching. "He's this close to solving the case. That usually means things will speed up and he'll need my help."

Jack shook his head. "How do you know it's almost over? From what you two told me yesterday, the killer could be several people, including someone in the cartel."

"That's Steve's style. He doesn't tell all he knows until he's ready to spring the trap."

Jack puffed out his cheeks and emptied them with a huff. "Enough shop-talk. Have you thought more about what we talked about last night?"

"What part? We talked about a lot of things."

"You know what part."

She looked to her left. He deserved an answer, but words refused to form. She needed to say something, so she spewed out the first thing that came to her mind. "How many houses do you think that one windmill is powering right now?"

His lips barely parted. "I'll take that as a no."

"Then you're wrong. It's not a no, but it's not a yes either. I need more time to think about it."

"How much time?"

Her first inclination was to tell him she wouldn't rush into something they'd both regret. Instead, what came out of her mouth was, "Two nights after we solve the case, I'll have an answer for you."

He extended his right hand. "Shake on it."

She did, and he teased her by saying, "Would you mind drawing up a contract on that?"

She teased him right back. "If I do, I'll put an escape clause in the fine print."

"In that case, forget it. You look honest... for a lawyer, that is."

She socked him in the arm.

The miles hurried by as they bantered back and forth about everything and nothing. Before she knew it, they were in the heart of Brownsville, looking for a parking spot close to the courthouse. Sunday morning meant there was no problem finding one. As they walked toward the courthouse, Heather's phone signaled an incoming text. She put a hand on Jack's arm to stop him from walking away from her. "It's from Steve. He says the DA dropped the charges on Kate and we're to pick her up at the county jail."

"How did he know that before me?"

Heather cocked her head. "I already told you. He's an omniscient medium who can tell the past, future, and everything that's happening in the world now."

"Or?"

"Or, Mike Moreno received a phone call from Steve and someone high-up with the Rangers told the DA Kate's arrest is bogus and she needed to be released before her hot-shot lawyer sued the city and county."

Jack wiggled his eyebrows. "I like the sound of that."

"Let's not press our luck. Where's the jail?"

"Not far."

When they arrived, Kate was pacing the sidewalk outside the building. Her hair was a bird's nest of tangles and her makeup was the worse for two days wear. She carried a brown paper bag that Heather thought contained paperwork and perhaps the jewelry she had on when Ramos arrested her.

Before Jack could push the unlock button, Kate pulled on the back door and almost lost her balance when it slipped from her fingers with a loud pop as it retracted. She slapped the window before Jack could find the right button and fix his mistake. "Sorry," he said when Kate tumbled into the back seat.

"Sorry for what?" asked Kate with venom in her words. "Sorry for not letting me in the car, not getting me out yesterday, or making me wait on the sidewalk for two hours?"

"You've been out that long?" asked Heather.

Kate didn't reply.

"We're so sorry," said Jack.

Kate held up her left hand as a stop sign. "Drive. Just drive."

This was a side of Kate Heather had never seen. Up to now she'd been the perfect hostess, a ready listener, and not one to raise her voice. Heather liked this facet of Kate's personality. Something, or someone, could push her only so far before claws came out. And who could blame her? Ramos had framed her for murder, thrown her in jail and transferred her to what was most likely a dungeon of a cell. Stripped of her own clothes and her dignity, Kate had limited interaction with Jack and then, contrary to what she was told by him, she was tossed out on the street on a Sunday morning.

Heather knew time could heal frayed emotions, but she wondered about the events of the last few days. A false arrest for murdering your ex-husband only added to the trauma Kate had already endured.

While Kate was in a jail cell, Heather and Jack had been dining at an exclusive restaurant, riding on the beach, building a fire, and counting stars. Kate and Steve should have had the opportunity to have that same experience. The ride to South Padre Island passed without a single additional word from Kate. All the while, the windmills kept turning.

Jack opened the door to his and Steve's apartment and Heather breezed past him. As expected, Steve sat in the recliner. He'd put on jeans and a shirt with a collar. She deduced he planned on having a more formal day.

"How's Kate?" asked Steve, as he lowered his feet.

"I believe eating nails and spitting sparks is the phrase that captures her state of mind," said Jack.

Steve pulled a hand across his mouth. "I was hoping you wouldn't say that. Was there any problem in getting her released?"

Jack continued to answer. "All charges dropped. She waited two hours on the sidewalk. I wish we'd been privy to that bit of information. Needless to say, it was a chilly ride back to the island."

"Sorry. The one thing I didn't expect on a Sunday morning was efficiency from the DA or the jail."

Heather made her way to the kitchen and retrieved two bottles of water from the refrigerator. She spoke loud enough for Steve and Jack to hear. "After Kate blew up, she gave us the silent treatment. Not another word the whole way."

Heather stopped on her way back to the living room. "Do I smell Chinese?"

"I thought the three of you might be hungry. I had it delivered. I put the oven on warm, but you need to check it."

Jack moved to join Heather in the kitchen. "I don't know about anyone else, but I'm starving."

Heather opened a cabinet and brought down three plates. "Do I need to take Kate a plate?"

"She has her own," said Steve. He rose from the chair and walked to the table. "I figured she's still pretty rattled after two nights behind bars, so I left a note on the bar. I hope she can read it. My hen-scratching leaves a lot to be desired."

Jack pulled silverware from the drawer and soon the trio sat at the table, scooping up helpings of fried rice and three different concoctions from white cartons. Heather and Jack used chop sticks while Steve shoveled his meal in with a spoon.

In between bites, Steve broke the silence. "I had a visitor this morning. Gloria Giles came calling."

Heather looked up from her plate. "How's the island's chief of police?"

"She's wearing a neck brace. Otherwise, it was an informative meeting. She's arresting Ramos tomorrow morning."

Both Heather and Jack put down their chopsticks. Jack was the first to react. "It's about time. What took her so long to figure it out?"

Heather cast her gaze past Steve to the sunny day outside. Something wasn't right. "Wait a minute. If she really thinks Ramos is guilty, why is she waiting until tomorrow morning to arrest him?"

Steve took a bite of egg roll. This was one thing he did that drove Heather to distraction. He'd wait until she asked a pertinent question and then fill his mouth so she'd have to wait for the answer. While he was chewing, she let out a huff and looked at Jack. "Pay attention, Jack. This is the master detective performing a dramatic pause. He does this before he says something profound."

"Nothing profound today," said Steve, with his mouth still half full. He continued to chew then swallowed. "Gloria said she's waiting because she wants to orchestrate the finale."

"What's there to orchestrate?" asked Jack.

"She didn't know that Ramos stayed most of the night with Connie. She also thought it might inconvenience a judge if she rushed, and she wanted to get the press rounded up."

Heather and Jack traded glances. "Something still isn't right," said Heather. "I can almost buy that Gloria needs to make sure Ramos was at the complex, but the other reasons are sketchy."

Jack added, "Judges have their lives interrupted all the time.

It goes with the territory. As for the press, they'd walk through hot coals on Christmas to get to a story like this."

Steve shrugged. "Maybe the wreck rattled Gloria more than I thought. She might be on pain pills and wants to make sure she doesn't slur her words on camera."

What Steve said made sense, but Heather thought it still had the faint smell of something not quite right. What did it matter? Ramos was going to jail. Still, she thought about challenging Steve on it, but Jack spoke up before she could.

"Heather has the photos of Gloria's SUV. She had an interesting encounter with a pistol-packing repairman."

Steve rested his spoon. "Tell me all about it."

For the next few minutes Heather and Jack gave a minute-by minute recounting of their trip to the out-of-the way repair shop and her encounter with the repairman.

"What did he look like?"

"Big, but clean," said Heather. "More like a weightlifter than someone who put a wrench to cars for a living."

"He looked like a bouncer to me," said Jack.

"Interesting."

Once again, Steve changed the direction of the conversation. "Are you ready to make an offer on the property?"

"Let me check my email. If my number crunchers got back with me, I should be able to knock out a contract this afternoon. It won't be the final one and will have plenty of escape clauses in it."

Jack looked at her. "She's big on escape clauses."

"Just for that, you can help me write it."

"Sorry. I'm a defense attorney and useless when it comes to commercial real estate. If you're going to bury your head in a computer this afternoon, so am I, but not in a contract. Remember? I have three trials waiting on me when we get home."

With lunch finished, Heather went to Kate's to check on her. A dirty plate in the sink and the sound of running water in

Kate's bathroom told Heather that her hostess was taking steps to put her life back in order.

When she returned, Jack was in his bedroom with the door closed and Steve was waiting for her at the table. She put her computer and satchel down and sat near him. He spoke in a voice low enough so Jack couldn't hear.

"Is Kate any better?"

"She ate, and I heard water running."

"Good. She'll feel better after washing jail off and taking a nap. How did you sleep last night?"

"Me? I slept fine. What's that got to do with anything?"

"You may not get much sleep tonight."

Heather pulled her head away from him. "What have you volunteered me for now?"

"You'll like it and you'll have company. It will be almost like a slumber party."

26

Connie came to the door wearing a leopard print yoga exercise outfit. It was the most conservative attire Heather had seen her in to date. Heather settled in a chair at a glass dining room table. She arranged two file folders in front of her and fired up her laptop. Steve took his place at the head of the table while Connie walked barefoot to the refrigerator. She returned to the table with a blender of some sort of frozen concoction and three glasses with salted rims. Connie filled the glass in front of Steve.

"Margaritas," said Steve. "Are they frozen or regular?"

"How you know?" asked Connie in her broken English.

"The lime. I smelled it when we came in. You must have a juicer."

"Frozen." said Connie as she filled the remaining glasses.

Steve took a sip. "Delicious."

Heather thanked her. Steve wasn't kidding. The freshly squeezed lime played off the salt on the rim of the glass. The slushy concoction was so much better than what came out of machines.

It must not have been Connie's first batch of the evening. Her words came out slurred, and she launched into business without inhibition. "You want to buy?" Connie pushed a scrap of paper across the table and Heather read it.

"Before we discuss numbers, Steve has a question for you," said Heather.

Connie's perfectly plucked eyebrows pinched together. "What question?"

"Did Ramos ever leave this apartment at any time on the night of Ricardo's murder?"

"I already told you. We drink too much. He fell asleep, and I watch Netflix." She looked for a reaction, but none came. "Now, make me an offer."

"Show her," said Steve.

Heather passed a folder to Connie and opened the one in front of her. "This is an intent to purchase agreement. It will be up to you to accept it, or not."

"How much?"

"Look at the bottom of page four."

Connie flipped the pages with purpose. Her gaze settled on the figure listed. "This is less than half."

"I told you it would be."

"If you pay cash, I agree."

"I'll pay in cash, gold, Bitcoin, or a combination of the three. But..." Heather let the sentence dangle in the air until Connie looked up. "There are certain conditions."

"What conditions?"

"You'll find them on the pages we skipped. To help you better understand, Steve and I will explain."

Steve smiled and spoke in a smooth, fatherly tone. "Connie, I need to tell you a little about me and Heather. I used to be a homicide detective in Houston. Heather was a detective in Boston."

Connie's eyes widened at the information. "You're both cops?"

"Not anymore, but we help the police from time to time solving murders. We came here for a nice quiet vacation and found ourselves in the middle of a murder. We wouldn't have gotten involved if the victim wasn't Kate's ex-husband. We knew the police would suspect her."

"Stupid cops!" Connie all but spit the words out. "Kate didn't kill Ricardo. She a nice lady who writes books."

Steve nodded. "You're right. She didn't kill him, but we had to find out who did to get her out of jail."

"You know killer?"

"I can't tell you who, but the person is involved with the men your husband used to work for."

Connie put one hand to her throat and picked up her glass with the other. After an over-sized drink, her eyes narrowed. "What does this have to do with me?"

"Everything," said Steve. "You know as well as I do that whoever killed Ricardo made a mistake. You're the one they meant to kill." Steve spread his arms wide. "Why else would you be willing to sell this for half its value?"

Heather jumped in. "You're in danger."

Connie didn't dispute the predicament she found herself in, but she wasn't ready to go down without a fight. "How do I know you're telling the truth?"

Steve leaned forward. "In about an hour, highway patrol officers will be here, and they'll spend the night here in your penthouse. You won't be here. You'll be with Heather in one of our apartments."

Connie took in a deep breath, and dry washed her hands.

Just in case Connie didn't understand the gravity of the situation, Heather explained. "We believe someone will come here tonight and try to kill you."

Steve lowered his voice to a whisper. "We might be wrong. There may not be people out to kill you. If you believe you're safe, then stay here tonight by yourself."

Steve couldn't see her, but Connie was shaking her head. "I go with you."

"In that case," said Steve. "There are other conditions that you'll need to agree to."

Heather thought Connie needed some good news to keep from being overwhelmed. "There are also some enormous benefits if you agree to our terms."

"What do you mean?"

Heather pointed to the contract with her pen. "Everything is in writing. Tomorrow afternoon, a Texas Ranger will take you to the airport in Harlingen. He'll put you on my private jet, and you'll fly to Conroe. My pilot will give you one hundred thousand dollars as a down payment for the complex. Rangers will have a new identity for you and take you to a very nice hotel where I've reserved a room for you. You'll be off the island and safe as long as you do nothing stupid."

"When will I get the rest of money?"

"We're flying home on Thursday. The money will be in my office waiting for you on Friday, if that's what you want. I'd advise against having that much in cash, but I can make it happen if you insist."

"What do you suggest?"

"Do you still want to go to Spain?"

"Yes."

"I'm used to transferring sizable sums of money all over the world. We can talk about your options tonight."

Steve took over. "There's something else we insist you do, or there's no deal. You'll need to tell the Rangers everything you know about the people your husband worked for. That starts tonight when a Ranger named Mike will be here."

"They'll kill me if I talk."

"They're already trying to kill you. We're keeping you alive."

"How do I know I can trust you?"

Steve folded his hands in front of him. "It's us or the cartel. Take your pick."

It didn't take Connie long to choose, but with conditions of her own. "I want two-hundred thousand in cash before I get on airplane."

"It's a deal," said Heather. "One last thing." She pointed to a clause in the contract. "This appoints me as property manager beginning immediately. You'll still own the complex until you receive all monies agreed to, but I'm running it."

"Why you want to manage?"

"That's not important for you to know. Sign on the last page and pack an overnight bag. You have a date with a Texas Ranger."

Heather's pen glided across the page as she added her signature to that of Connie's on the one-of-a-kind agreement. A knock on the door caused both women to jerk their heads up. Heather snapped open her purse and retrieved her pistol.

"See who that is," whispered Steve.

Heather kicked off her shoes and quick-walked to the door where she looked through a peep-hole which gave her a fisheye view of Gloria Giles. Heather hot-footed it back to Steve and whispered, "It's Gloria."

"I'm coming," said Heather in a loud voice as she scraped the chair across the tile floor. Steve lowered his voice. "Connie and I will go to the bedroom and be quiet until you come get us."

Heather held her right index finger against her lips, giving Connie the signal not to talk. Steve and Connie went to the master bedroom and closed the door. The last things to do before answering the door was to put glasses and blender in the freezer and put the contracts back in her computer bag.

A second, more insistent knock sounded. Heather scurried to the door and opened it. Gloria's eyes opened wide, when she saw it was Heather, but only for a few seconds.

"What are you doing here?"

It was time for a lie and it needed to be convincing. "Sorry about the delay in getting to the door. I've been inspecting the penthouse. Since I'm planning on buying the complex, I wanted to see if it lived up to Connie's description."

"Is she here?"

"I'm surprised you didn't see her on your way up. She went shopping and told me to take my time looking." Heather pointed to her computer. "Since it's nice and quiet up here, I thought I'd take advantage of the time alone and knock out the preliminary purchase agreement. It's the first step."

Gloria cast her gaze to the table with the lap top on it and Heather's chair pulled out. "No problem. It was just a follow-up question for Connie. It can wait until tomorrow."

It seemed like ten, but it was closer to five minutes when Heather turned the knob of the bathroom door and Steve spoke. "Can us scared rabbits come out of our hole?"

"What did she want?" asked Connie, her voice catching.

"It was just a follow up question. Expect her back tomorrow."

"But I won't be here," said Connie.

"You'll be here tomorrow morning."

"Where will I sleep tonight?" asked Connie.

"In my bed," said Steve. "I'll be in the living room."

Heather tilted her head. "What about Jack?"

"He has his own room."

Connie ran her hands down the faux leopard skin outfit. "Are you afraid I'll visit your boyfriend?"

Heat rose into Heather's face, but she didn't want to admit a little green monster named jealousy whispered a warning in her ear. "Nothing of the sort, but you're in danger, and I always carry a pistol. I'll sleep on the couch. Besides, I'm sure Kate wants to be alone after what she's been through."

Steve stood outside the doorway. "Get her packed and out of here before we have any more unexpected visitors."

Before they could pack, Steve's phone buzzed with an incoming text. A mechanical voice identified the text came from Mike Moreno. "Twenty minutes out."

Steve instructed the phone to reply to the text. "Penthouse unlocked. Contract signed."

27

Mike Moreno, along with two men and a woman, piled out of an unmarked SUV as Heather looked down from the patio balcony of Steve and Jack's apartment. They'd parked between a pickup and a minivan, on the far side of the parking lot. Everyone wore jeans and carried a variety of suitcases and bags. They looked like a couple and two single guys coming for a week on the beach.

Thirty minutes later, Heather opened the door to let Mike in. "Two cameras mounted," he announced. "One in the hall and one facing the door from the inside of Ms. Diaz's apartment." He unzipped a large black bag and took out a laptop. "I need to fire this up and make sure the cameras are working." The computer went through its normal come-to-life procedures and showed a full screen of the hallway and door of the penthouse. Mike manipulated the mouse and a second image on a split-screen came up, this one from inside Connie's.

Mike got on his phone. "Hall camera looks good. Move the one on the inside more to the left." The image on the screen jiggled and shifted. "That's good. Unpack and get into body armor. Two people with eyes on your screen at all times."

The phone's speaker was on. "Is it all right if we finish the margaritas we found in the freezer?"

"Sure," said Mike. "I hear there's plenty of work in the tourist shops around here." He disconnected the call.

"Sorry to bust in like that," said Mike. Steve made introductions and told him they'd already had one visitor in Connie's penthouse this evening.

"Who?"

"Gloria Giles paid us a visit before we could get Connie out of there."

"What did she want?"

"To talk to Connie. She said it was a follow-up question that could wait until tomorrow morning."

"Did Gloria say anything about arresting Detective Ramos?"

"It didn't come up."

"Good. Where's Connie? I need to have a long talk with her."

"In my bedroom. First door to the left down the hall."

"I'd better come with you," said Heather. "She has a thing for dark, handsome types."

"Is there someone who can monitor the screen while we're out of the room?"

"Jack's here. I'll get him."

Heather scampered to Jack's bedroom and told him what she needed. He looked up from a yellow legal pad. "I thought they were bringing a female trooper."

"They did. She's in the penthouse, waiting with the other two."

Jack put the legal pad down. "How long will you be?"

Heather tilted her head. "I have no idea. As long as it takes, I guess."

Jack sighed. "I thought we might sneak away and get something to eat."

"Steve wants me to go with him to check on Kate later on and there's no telling when things might kick off in the penthouse."

The muscles in Jack's jaw flexed. He threw his pen down on the legal pad and stood. "I should have known better than to ask."

She blocked his path and put her hands on his chest. "Have you been in here sulking?"

"What if I have?"

"Why are you making a big deal of us not going to dinner when we have important things to do here?"

He took her by the wrists and gently lowered her hands. "Since you make up half of the great detective team, figure it out yourself."

Stunned by his words, she watched as he stepped around her and went toward Steve and Mike's voices.

"I don't have time for this," mumbled Heather. She knocked on Connie's door and walked in on her as she lay in bed, watching television. Spanish flowed from the speakers, but the unspoken language of a steamy romance didn't need interpretation. Heather found the remote and switched it off. "It's time for you to answer some questions."

Mike appeared at the door, pushing one of the roller chairs from the dining room and pulling another. Connie might as well have been a cat looking at a bowl of cream when she saw the handsome lawman. She all but purred and slithered up in the bed, coming to rest in what Heather would describe as a B movie pose intended to portray seduction. The fluttering eyelashes lasted until Mike informed her of her rights and that lying to him could result in criminal charges.

An hour and a half later, Heather and Mike left Connie to wash the running mascara from her face.

"That was a good start," said Mike. "I'll need to check out what she said and see how many lies she told. Another Ranger will pick her up from the airport in Conroe tomorrow evening and hit her with a second round of questions."

"I'm supposed to meet with her in my office on Friday," said Heather. "Will you have all you need by then?"

"We should. If not, we'll take her passport until we do."

"She'll have plenty of money to console her."

"By the way," said Mike. "Thanks for being her attorney while I questioned her. I wish all attorneys allowed their clients to speak so freely."

"If I'd left you alone with that cougar, you might have come away with claw marks."

The handsome man grinned. "Double thanks for that."

Steve stood as soon as Heather pushed her chair under the table. "Are you ready to go?"

Jack fidgeted in his chair but said nothing.

"I'm ready."

"Where are you two going?" asked Mike.

"Kate's," said Steve. "We haven't checked on her since Heather and Jack brought her back from jail."

"You'd better step lightly," said Jack. "She wasn't in a very good mood when I last saw her."

KATE'S APARTMENT HAD A CAVE-LIKE FEELING WHEN HEATHER and Steve arrived. The closed vertical blinds and curtains gave the living room a closed-in, almost cocoon vibe. Heather wondered if Kate was attempting to reclaim a sense of safety, and looking at the outside world was a bit much for her to handle.

"We wanted to check on you," said Steve after Kate snapped open the dead bolt and let them in.

"I'm much improved."

"We won't stay long," said Steve. "I know you need time by yourself to process all that's happened."

Kate turned away without responding. She went to the living room and sat on a chair that was infrequently used. Its diminutive size took up an odd-shaped open space to the right of a television mounted on the wall. With legs crossed and hands on the plaid fabric of the armrests, she waited.

Steve went to the recliner and settled himself with feet flat on the floor. "Have you eaten anything since you got home?"

"I ate after I showered. Thank you for the Chinese."

"One meal a day won't keep you going. We could have something delivered for dinner."

All the while she had a light grip on the chair's arms, as if she needed to make sure it wouldn't shift beneath her. "No, thanks. I overdid it on Chinese. If I'm hungry, I'll get a bowl of cereal."

"Heather won't be spending the night here," said Steve.

"That's fine," said Kate, her voice sounding more confident. "I'm used to being alone."

"I know what you mean," said Steve. "If I'm not working on a case or have something I can't do by myself, I often prefer it."

Long seconds of silence followed. Kate finally shifted in her chair. Steve must have waited for her to make this little move before he spoke. "Don't blame Jack for you staying in jail for two nights. I'm to blame. I could have had you released yesterday, but it was too dangerous for you to come back to the island."

Kate's fingers dug into the arms of the chair. "Am I still in danger?"

"Not any more. The police will soon make arrests that will put Ricardo's killer behind bars for a long time. You were being used as a scapegoat. All that has changed. The killer has someone else to place the blame on. You're as safe as any other person who's living on the island."

Kate released her grip on the chair. "I want to go to Florida."

"I know. When would you like to leave?"

"Tonight, if I could."

Steve shook his head. "There's going to be activity tonight and tomorrow. A Texas Ranger is in my apartment. He'll need to interview you. It's a complicated case and it may take a few days before you can leave."

Kate let out a huff. "I have a six-month lease."

"Where do you want to go?" asked Heather.

For the first time since she sat down, Kate's gaze shifted to Heather. "To Florida. I want to see my parents. I've limited my contact with them through the years because I was afraid Ricardo would use them to find me." She let out a sigh of regret. "As things turned out, I made it easy for him."

"Leave it to me and Heather," said Steve. "We'll get you to Florida as soon as possible."

"What about my lease here?"

"I'll cancel it," said Heather with a shrug that communicated it was no big deal. "It's something I can do as the new manager of the complex."

Kate's response was an open mouth followed by a this-is-too-good-to-be-true stare.

Steve rose. Kate and Heather followed his lead. "Heather, do you need to get anything before we go back to my place?"

"Only my toothbrush."

"Go get it while I say goodnight to Kate."

Heather took her time. When she returned, Kate had Steve's hand in hers. Or was it the other way around? The only thing Heather heard was Kate saying, "I'm sorry." Steve replied, "I'm sorry, too."

They separated, and Steve walked to the door. "You'll be safe tonight, Kate. But it's always a good idea to use the dead bolt."

The click of metal into a slot reminded Heather of something she'd seen portrayed in a movie. What she didn't know was whether the movie starring Steve and Kate was at the end of a scene, or if it was right before *The End.* Time would tell.

Steve remained silent until they reached the door to his apartment. "You, Jack and Mike need to take turns watching the monitor. Jack's room has two beds. I'm taking one of them."

"You don't want to stay up for the action?"

"Tell me about it in the morning."

No matter what Steve said, Heather doubted he'd sleep much, if any.

28

Once inside, Steve didn't stay but a few minutes before informing Jack of his intention to retire to the bedroom for some alone time and perhaps a nap on the spare bed.

"I plan to go out for a bite to eat, even if I have to go alone," said Jack.

After Steve left, Heather caught Jack's attention and motioned her head toward the patio. Once outside with the door shut, she stared at him. "What's up with you?"

Jack went to the railing and looked into the night. "What do you think is wrong?"

"I'm not sure, but you're acting like a petulant child. Sulking isn't very becoming on you."

He shrugged. "And being obsessed isn't your best look."

Heather wanted to give him a quick kick in the seat of his pants, but stuffed down her anger. If it was a battle of wits and words he wanted, that suited her Irish temper just fine. "Give me your best shot, counselor."

Jack spun around. "What will you be doing for the next two hours?"

"What?"

Jack lowered his voice and repeated the question. "For the next two hours, what will you do?"

"How should I know? Hit men don't keep regular hours or advertise when they'll show up."

"Perhaps not, but they're not much on taking unnecessary chances. Look at the parking lot. People are coming and going to places where they can have an enjoyable meal and spend time together. That means there's a high probability that someone would see the guy you're waiting for in the parking lot. That translates to witnesses that could identify and testify against anyone who was stupid enough to come on this property until the wee hours of the morning."

Heather shook her head. "You're talking probabilities. The only way to be sure is to keep watching the monitor all night. Until dawn if necessary."

"That's not your job. Why can't Mike watch the monitor for two hours? That's all I'm asking."

"Why are you pressuring me to go out tonight?"

"I just am."

Heather wasn't buying it. "You're putting me through some sort of test, and I don't like it."

Jack threw up his hands. "Perhaps I am testing you. So what? You've been testing my patience for months." His voice raised. "I thought we were coming here to see if we have a future together. And don't pretend that you haven't tested me twice as much as I have you."

"How?"

Jack held up an index finger. "Number one: You broke your promise to play golf with me once a week. Number two: You regularly break dinner dates with me because you're working on the next big deal. Three: This trip. Coming here wasn't about seeing if we had a future. The main reason we came here is because you heard a rumor about a hot deal with this complex."

"That's not right." She tried to continue, but he spoke over her.

"That's the main reason you came. Otherwise, Steve could have come by himself."

"I didn't know there was going to be a murder and Connie would be so desperate to sell. How was I to know I could get the complex for half price?"

"You're going to make millions of dollars more. Congratulations." Jack took a step forward. "It doesn't matter. If it wasn't this complex, you would have spent your time researching other properties or on the phone working some other deal. Don't deny it."

She couldn't, so she didn't. That one hit home. But she wasn't about to let him have the last word. "I'm committed to seeing this case through."

"I know you are, and I expect you to. All I asked you for was two hours. Ask Steve or Mike if they can do without us until ten o'clock and see what they say."

If there was one thing Heather couldn't abide, it was being told what to do. She set her jaw. "I'm staying here. There's a potential victim in one bedroom, a blind man in the second, and a Texas Ranger staring at a boring view of a hallway and the inside of a penthouse."

Jack took in a deep breath and looked down at her. "Enjoy your evening, Heather. I'm not sure when I'll be back."

She considered asking him where he was going, but thought better of it and stood aside as he slid the door open. Instead of following him in, she slid the door back in place and put a wall of glass between them. Moving to the rail she looked to the dunes and the distant churning surf.

She watched from above as Jack climbed into the golf cart, turned on the LED lights, and chugged away. She wondered if he would be on the flight out tomorrow while she and Steve finished here.

Back inside, she went to Jack's room and threw herself face down on his bed. Steve lay propped up on the bed next to hers. "Another fight?" he asked.

"You already know."

"I guess I did." His voice had a melancholy ring to it.

She didn't mean to sound like a love-torn teen, but truth be told, for all her education and sophistication, that's what she was. She'd never ventured into the deep waters of romance. "What am I supposed to do?"

"Give it time."

"How much? What if he moves on?"

"Then you'll have to start over with someone else."

"What about you and Kate?"

"I'm already as content as I'm going to be."

She rose from the bed, went to the bathroom to wash her face, but stopped at the door. "Do you want me to wake you when we see something on the monitor?"

"I won't be asleep. Order me a burger, fries and a chocolate malt. See if Connie, Mike and his crew have eaten."

Heather sighed. "Jack will probably dine on oysters Rockefeller tonight and I'm eating burgers with a mob queen and a cop."

Steve chuckled. "You wouldn't have it any other way."

She closed the door. Steve was right. There was something about catching killers with him that added a missing piece to her life. She couldn't explain it to her satisfaction, and it sounded hokey when she tried. Being a part of dispensing justice was a reward in itself, as if part of some master plan to save humanity from spinning out of control.

She shrugged off the mysticism and went to Connie's room to take her order of a cheeseburger, onion rings, and a diet soda. She said she needed to watch her calories.

IT REMINDED HEATHER OF TOO MANY GREASY MEALS WHEN she was a cop in Boston, but there was something familiar and comforting about having a burger and sharing an order of onion rings with Mike. Connie joined them, ate every bite, and fell asleep in Steve's chair about twelve-thirty. The clock on the microwave silently moved from one number to the next, never in a hurry and never slowing down. Waiting for something to happen was one part of being a cop and a private detective that Heather never enjoyed, but she knew it was a necessary part of doing the job. Sometimes it paid big dividends, but it usually came after hours of second-guessing. Would the boredom result in anything but a lost night's sleep? Once again, time would have the answer.

Steve dined in his room and didn't come out with his bag of trash until one-thirty, just prior to Heather's phone ringing. She caught the call on its third ring.

"Heather, come get me."

Jack's words rode on a surfboard of alcohol. She'd heard the same slurred pattern a thousand times on the streets of Boston, close to the time the bars closed.

"Where are you?"

"At the place we ate."

"Which place?"

"Next to the toy boats, the place with the pie. Come get me. Zeke took my keys from me."

"Good. You sound like you tried to drink all the booze they had."

"I'm not in that bad of shape, but Zeke's right. I don't need to be driving."

Heather was considering what to do when Mike's phone came to life. Jack was speaking in one ear while she listened to Mike with the other.

"I see nothing," said Mike.

Heather interrupted whatever Jack was saying in mid-sentence. "Things are going down. I'll be there as soon as I can."

"You can't come get me now?"

"Hold on. Let me see if it's really our guy. If it isn't, I'll come get you. If it is, call a cab."

"Never mind," said Jack with frustration salting his words. "I'll walk. It's only a couple of miles."

The phone Heather was holding went silent. She wasn't upset that it did. A two-mile walk might be just what Jack needed to sober up. She listened to Mike's side of the conversation.

"That may be our guy. Is everyone in place?" A few seconds passed. "I'll come up as soon as I see him in the hall."

Connie stirred in the chair, stretched like a cat waking up from a nap, and yawned. "What's happening?"

Mike answered the question, but directed his words to Heather. "A trooper is on the balcony with night vision. A lone man wearing all black is coming up the boardwalk from the beach. She lost sight of him when he reached the edge of the building. It could be our guy."

Mike was already on his feet as he spoke the last words. He unzipped his black bag, donned a tactical vest, grabbed a helmet, and put it on. The last items he took out of the bag were a black rifle and a thirty-round clip. He inserted the clip, seated a round in the chamber, and checked to make sure the weapon was on safety.

It seemed like an eternity before a figure appeared on the computer screen. Instead of coming from the elevator, the suspect appeared out of nowhere and was at the door of Connie's apartment. Mike made for the door, speaking into a microphone as he left.

Connie was out of her chair, looking at the computer screen. Steve appeared like a ghost from the direction of the bedrooms. Heather gave both Connie and Steve an explanation of what was going on. "Whoever it is, he took the fire escape stairs up and didn't use the elevator. He made it to Connie's front door before the hall camera picked him up."

"Do you recognize him?" asked Steve.

"Ski mask," said Heather.

"Look," said Connie. "He has a key to get in. How'd he get it?"

"We're looking from inside now," said Heather.

"Why does it look so funny?" asked Connie.

"Night vision camera. I bet they rigged the switch by the door not to work, just in case he turned on the lights."

"Is that a cop standing behind the door?" asked Connie.

Heather didn't have time to answer before the door opened and light from the hallway flooded the entry. The officer standing behind the door kicked it shut. What happened next was a tangle of bodies as two state troopers made quick work of taking the would-be killer to the ground. The third trooper stood with a shotgun at the ready. Handcuffs went on the dark-clad figure's wrists and two of the troopers ran hands over every inch of the suspect.

The door opened again, but not before the captors pulled their night-vision goggles up and away from their eyes. The shotgun carrying trooper went to a far wall and flipped a switch. What looked like instant daylight gave a new and not so otherworldly view of the scene. Both officers handed Mike pistols they'd taken off the man. As the search continued, they added a knife to the collection.

They stood the man up and pulled off the ski mask. Mike had his phone in his hand. Heather's phone rang. "Does Connie know this guy?"

Connie was shaking her head.

"Bring him closer to the camera," said Heather.

Connie hesitated. "I think I saw him once on a cruise."

"I saw him yesterday," said Heather. "He's the guy that told me to leave the back lot of the car repair shop in Port Isabel."

"Thanks," said Mike. "That's plenty for a search warrant."

Mike returned to Steve's apartment about twenty minutes later with news. "He lawyered-up as soon as I read him his rights."

"Did all three of the troopers take him to jail?" asked Steve.

"Just the two men. I told Sylvia she could stay in the penthouse and get some sleep. I'll take Connie up with me and I'll grab some shut-eye on the couch." He looked at Heather. "What time do you want me in the morning?"

"No rush," said Steve. "Gloria will be busy arresting Ramos and making sure she's on television. She won't be here to gloat until tomorrow afternoon."

Mike and Connie left, and Steve went to bed. Heather thought about calling Jack, but decided against it. She didn't know why she didn't feel an urgency to save him from an early morning walk home. Instead, she went to the patio to wait. The ever-present Gulf breeze had a chill to it. She grabbed a fleece throw off the back of the couch and returned outside. Thirty minutes later, after some deep soul-searching, she saw Jack walk across the parking lot. She hoped he wouldn't be in the mood to talk.

The door to the apartment opened as she sat on the couch. Stating the obvious she said, "You made it."

"Yeah," said Jack. "I'm in no shape for anything but a bed. I'll see you tomorrow."

Heather had dreaded a long, emotion-draining talk at two-thirty in the morning. Jack had unilaterally postponed the discussion, which was fine with her. One more day's work, and they could be alone and come to some sort of agreement. Would it be to go their separate ways, to commit to something more permanent, or something in between? Her heart and head pointed in different directions.

One thing was certain. She needed to get some sleep. One hit-man was in custody, but was this the last threat? Something about the cagey way Steve smiled didn't sit right. Heather turned off the lights, left the apartment, and went down the hall to Kate's. She slipped in as quiet as a shadow, kicked off her sandals and covered herself with the throw that was still wrapped around her shoulders. As tired as she was, the couch was all the bed she needed. The last thing she did was put her pistol under her pillow.

29

Heather groped for her phone, not counting how many times it rang before she focused enough to find her purse and swiped the face. The voice that came out of her mouth sounded raspy, like that of a grandmother with a two-pack-a-day smoking habit. "This better be good."

"Wake up, sleeping beauty."

It was Steve's voice, sounding much too chipper in the predawn darkness. "Come down the hall. I have a job for you that can't wait."

"Neither can my bladder. I'll be there in five."

"Coffee will be waiting."

The cold water on her face did little to bring her to life. She pulled her hair into a ponytail, noticed a new line by the corner of her left eye, told it what she thought about wrinkles, and grabbed her purse on the way out the door.

Steve met her in the hall. "Go to the parking lot and see if anyone is watching the building. Get where you can see the exit door closest to the penthouse."

She spoke through a wide-mouthed yawn. "You always have something for me to do when I'm having a pleasant dream."

Steve didn't respond other than to say, "I hope you parked the rental close enough you don't have to hide behind cars."

"Is there anything else I'm supposed to be watching for?"

"You'll know it when you see it."

She groaned and spun to leave.

"Don't forget your coffee." He extended a hand with a tall travel mug. It didn't earn him a thank you. That might come later, as long as she saw whatever he was sending her to look for.

She checked the vehicles in the parking lot closest to the penthouse and came up with a big, fat, nothing. She ended up at the SUV they rented many days back. It was well away from the exit door nearest the penthouse, but was on the first row with an unobstructed side-view of the entire complex.

Sips of coffee did little to stifle her yawns, but it helped to keep her eyes from slamming shut. After thirty minutes, an aging car entered the lot. The driver found an empty spot four cars down from Heather and backed into it. He, like her, parked facing the building. The glow of a lighter and the red tip of a cigarette were visible, but she couldn't get a good look at the driver.

Dawn broke, which meant it would still be several hours until people started stirring. She'd never been more wrong. The first car to arrive was the downtrodden Crown Vic assigned to Detective Ramos. It rattled by and brakes squealed the vehicle to a stop in a fire lane. Ramos pushed the squeaking door open, tumbled out, and went into the building. Heather called Mike to give him an update. Then she called Steve.

"Did you know Ramos was coming here?"

"I thought he might. Did you call Mike?"

"Yeah." That's when Heather noticed the cigarette smoker had stepped out of his car with something black in his hand. "What about the guy filming everything with his phone?"

"Good," said Steve. "Stay where you are. Things are about to get interesting. Make sure you film what happens."

Three city police vehicles and Gloria's SUV entered the

parking lot and blocked Ramos' car, front and back. Everyone was wearing full tactical gear except Gloria. She had on the vest, but no helmet. Her blond hair caught a gulf breeze, lifted, and fell.

It wasn't long before Ramos exited the door and ran headlong into drawn pistols and rifles. The man filming discarded his cigarette and moved up to capture the entire episode on his phone. Amid shouts of protest from Ramos, the officers had him cuffed, searched, and in the back seat of Gloria's SUV in less than a minute. The parade of vehicles left as a seagull swooped and rose, laughing at the scene.

Heather once again called Steve. "The show's over. Can I come back in now?"

"Did you get a picture of the guy filming everything?"

"Him and his car."

"Send them to Mike and come back in. You can join me and Jack for breakfast. I have another job for him."

"I doubt he'll be thrilled to hear it."

"That's what I need you for. Your powers of persuasion work on him."

"Don't count on it today."

Steve had the door open for her when she arrived. Instead of meeting in the hall, they stepped into the kitchen, where Steve had a fresh mug of coffee waiting. She thought he'd poured it for her, but soon found out that wasn't the case.

"Take this to Jack and get him up. I need you to talk him into going to the city jail and representing Ramos."

Heather took a step back. "Now I'm positive he won't like it."

"Be persuasive. Use your imagination."

"He was really mad at me last night."

Steve dismissed the excuse with a flip of his hand. "He hasn't written you off yet. If he had, he wouldn't have tried to drown his troubles last night. Did he pack his suitcase?"

"He might have when he got home."

"He didn't. I would have heard him."

"You're not convincing me."

"Tell Jack all he has to do is go to the jail, tell Ramos not to talk to anyone but him, and get the future ex-detective's side of the story."

Heather refilled her travel mug. "I'll try, but I'm not guaranteeing anything."

Jack lay face down on the covers, still wearing the shorts and Hawaiian shirt he had on after walking back to the complex. At least he'd taken his sandals off. She noticed his left heel had a substantial blister on it. Regrets for not agreeing to go out for dinner with him bubbled to the surface. He was right. They would have been home in plenty of time for the capture of the hitman. She relived watching the video and realized Mike hadn't invited her to do anything.

She gave Jack a long look as he slept and concluded that her mouth needed a gag, and her Irish temper had to be tamed. No more excuses. If he wasn't through with her, she'd need to make some serious changes.

Heather placed both cups of coffee on the nightstand, leaned down, and kissed his cheek.

No reaction.

She tried again, this time with a triplet of kisses.

Still nothing.

She lay on top of him and repeated the kisses.

He opened an eye. "I'm going to start at a hundred and count backward. You have until I get to three to stop what you're doing."

She pushed herself off of him and stood. "Coffee's ready. You need to shower and shave. There's a client waiting for you at the city jail."

He cracked an eye open but made no other movements. "I'm on vacation. Tell them to call someone local. Better yet, you go down and represent them."

"Steve wants you to go."

He rolled over to his side. "Like I said, I'm on vacation."

"He sent me to convince you. Name your price."

Jack pushed a trio of pillows against the headboard, sat with his shoulders against them, and reached for the mug of coffee. He considered her words as he took the first sip. Still holding the mug, he said, "I'm not sure you're willing to pay what I'd charge. I'll need some sort of surety."

Heather nodded. "This complex is worth about forty million dollars, give or take a million or two. You know that I'm getting it for less than half. I'm going to sell it as soon as I get a fair offer. I'll give you half the profit. That will be payment for what you've done in helping Kate and for spending an hour with Ramos getting his side of the story. After that, you can pass Ramos on to a local attorney."

Jack's head dipped, and his mouth hinged open. "Ten million dollars for three days' work?"

"It includes a settlement for pain and suffering. Take it or leave it," said Heather.

Jack took another sip of coffee. "As generous as the offer is, I make a decent living and have almost everything I want. That's not the reason I came down here. I wanted to spend time with you."

Heather couldn't help but admire his character. She paced across the bedroom, rubbing her chin. "You're a tough negotiator, Jack. I'll make a counteroffer. You and I will go back to our previous agreement. We each commit to play golf together once a week and each week we'll have at least one dinner together. I'll put the entire profit from the sale of this complex in escrow. The first person to break the contract will forfeit their half."

"How long is this contract for?"

"Six months, with option to renew if both parties agree."

"What if one of us wants out after six months?"

"We split the profit."

Jack looked at her. "No escape clauses?"

"None, and it will be in writing."

Jack extended his hand for her to shake. She did the same and he pulled her down to sit by him on the bed. "Pleasure doing business with you, counselor."

"And it's a pleasure doing pleasure with you, sir." She removed herself from the bed. "Get showered, shaved, and dressed. They took Ramos away twenty-five minutes ago. Get to him before he calls another attorney."

She was at the door when she turned to see Jack unbuttoning his shirt. "By the way, you and I are having our first weekly dinner by ourselves tonight."

30

Kate brought her mug of coffee while Heather dug a spoon out of the silverware drawer. "I talked to Steve last night. He reminded me you're eager to get to your parents in Florida. When do you want to leave?"

"Yesterday."

Heather noticed a hint of a smile. "I'm glad to see your sense of humor is returning. Getting a good night's sleep helped you, but getting on an airplane yesterday might be a little tricky. Why don't we all fly out together on Thursday?"

Kate walked halfway into the living room, and turned around. "Was this your idea or Steve's?"

"It was mine to buy the complex. Connie and I hammered out the terms."

A touch of suspicion laced Kate's next words. "And Steve?"

"He wanted us to all fly back together. After Steve, Jack, and I get dropped off in Conroe, you'll fly on to Florida. That way you won't need to fly commercial. We'll be on my corporate jet. I'll need to notify my pilots so they can submit a flight plan, but there's plenty of time for that."

Kate's lip quivered. Heather held up a hand to stop her from trying to respond. "It's a fair trade. You didn't charge me for staying here with you, and you gave me a tip that's worth millions."

Kate's emotional ship seemed to be under its own power again. She even inquired about why Steve decided it was best for her to stay locked up in jail an extra night.

"Like he said yesterday, it was too dangerous for you to come back to the island. Early this morning, they arrested Detective Ramos for killing your ex. It all took place just after dawn in the parking lot."

Kate's hand went over her heart. "Ramos? He killed Ricardo?"

"They arrested him for it." Heather paused. "That's not all that happened while you slept last night. State troopers and a Texas Ranger caught a guy we think to be a cartel hitman trying to get to Connie. He even had a key to her top floor apartment."

"When did that happen?"

"About one-thirty this morning."

With eyebrows pinched together, Kate asked, "I thought you said Steve kept me in jail until it was safe for me to come here. Now you tell me a murderer and a hit-man came on the property while I was alone. That doesn't sound very safe to me."

"You underestimate Steve. He'd never put you in danger."

Seeing no reaction, Heather went on. "Gloria Giles is coming by this afternoon. I think she wants to apologize for believing Ramos and not checking on his investigation like she should have. I guess we have to give her a break. After all, she didn't come out of this unscathed. She has a sore wrist and neck to prove it."

"What time will she be here?"

"After she gets through talking to the press. Steve thinks it will be early afternoon. She doesn't know it, but we've planned a little celebration luncheon for her in the penthouse. Connie wanted to do something special for her because she came to arrest Ramos herself. The video has already gone viral."

Kate finger-combed her pillow-flattened hair. "I'd better make myself look presentable if I'm going to a brunch."

"I'm under strict orders from Steve to make sure you understand you don't have to come. He thought you might like to hear all the facts first-hand from the principal characters." She chuckled. "His words, not mine. You've been a good influence on his word choices. He's taken to calling suspects possible antagonists and witnesses minor characters."

Kate smiled widely. "His stories really are getting better. I wonder if parts of this case might end up in print."

Heather shook her head. "He doesn't think so unless he can do something about the ending."

"He's right." She took steps toward her bedroom. "It needs a twist."

"PERFECT TIMING," SAID HEATHER AS THE DOOR TO STEVE'S apartment opened wide and Gloria stepped in wearing a fetching black business suit, low heels, and a black purse dangling from her right hand. The tan, padded neck immobilizer didn't match the look she was going for, but it added an element of sympathy. It was the same power apparel they'd been looking at on local news and YouTube. Steve made his presence known by saying, "I've been listening to the reports. Congratulations on the arrest."

Gloria gave a nod to the compliment and said, "Thanks, but I can't take all the credit."

"Good leadership brings about excellent results," said Steve. "I would ask you to sit, but we have a celebration party planned for you and there's not enough room here."

Gloria tilted her head. "A celebration party?"

"Actually," said Steve. "It's a triple celebration. First, your arrest of Ramos. Next, Heather is purchasing this complex from Connie Diaz. Finally, Kate is now above all suspicion and we have you to thank." He issued a wide smile. "We're off to the penthouse."

Heather joined in. "Have you ever been to the penthouse? Connie's late husband spared no expense, and the view is breathtaking."

Gloria's eyes widened a little. "I only saw the entry yesterday. I always wondered what the entire apartment looked like."

Steve took a step toward Gloria. "I have to hear how you put the pieces together. Lead me while Heather carries supplies for the party."

Heather looked at the counter that held two platters of food and a cloth shopping bag. "Darn. There's more than I can carry in one trip and everyone is waiting." She gave Gloria what she hoped would be a pleading look. "Could you be a dear and carry the cheese tray for me?"

"Sure."

Steve sidled up to Gloria. "Hook your right arm into my left. That leaves my right hand free to use my cane."

Gloria shifted her purse to her left hand, but realized she still had to carry a large tray of cheeses. She was about to speak when Heather said, "Put your purse in the bag and I'll carry it. There's plenty of room, just paper goods."

They started down the hallway and ran into Jack coming off the elevator and Kate coming out of her apartment. Dual conversations broke out. Heather peppered Jack with questions as Steve, Kate, and Gloria boarded the elevator with Steve stringing one sentence onto the last one.

"Send the elevator back down," said Heather. "Jack and I need to discuss some boring legal stuff."

Soon, the five were standing in the spacious living room of the penthouse with Connie. For the occasion, the hostess wore designer jeans, a summer knit top, and sandals with gold straps. Heather thought Connie selected the outfit for travel more than brunch.

Connie asked Gloria if she'd prefer a bloody Mary, a mimosa, or champagne.

"I shouldn't," said Gloria. "But it's not every day I get to make such an important arrest." She took a flute of champagne to the massive windows and looked over the dunes to the Gulf.

Heather put Steve in a chair and asked Kate to help her put out the food. It wasn't long before multiple conversations began. Talk flowed freely, as did the wine for Connie and Gloria. Heather and Kate sipped a mimosa and Jack made himself a virgin bloody Mary, saying he didn't want a repeat performance of last night's overindulgence.

Once the plates were almost empty, Steve spoke loud enough for everyone to hear. "Heather, you and Jack need to tell us the complete story about Jack having to walk home last night."

The two, sitting side-by-side, gave each other a questioning glance. Who would open the conversation? Heather took the lead. "Last night, Jack wanted to take me out to dinner. I declined because Steve found out someone planned to kill Connie."

Jack chimed in. "I thought the chances of someone coming to kill her before the wee hours of the morning were next to zero. It was silly. I wanted us to go out to eat, and she wanted to stay in." He looked down at his flip-flops. "We had quite a fight. I left and tried to drown my troubles."

Gloria spoke up. "Wait. What did that story have to do with someone trying to kill Connie."

Steve gave the answer. "Heather didn't go with Jack because a Texas Ranger and state troopers were here and arrested a guy about one-thirty this morning. She didn't want to take a chance on missing the action." He then asked, "You didn't know, Gloria?"

Gloria drained her glass and took her time responding. "The Rangers can be a secretive bunch and some of them still don't like the idea of a female chief of police. Do you know who they arrested?"

When Steve didn't answer, it meant he intended Heather to. "Jack and I went to check on the damage to your car on our way to pick up Kate from county jail. The guy that came to kill Connie worked at the repair shop in Port Isabel. He's a big guy who carried two pistols and a knife on him."

Steve shook his head. "I lost sleep trying to figure out why he carried two pistols. It was right before dawn this morning when it finally came to me."

The room went silent until Gloria said, "Don't keep us in suspense. Why did he?"

"He was going to make it look like a suicide and leave one gun here in the penthouse."

Heads nodded and Gloria added, "That makes sense." She turned to Connie. "Would you mind if I had more bubbly? I'm hearing more and more reasons to celebrate."

Connie took the bottle out of ice, wrapped it in a white, cloth napkin, and filled Gloria's glass.

Small talk followed until the sound of the bottle going back into the ice reached Steve's ears. He raised his voice to overcome the chatter. "I wonder, Gloria, did you ever suspect any other people of killing Ricardo besides Kate and Ramos?"

"There wasn't anyone else. Kate was the logical choice until I discovered it had to be Ramos."

"But there were others," said Steve. "Heather and I did some snooping the first day and found three people with motives." He held up two fingers. "There's Miguel Sosa and his fiancé, Sarah Childs. He's the captain-in-training on Ricardo's catamaran and she more-or-less runs the business. Ricardo promised them they could purchase his boat. They discovered he was backing out on his commitment. Plenty of motive there."

Gloria shrugged. "Motive doesn't mean they had means or opportunity."

"Did anyone check?"

Gloria played off the question with a laugh, followed by, "Ramos certainly didn't. He already had Kate to take the fall."

"Good point. There's one more person—Joy Day. She runs the novelty boat business and was Ricardo's significant other for years. The sun took its toll on her and Ricardo traded her in on a newer model."

Connie sheepishly raised her hand. "My husband started hosting moonlight cruises for his business associates. That's where I first met Ricardo. After my husband died, I sort of had a fling with Ricardo. He was very handsome and much more manly than my husband."

Kate blinked several times, but said nothing to contradict Connie.

Steve leaned forward. "That gave us one other suspect."

"And who is that?" asked Gloria, with the first hint of a champagne-induced slur to her question.

Steve's head turned until it faced their hostess. "Connie, of course. She just said she was his lover. What she didn't say was Detective Ramos came to visit her on a regular basis, too."

"Ricardo was a very dangerous man," said Connie. "A terrible temper."

The room went quiet, which made the knock on the door all the more foreboding.

31

Connie opened the door. "Zeke. Heather told me you were coming with paintings. What did you bring?"

His hair was in a tight man-bun and he walked in with confidence. Zeke looked up at the can lighting in the ceiling, nodded, and set up his easel.

"Don't unwrap the first two I selected," said Heather. "Show us your most recent one. I have a feeling it's something special."

Heather took the two paintings from him she'd picked out for her and Jack and stood them against the wall. There was no hint of the introverted painter today. Zeke was in full sales mode as he set the painting on the easel. "I painted this during the terrible thunderstorm last week. I caught the image in my mind as I sat on my balcony, getting soaked. It's the exact moment lightning streaked from the sky and struck nearby."

Heather bent down to look at the finished product. Both images looked blurred by rain, but one thing was undeniable. She stood up straight. "I believe the shadowy figures on the parking lot are Ricardo and the person who shot him. The killer has blond hair."

"Wait a minute," said Jack. "If this painting is accurate, that means Ramos didn't kill Ricardo. His hair is black as pitch."

Zeke lifted his chin. "The hair I saw was blond. Impressionists paint to distort colors and objects. I'm a realist. I paint things as they are, capturing the moment in time exactly as it is."

"I'm not doubting you," said Jack. "Just the opposite. I'm speaking as an attorney who specializes in criminal defense. Your testimony will go a long way to putting doubt in a jury's mind."

"Horse apples," said Gloria. "I have Ramos dead to rights, and he won't skate out of this because some painter thinks he saw something in a driving rainstorm."

The room became a riot of opinion-spiced conversations, this time more heated.

Steve stood and remained silent until everyone stopped talking. He sat back down. "Since we're engaging in speculation, let me offer the group one more suspect that no one has mentioned. This may seem like a stretch, but I want you to look at things from a different angle." He waited until no one moved except to breathe. "What if Ricardo wasn't the intended victim?"

Gloria laughed out loud. "You're grasping at straws, Steve."

A sly smile crossed Steve's face. "But what if the *real* victim was someone else?"

"Who?" asked Gloria.

"Connie."

"Give us a motive," said Jack.

Steve leaned forward. "The cartel paid for this complex and Connie wouldn't sign it over to them after her husband died."

Gloria wasn't buying it. "The city hired me to keep a tight lid on the cartel's operations here on the island. Believe me, if they were going after this property, I'd know about it."

Steve leaned back in his chair, giving a good impersonation of a professor about to lecture a group of wide-eyed students. "You're probably right, but Heather and I did some research on Ricardo, and we believe the cartel was after his business. Let's think about that. Ricardo was making a good living, working as much as he wanted by conducting sunset cruises. He started doing a few moonlight cruises, and they turned out to be even more profitable. However, they also attracted an undesirable clientele. One thing about the cartel, if they see a business that makes money, or, better yet, is a way for them to launder money from other sources, they'll try to take over that business. That's the position Ricardo found himself in. That's why he backed out of the deal to sell the business to Miguel and Sarah."

Steve waited a long three seconds. "Gloria, did you know the cartel was putting pressure on Ricardo to sell?"

She had the champagne to her lips when he asked, so she grunted out a negative answer.

Steve turned toward Kate. "You know Ricardo better than anyone here. What would he do if someone was trying to take his business from him against his will?"

"He'd erupt at first. Coming from Cuba, he knew what oppression was." She took a breath. "But he could also be pragmatic after he calmed down. I think he'd make the best deal he could and move on."

Heads nodded as Steve continued. "That's possible, but there's someone else who's feeling more heat from the cartel than Ricardo did." He knew where Connie was sitting and pointed at her.

Connie hung her head. "He's right."

Heather chimed in. "If you can launder money in a small business like Ricardo's, think what you can do in an apartment complex."

"And the cartel wanted it back," said Steve. "All they had to do was get rid of Connie."

"I wouldn't sell to them. My husband left this to me."

"Connie had no motive to kill Ricardo," said Steve. "They were both being squeezed by the same people."

"That's nothing but wild speculation," said Gloria.

The corner of Steve's mouth pulled up. "What motive did Ramos have for killing Ricardo?"

"A lover's triangle, and he's tied up in the cartel. They told Ramos to kill him so they could get the sunset cruise business."

"I thought you said you knew everything the cartel was doing on the island," said Steve in an even tone. "Now we're learning you didn't know about them going after Ricardo's boat and business or them coming after Connie to kill her." He kept going. "Now that I think about it, you promoted Ramos to detective and didn't know about his involvement in the cartel?

"There's one more thing we've discovered," said Steve. "Ramos was with Connie in this penthouse all night. Neither of them left. While they were here, someone else killed Ricardo in the parking lot."

"Can you prove anything you've said?" asked Gloria.

"We can," said Steve and Heather at the same time.

Gloria shook her head. "I'm not buying this. Ramos was a jealous lover, and that's what's going to put him in prison."

"I'll lay money against that," said Jack. "There's the painting and testimony of Zeke that it was a blond in the parking lot. Connie will testify that Ricardo left after trying to come see her. Ramos didn't follow him. You don't even have the murder weapon."

The muscles in Gloria's jaw flexed. She picked up her glass and drained it. Connie was quick to refill.

"There's other things about Ramos that make me scratch my head," said Steve. "Why didn't he make any effort to interview other witnesses? Even if he planned to frame Kate, he did nothing to make it look like a thorough investigation. And why did he wait so long to begin the investigation? Everyone that watches television knows the first forty-eight hours after a killing are critical to a positive outcome."

"He's lazy," said Gloria.

"Then why did you promote him?" Steve held up a hand. "Sorry, I revert to my old ways of asking questions."

Jack scratched his chin. "I talked to Ramos this morning. His defense will be that Gloria told him not to begin the investigation until he had a file folder complete with the interviews conducted here."

"He's a liar and lazy," said Gloria. "I never told him to slow-walk the investigation."

"What about the gun?" asked Heather.

"What gun?" demanded Gloria.

"The pistol planted in Kate's recliner that was meant to incriminate her."

Steve shoved his hand down the side of the chair to demonstrate. "I found it in the chair and we turned it over to Mike Moreno."

"It's a nine-millimeter," said Heather. "And ballistics shows it's the gun used to kill Ricardo."

Gloria was on her feet. "Are you two telling me you found the murder weapon and didn't turn it over to me? I should arrest both of you right now."

"That wouldn't be smart," said Jack. "Who were they supposed to call? Ramos was in charge of the case. He wasn't interested in anyone but Kate. And from all appearances, you were fine with that. They bagged it, tagged it, and called a Texas Ranger. I'd say an arrest of Steve or Heather would be fertile grounds for litigation."

"Then I might need to add you to the list of those obstructing an investigation."

Jack laughed. "I'll write that threat off to you having too much champagne."

It was Steve's turn. "One more thing about Ramos that puzzles me. We have a video of him collecting an envelope from Joy Day. What was he doing?"

Jack spoke up. "Ramos told me today that Connie's husband started that business. She gave it to him to manage because she didn't want to mess with it."

Steve kept his head still. "Is it true, Connie? Did you give Ramos that business?"

"Yes."

"Let's put this together," said Steve. "Connie gave Ramos a legal way to make money on the side, by taking over the lease to the novelty boats and dock. Connie thought Ricardo was too dangerous to spend any more time with. I can't see Ramos having a motive for wanting either Connie or Ricardo dead. That leaves us with looking for someone else."

For the first time, Kate spoke up. "Then who do you suspect?"

Steve allowed a long pause. "I wonder if it's Gloria Giles."

A pink blush rose from Gloria's neck up to her cheeks. "Tell me, Mr. Former Cop, I wonder how silly you'll look when you can't prove any of this?"

Steve raised his shoulders and let them drop. "I wonder about a lot of things. Like why you made up that story about being run off the road and hitting a telephone pole."

Heather broke in. "There's not a scratch on the back of the car or on anything except the hood. I took photos."

Steve immediately added, "I'm curious about your account of kicking the kids from Mexico out of the restaurant, and why you didn't call for backup when you said teens cornered you in the store."

Gloria scooted to the edge of the couch. "I've had enough of this trip to Fantasyland, Mr. Smiley. I suggest you and your entourage leave police work to the professionals."

Steve ignored her. "It all started when you picked on the wrong group of kids in the restaurant. You didn't know who their parents were, but you soon found out. Connie's husband was there and had you dead to rights. You were going to lose your job and everything you owned. To avoid that, all you had to do was look the other way when the cartel started to move in on businesses. One thing led to another and they had you in their net. You were supposed to kill Connie, but you messed up. Instead of Connie leaving the building, it was Ricardo. You couldn't tell in the driving rain with his head covered by the hood of the rain pancho."

"She called and told me to meet her in the parking lot," said Connie. "Ricardo came to the door right after that. Ramos was already here and I'm afraid of storms. Ricardo left when I told him to go. He was supposed to tell Gloria I was too drunk to talk to her. It was raining so hard I gave him my pancho."

"Ramos gave me the same version of the story this morning," said Jack.

Gloria picked up her purse and sat it on her lap.

Steve kept talking. "The night you came to see us, you said it was kids in the store that blocked you in. They weren't kids, but a couple of big men. I bet one of them was the guy Heather met at the repair shop. They wanted to send you a reminder that you owed them a big favor."

"You've lost your mind."

"No, Gloria, you lost your way."

She was on her feet with a pistol coming out of her purse before anyone could react.

Kate gasped. Zeke fell on the floor, covering his head.

With the pistol pointed at Connie, Gloria said, "I may have lost my way, but I'm dead if I don't take care of her. Believe me, I'm a lot more afraid of the men that were in that store than going to prison."

Heather, having already reached in her pocket, pulled out a fist full of cartridges. "You not only lost your way, you lost these on the way up to the penthouse."

Mike Moreno and the female state trooper poured out of the master bedroom with pistols drawn.

Gloria looked down the barrels of the two pistols, let hers drop to the area rug, sat down, and drank the last champagne she would have for the foreseeable future.

Heather turned her attention to the Texas Ranger. "Be sure to pick up the couple that runs the office downstairs on your way out. You'll find they've been laundering cartel money through the complex."

Steve chuckled. "You didn't tell me about that."

"Turnabout's fair play. You never tell me everything."

32

Steve shifted in the leather seat. The flight in the private jet from the airport in Harlingen had been smooth and quiet, with Heather and Jack sleeping most of the way. Their fatigue was most likely caused by both of them concentrating on work during the day followed by late nights taking rides in the golf cart to the far reaches of the beach.

Upon landing at Conroe's Regional Airport, the couple went to the terminal to grab a quick bite to eat. After overseeing the refueling, the pilots took a break, leaving Steve and Kate on the plane by themselves.

The days following the arrest of Gloria Giles were spent writing. Kate let her feelings be known in no uncertain terms about how frightened she was when Gloria brandished a pistol. After that, their conversations were cordial, but cool.

Steve considered his options and decided to make an attempt at thawing at least part of the chill. "I hope we're not going to part on such bad terms. I'm sorry. I thought you knew I'd never place you in real danger."

"You're blind. How could you know if Heather had unloaded Gloria's gun?"

This was a good start. The tone of her voice held regret, but also a ray of hope. The reference to his disability was a low blow, but he could take much more than that.

"We worked it out ahead of time. If she couldn't unload the pistol before we got to the penthouse, I had an excuse ready for you to return to your apartment. When Heather didn't say anything, I knew you'd be safe."

A sniffle from Kate told him she was thawing fast. It was time to update her on unresolved items. "Let's talk about some good things that happened."

"Like what?"

"Like a handsome young couple is getting married and has a wonderful future ahead of them."

"Jack and Heather are getting married?"

Steve let out a laugh. "Heavens, no. They enjoy each other's company, but I think this trip convinced both of them they're a long way from a permanent relationship."

"Then who are you talking about?"

"Miguel and Sarah from the sunset cruise. It was very generous of you to sell the catamaran to them at such a low price."

"I don't want anything to remind me of Ricardo."

"Heather, Jack, and I went to see them. We recommended they give big discounts to first responders on their cruises. A steady stream of cops on board should help keep the cartel away."

"They were both so good with customers," said Kate. "Especially in helping you on the boat. I'm glad everything is working out for them."

Steve didn't want the conversation to lag, so he moved on to the next piece of unfinished business. "It turns out Detective Ramos is what he seemed to be—mostly honest and incompetent. He didn't want to pay taxes on the money he received from the novelty boats so he insisted on cash payment from Joy. Gloria used him as a back-up fall guy when she couldn't pin Ricardo's murder on you."

"Didn't the cartel own the novelty boats and the dock?"

"It turns out I was wrong about the cartel taking over that business. It's always been legit and was operated by Connie's husband. Heather tacked it on to the purchase of the complex and sold it to Joy for next to nothing."

"What about Connie? Was she able to help the Rangers?"

"Her husband kept her in the dark on most of his business dealings except for the apartment complex. Heather and Jack have been spending half days pouring over his financial records. It turns out he had several legitimate businesses. Heather's buying them all at fifty cents on the dollar."

A softness came into Kate's voice. "I did enjoy the ride we took on the duck boat." Her deep exhale seemed to push away some of the bad memories, leaving room for the good ones to take their place. "What else did I miss while I was sulking?"

"Not much more. Connie is in a fancy hotel in The Woodlands. It's an upscale community north of Houston, close to Bush International Airport. She's cooperating with the Rangers, but she didn't know as much as they were hoping. Heather's meeting with her tomorrow to sign all the sale documents. After that, Connie will leave the country. I heard she's changed her mind about getting back into television and movies or even moving to Spain. I told Mike Moreno I didn't want to know where she's going."

"What about the complex? Will Heather keep it or sell?"

"She already has potential buyers lined up." Steve chuckled. "Her father is one of them. She can make more money in one day than I made in twenty years. But in this case, both she and Jack will come out with a big stack of chips. She's splitting the profit with him."

"That's very generous. And what about Gloria Giles? Is a long prison sentence in her future?"

"Her attorney will try to get a change of venue for her trial. The authorities have her in protective custody at the jail, trying to keep her alive until the trial. They may have their job cut out for them. The cartel can be a pretty determined lot."

Steve heard the fuel truck pull away from the airplane. "That pretty much covers everything, except for you and me."

Kate cleared her throat. Her words came out soft and halting. "I've been thinking. I can't..."

Steve cut her off. "Let me talk first. We can't live in the past, but that doesn't mean what's gone before doesn't affect our futures. You've been through something this past week that will take you a long time to get over. It would be unfair of me to expect anything from you. That's why I've decided to find a new writing coach, someone whose focus is detective fiction."

Kate sat silently. Her hand found his, and she squeezed it. "You're quite a man, Steve Smiley, but I can recognize subtext a mile away. Your words aren't matching what you really want to say, but the meaning is clear as glass. You know I need time by myself. I need to write in order to process what happened." She paused. "And I know you'd rather be with your memories of Maggie than with anyone else."

Steve nodded. "How long?"

"A while. Don't expect to hear from me for the next year." Kate grabbed his hand. "And no murders when we see each other again, if you don't mind."

"I'll try, but they seem to come looking for me."

A silent few seconds passed before Steve said, "I have a present for you. Look under Heather's seat."

The sound of Kate tearing off wrapping paper reached his ears. Her laugh flowed as a mixture of joy and hope.

"I had Zeke do a rush job of painting it for you. I thought about a beach scene, but this seemed more our speed."

Kate's laugh bubbled over. "It's perfect. Not every man gives a woman a commissioned painting of two friends taking a ride in a boat that looks like a bathtub toy."

Steve smiled. "And it's not every woman who would appreciate it."

The Name Game Murder

One recluse millionaire. One murder... so far.

Life between cases is downright boring for blind PI Steve Smiley. When an insurance investigator looking for a missing millionaire is convinced the man is alive, Smiley doesn't hesitate to join the hunt.

With no murder weapon and no body, Smiley suspects the man faked his own death. But the trail of multiple passports turns cold... until a body is found in a burned-out Texas truck. Dental records confirm it's the missing man. A bullet in his back confirms he was murdered. But why would someone want to kill a video game developer?

Then the killer takes a shot at the man's widow. With both her life and Steve's reputation on the line, can he stop the killer before he strikes again? Or will this be the one game Steve loses?

Scan the above image or go to bruchammack.com/books/the-name-game-murder/

From The Author

Thanks for reading *Murder In The Dunes*. I hope it satisfied your appetite for a good mystery and kept you turning the pages to find out 'whodunit.' I would be very grateful if you would take a minute to leave a review at your favorite retail site, Bookbub or Goodreads. Reviews are the lifeblood of books and you, the reader, can keep that lifeblood flowing!

I have a great community of mystery lovers that are the first to hear about new releases, discounts and other mysteries I've enjoyed. I'd love for you to get in on the fun and join my Mystery Insiders reader community. After you sign up I'll send you a *reader exclusive* Smiley and McBlythe mystery novella!

You can also follow me on Amazon, Bookbub and Goodreads to receive notification of my latest release.

Thanks again for reading!
Bruce

Scan the image above or go to brucehammack.com/the-smiley-and-mcblythe-mysteries-reader-gift/

About The Author

Drawing from his extensive background in criminal justice, Bruce Hammack writes contemporary, clean read detective and crime mysteries. He is the author of the Smiley and McBlythe Mystery series, the Star of Justice series and the Fen Maguire Mysteries. Having lived in eighteen cities around the world, he now lives in the Texas hill country with his wife of thirty-plus years.

Find out about his latest release, sign up for a free short story and see his entire catalog of books at brucehammack.com

www.ingramcontent.com/pod-product-compliance
Lightning Source LLC
LaVergne TN
LVHW041626060526
838200LV00040B/1462